Berkley Sensation Titles by Christine Wells

Sweetest Little Sin

CHRISTINE WELLS

B

BERKLEY SENSATION, NEW YORK

THE BERKLEY PUBLISHING GROUP
Published by the Penguin Group
Penguin Group (USA) Inc.
375 Hudson Street, New York, New York 10014, USA
Penguin Group (Canada), 90 Eglinton Avenue East, Suite 700, Toronto, Ontario M4P 2Y3, Canada
(a division of Pearson Penguin Canada Inc.)
Penguin Books Ltd., 80 Strand, London WC2R 0RL, England
Penguin Group Ireland, 25 St. Stephen's Green, Dublin 2, Ireland (a division of Penguin Books Ltd.)
Penguin Group (Australia), 250 Camberwell Road, Camberwell, Victoria 3124, Australia
(a division of Pearson Australia Group Pty. Ltd.)
Penguin Books India Pvt. Ltd., 11 Community Centre, Panchsheel Park, New Delhi—110 017, India
Penguin Group (NZ), 67 Apollo Drive, Rosedale, North Shore 0632, New Zealand
(a division of Pearson New Zealand Ltd.)
Penguin Books (South Africa) (Pty.) Ltd., 24 Sturdee Avenue, Rosebank, Johannesburg 2196,
South Africa

Penguin Books Ltd., Registered Offices: 80 Strand, London WC2R 0RL, England

This is a work of fiction. Names, characters, places, and incidents either are the product of the author's imagination or are used fictitiously, and any resemblance to actual persons, living or dead, business establishments, events, or locales is entirely coincidental. The publisher does not have any control over and does not assume any responsibility for author or third-party websites or their content.

SWEETEST LITTLE SIN

A Berkley Sensation Book / published by arrangement with the author

PRINTING HISTORY
Berkley Sensation mass-market edition / May 2010

ISBN: 978-0-425-23480-8

BERKLEY® SENSATION
Berkley Sensation Books are published by The Berkley Publishing Group,
a division of Penguin Group (USA) Inc.,
375 Hudson Street, New York, New York 10014.
BERKLEY® SENSATION and the "B" design are trademarks of Penguin Group (USA) Inc.

PRINTED IN THE UNITED STATES OF AMERICA

10 9 8 7 6 5 4 3 2 1

For Maisie, who loved books and wrote in the margins.

ACKNOWLEDGMENTS

Every time I write an acknowledgments page for a novel, it strikes me anew how lucky I am to be surrounded by people who share my passion for writing and books. To my editor, Leis Pederson, thank you for your insights and your support; to my publicist, Kathryn Tumen, and all at Berkley who work so hard to bring my novels to the shelves, my deepest gratitude.

Thanks also must go to Jessica Faust for guiding my career and to Kim Castillo for being this "author's friend" in every sense of the word. I must also acknowledge the wonderful work artist James Griffin and the Berkley art department have done on my beautiful covers.

To my agent, Helen Breitwieser, thank you for your enthusiasm and expertise. I love working with you. To Anna Campbell, I value your friendship and your "junior pen of death" more than you'll ever know. To Denise Rossetti, who helps unravel the knottiest of plot problems, my everlasting thanks.

To the Romance Bandits, who are more like sisters than colleagues, I'm so proud to be one of you, and to the fabulous Bandita Buddies, thank you for helping us build such a warm, welcoming community on the Internet. To all my friends in Romance Writers of America and Romance Writers of Australia, the Beau Monde and BRRAddicts, your passion, hard work, and talent is a constant inspiration.

To my family and friends—Jamie, Allister, Adrian, Cheryl and Ian, Michael, Robin and George, Vikki, Ben and Yasmin, my love and gratitude for your support, love, and friendship.

One

London, 1817

IN the deepest hours of a damp, dismal night, a glossy black barouche slowed outside a Mayfair house. The carriage's door swung open. Without stopping, the vehicle ejected a long black bundle and sped away, wheels kicking up an arcing spray of water in its wake.

The bundle hit the pavement and rolled a couple of times before coming to rest against a boot scraper at the foot of a flight of shallow steps.

As the iron instrument dug sharply into his ribs, the Marquis of Jardine gave a soft groan. His body was a mass of unidentified agonies. His head pounded with a vicious, fiery pain, as if a blacksmith had plunged it into a furnace, then set to work with an anvil.

The flagway was damp from a recent downpour. Jardine sank his lean cheek into the blessed cold, relishing the wet shock that distracted him, if only for a second, from the pain. They'd damned near killed him this time. Hell, but he'd had enough of this game.

Buttery light waxed over him as a door opened above and footsteps clattered down the stairs. Pride urged him to launch to his feet, but he couldn't summon quite enough will for that.

He bared his teeth in a ferocious snarl of a smile. The pain had been worth it, hadn't it? Because at last—*at last*—he'd found the missing piece of a puzzle that had eluded his grasp for years.

When his footmen hauled him up between them, his legs couldn't seem to do the job they were paid for. He was a tall man, with long, loose limbs—an awkward burden—and it was bloody ridiculous that he couldn't seem to rely on his own two feet. His footmen half dragged, half carried him up several teeth-chattering flights of stairs, then heaved him through a doorway and tumbled him onto his bed.

The exquisite pain of this process sent Jardine reeling toward unconsciousness. He longed for that relief, wished they'd just kill him and be done with it.

But no, there was a reason—a damned good reason—he needed to hang on to his wits. Vital importance. The fate of nations—no, *his* fate, come to that—was teetering in the balance, dangling by a thread. And he must do this thing, take care of this utterly crucial piece of business. . . .

Louisa.

His body arched off the bed, riding another wave of pain. A tidal wave of agony that swept a man up and dashed him against a cliff of jagged rock.

The fuzz of black dots at the edge of his vision swarmed and thickened. He groaned and someone nipped in with ruthless efficiency to tilt a noxious mixture down his throat.

Torpor spread through his limbs, his brain. The light dimmed, then snuffed altogether.

"No, no," he muttered. "Don't let me sleep."

Then he fell, spiraling into darkness.

LADY Louisa Brooke moved through her brother's ballroom with a smile fixed beneath her loo mask and a tight knot of apprehension in her breast. She'd waited for a sign all day, but none had come. She'd thought perhaps tonight . . . but he avoided entertainments when he knew she'd be there, treated her like the scantest acquaintance when they met unavoidably, as they often did in town.

He wasn't here tonight. Despite the anonymity of the masquerade and the crowded state of her sister-in-law's ballroom, she knew it. She'd sense his presence if he were here.

Thoughts of feigning a headache and making her excuses flitted through her mind, but she dismissed them. No one would believe the staid Lady Louisa was subject to invalidish megrims. They'd question her and fuss. That would be worse than enduring the attentions of her legion of suitors.

A small huff of exasperation escaped her lips. There were times when one simply despaired of the male population. Years ago, when she'd no dowry and no prospects, the beaux of the beau monde wouldn't touch her with a barge pole. Now that her brother had succeeded the distantly related Duke of Lyle, they swarmed like flies around a rotting sheep's carcass.

She grimaced. An apt simile. She was alone, abandoned, and moldering into dust. A dried-up old maid.

Firmly, she steered her mind away from the perilous waters of self-pity. She despised people who wallowed and bemoaned what couldn't be helped.

"Don't curl your lip like that, darling." Kate, Duchess of Lyle, magnificent in a confection of emerald green and dyed ostrich feathers, handed her a glass of champagne. "You'll scare off poor Mr. Radleigh."

Accepting the glass, Louisa bared her teeth. "If only."

She glowered across the ballroom at the tall, fair-haired man who had wisely chosen to dress in a plain black domino tonight. "The gentleman is persistent."

Tilting her head, Kate surveyed her guest as he paused to exchange greetings with a matron in bombazine and an enormous turban. "He's rich, they say."

"Mmm. Quite unique."

"Unique? How so?"

"He's the only one of my suitors who doesn't want my money." Louisa paused. "I wonder what it is he does want."

Kate gave a gurgle of laughter. "Well, could it be . . . um, don't be shocked, darling, but could it possibly be . . . *you* he wants?"

The idea made Louisa slightly nauseous. Only one man had ever wanted her. And he was . . . Impossible. Dangerous. Devastating.

Not here.

Repressing a shiver of equal parts fear and yearning, she shook her head. "There must be some other reason. Radleigh's probably in the market for a pedigree. It's the one thing he *doesn't* have. Only think how marrying the sister of a duke would enhance his standing in the ton."

Kate screwed up her pretty mouth in a moue of disapproval. "Cynical, Louisa. And shockingly dismissive of your charms. I won't allow it."

Louisa said nothing, smiling a little at her friend's staunch support.

"Mr. Radleigh is not so very bad, though, is he?" Kate continued to speculate. "His bow is all it should be."

They both watched Radleigh flourish in the direction of Louisa's approving mama. Quite an accomplishment to make an elegant bow when one was that large and powerfully built.

Turning Mama up sweet, Louisa thought. It was hardly necessary. At this juncture, Millicent Brooke would be perfectly happy to marry off her difficult daughter to any gentleman in possession of good character and all his teeth.

Dispassionately, Louisa remarked, "Mr. Radleigh's figure is pleasing enough, I daresay. And his features are attractive, if you admire fair men." She didn't.

"He seems amiable." Kate nodded. "And there is that fortune." She flicked open her fan with her characteristic restless elegance and plied it rapidly. "There is only one thing wrong with him, as far as I can see."

"What's that?"

Kate's voice was gentle, compassionate. "Well, he's not the Marquis of Jardine, is he?"

The stab of pain, excitement, and terror stole Louisa's breath for a moment. What terrible power in a name. Particularly when spoken aloud, unexpectedly, as if Kate read her thoughts, sensed the anticipation that lent an added tension to Louisa's erect posture tonight.

Before Louisa could respond, Kate's wandering gaze snagged on some point in the crowd and her fan stilled.

"There's that horrible Faulkner. Look! The man dressed as Mephistopheles over there." She snorted. "An appropriate guise, indeed. Can you *believe* Max would invite him here?"

Glad of the distraction, Louisa craned her neck to see. "Yes, of course. Why wouldn't he?" Faulkner was the head of the secret service and her brother's former superior. Max had retired from the service upon inheriting the dukedom, but obviously, he hadn't cut the connection.

"Well! Faulkner needn't think he can lure Max back into the fold." Kate vibrated with fury Louisa understood only too well. "Max is finished with all that cloak-and-dagger nonsense. He gave me his word."

"I'm sure it's a purely social connection," said Louisa soothingly.

If her brother had given his word, he would keep it. On the other hand, Faulkner struck her as the kind of man who never did anything without a purpose, and that purpose was usually Machiavellian. Kate had good reason to be suspicious.

But was Faulkner here for Max or for Louisa?

After the affair of Kate's stolen diary, Faulkner had required Louisa to sign a paper in which she gave her oath not to reveal any official secrets she'd learned in the course of her involvement. She'd discovered nothing while translating the diary, save the extent of Kate's rather risqué fantasies. However, Louisa had signed rather than pass that potentially embarrassing information to Faulkner.

And then he'd asked her for one small favor. . . .

One small favor often led to other, larger ones, in Faulkner's line of business.

Apprehension skipped down Louisa's spine. Yet, mingled with that emotion was a healthy dose of intrigue. She murmured to Kate, "Tell Max you don't want Faulkner here. He'll take care of it."

"Certainly not!" Kate declared. "I shall deal with him myself."

She would, too. Amusement curved Louisa's lips as she watched Kate sally forth. The last she saw of her sister-in-law was the jaunty bob of her ostrich plume as she wove through the crowd.

Turning to hand a footman her empty glass, Louisa had no doubt Kate would succeed in ejecting Faulkner. She wished, however, that Kate hadn't chosen this moment to desert her. Not with her mother and Mr. Radleigh heading this way.

Millicent Brooke had dressed as a fairy princess this evening. Her blond hair was swept up and surmounted by a diamond tiara that passed for a crown. Affixed to the back of her diaphanous pink gown was a pair of spangled gossamer wings. It was a costume for a girl, yet Millicent did not look at all ridiculous.

All evening, Louisa had watched her mother flit about

the ballroom like a pretty pink butterfly, her youth and spirits reclaimed with the restoration of the family's fortunes. Max had been absurdly generous with his new inheritance, and Louisa couldn't be sorry for it in her mother's case.

Millicent craved the kind of existence that filled Louisa with restless, screaming boredom. The endless social round, the gossip and parties, these were her mother's lifeblood. And having arranged her own second marriage successfully, Millicent was more eager than ever to have her spinsterish daughter off her hands.

Their lot after her father's death had been a frugal and largely joyless one, though Louisa had done her utmost to see that Millicent wanted for few of life's necessities. She'd even scraped together funds for a few treats along the way.

She didn't at all begrudge her mother's newfound joie de vivre, nor her desire to remarry. But she wished Millicent hadn't taken it into her head that Louisa's nuptials must come first.

Despite her mother's fragile air, she had all the subtlety of a sledgehammer.

Louisa waited, a fond, reluctant smile on her face as her mother bore down on her with Mr. Radleigh in tow. And "towing" was the operative word. Millicent literally dragged him along by the hand.

You don't need to lead any more lambs to the slaughter, Mama. There are plenty of willing sacrifices here.

The gentleman appeared not at all disconcerted by Millicent's eagerness. He bowed to Louisa, his hazel eyes gleaming with ill-concealed satisfaction.

"My dear!" Laughing gently, Millicent Brooke kissed Louisa's cheek and took her hand. "Mr. Radleigh has the most *thrilling* plan for our entertainment this summer. A house party! Only think how delightful."

Louisa murmured something noncommittal, but her mother overrode her.

"We shall be pleased to attend, shan't we, darling?"

To cap Louisa's embarrassment, her mother joined Radleigh's and her hands together, as if she were the vicar at their nuptials.

She resisted the urge to tug her hand free. "Oh, but, Mama—"

"Of *course* we will attend, Mr. Radleigh. Louisa was saying to me only the other day how she longed to see your house. She has quite a passion for the Oriental."

Everyone knew Radleigh had bought an estate in Derbyshire. The house was a curiosity, a strange mishmash of architectural styles. One wit had quipped that it was as if a Mogul palace had mated with an English country house and spawned a particularly hideous child.

Radleigh tilted his head to consider Louisa as a scientist might observe an interesting specimen. Candlelight rippled over his hair. It was an unusual, yellowish blond, like the color of a beaten egg, gleaming with pomade. Louisa gave in to impulse and tugged her hand free.

But his smile, she granted, was charming. "You must visit Ferny Hall, and we shall see if we cannot satisfy your . . . *passion*, Lady Louisa."

His mouth twitched, undoubtedly with amusement at the double entendre. Schoolboy humor. Louisa stared back at him, her face scrupulously blank.

She didn't like the warm turn of his conversation, much less did she approve of the position he and her mother had placed her in with this invitation. If she agreed to attend Radleigh's house party, he would take that as encouragement that she favored his suit—and rightly so. It was exactly what Millicent counted on.

She offered Radleigh a rueful grimace. "It does sound delightful, but we have many previous engagements, have we not, Mama? I'm afraid we can't possibly—"

"Nonsense!" trilled Millicent, her pretty lips drawing into a pout. "What engagements, pray?"

Louisa turned an incredulous look on her mother. *What engagements?* They always made the same circuit of country house visits during the summer. It was understood.

Millicent patted Mr. Radleigh's arm. "Of course we shall attend," she said. "To be sure, I'd so like to meet your sister, Mr. Radleigh. She is not with you in London, I take it?"

"No, Beth remains in Derbyshire. I will bring her to London and do the thing properly next spring."

He held out his arm, abandoning the subject of the house party now he had Millicent's acceptance. "Lady Louisa, I believe this is our waltz."

Her smile fixed, she placed her hand on his arm. She'd have words with her mother later.

The waltz had already struck up while they were talking. Radleigh swept them into the whirl of couples with an ease that surprised her. His style was polished, his movements precise. He held her at exactly the correct distance from his body, for which she was grateful.

Despite his respectful manner, there was something in him, something in his eyes, perhaps, that disconcerted her, kept her on edge. Something she didn't quite trust.

Well, what did it matter if she trusted him or not? Even if he aspired to her hand, he wasn't a contender for that dubious honor. There would never be any man for her but Jardine.

If only he would come . . .

"You look troubled, Lady Louisa. Is something wrong?"

Immediately, she wiped her face of expression. Mortifying to be caught mooning like that!

"Not at all." She swiftly changed the subject. "Do you leave London as soon as Parliament closes, sir?"

"No, I have business that will keep me here until August." He gazed into her eyes with disconcerting directness. "I wish for your company at this party more than I can fully express in a crowded ballroom. Do say you'll come."

She didn't immediately reply. There was a warmth in his voice that disturbed her, almost repellent in its calculated charm. She glanced at his face, to see his mouth pulled into a hard line. The angry grimace lasted for a bare instant, but the sense that his charade of mannered persuasion did not come easily to him assailed her.

"Our engagements . . ." she said vaguely. "I am sorry. They really do not permit."

After a slight inner struggle that again showed in a tautening of Radleigh's features, he fashioned his lips into a smile. "Do you shoot, Lady Louisa?"

"No, not at all," she said, refusing to give him any opening to cajole her further.

In fact, her father had blooded her on the hunting field when she was barely ten years old and taught her to shoot in her teens. After his death, there had been times when the loss of one laying hen to the wily fox had been devastating to her small household and pheasant for dinner a luxury. She'd honed her skill out of boredom as well as necessity. Thank goodness those days were past.

Radleigh seemed a little taken aback. "That is, indeed, a pity. Everyone comes to my house to shoot." Then a slow smile spread over his features. "Perhaps I might have the honor of teaching you?"

She suppressed her own smile. "Oh, *would* you? I've yet to convince my brother to take me to Manton's."

A crease appeared between his brows. "I am pleased to hear your brother has such good sense. It would be most improper for you to go there."

He spoke as if it were a brothel, not a shooting gallery. Louisa stifled a sigh. She ought to learn to mind her tongue.

Suddenly, she felt too hot in the crowded ballroom. The pins that held her complicated coiffure in place dug into her scalp; the lace at her bosom itched. Her stays constricted her torso and limited her movements to the point of discomfort. She felt confined, trapped in this garb, in this life, and the silent scream of tedium welled up in her throat.

She did her best to force it down and expended considerable tact to maneuver the conversation to neutral waters. This absurd panic happened to her occasionally, but it was more acute tonight. Perhaps because tonight, she waited for *him*.

Finally, the dance ended. Radleigh released her and she managed to regain her equilibrium.

Louisa curtseyed in response to Radleigh's perfectly constructed bow. She slid a glance to the clock on the mantel.

An hour till midnight.

She had to get away.

Louisa excused herself from Radleigh on the pretext of a prior arrangement to take supper with friends and escaped.

With a quick look over her shoulder, she slipped out to the terrace overlooking the square. Now, at last, she could breathe.

The air was fresh with the scent of recent rain. Alone on the small balcony, she gazed out into the night.

Thick clouds slid apart like curtains in the stiffening breeze, revealing a glint of the heavens. The vastness of that space called to her, reached out to envelop her in its cool embrace.

She didn't know what she wanted; she only knew that it was not to be found in a London ballroom. Restlessness pervaded her body, her soul, and it wasn't only because Jardine would come to her tonight.

This wasn't the ennui expressed by half of her acquaintances, fashionable idlers who delved ever deeper into depravity or extravagance to relieve the boredom of having too much money and too much time on their hands. It was a desire, a need, for something other, something different. Something *more*.

Lost in her thoughts, she jumped when a sound behind her pierced her reverie. Quickly, she turned, to see the heavy curtain at the window swing open.

A man stepped out of the ballroom.

Two

"Lady Louisa." The graveled voice was oddly familiar, but his face lay in shadow.

The figure moved toward her, and she would have been startled if she hadn't seen him in that devil's costume earlier.

Faulkner. So Kate hadn't succeeded in ousting him from her ballroom, then.

"Good evening, Mr. Faulkner," she said, as coolly as she could manage.

The wrought-iron rail was cold and hard at her lower back. Catching herself in retreat, she moved away from the balustrade. "I came out for a breath of air, but I should go—"

He grasped her elbow as she tried to slip past. "I think you'd prefer me to say what I have to say out here. Never fear. Your reputation is safe with me."

She halted. It wasn't her reputation that concerned her. His manner gave her a twist of unease, an unwilling thrill of anticipation.

But the mere fact he didn't hesitate to manhandle

her told her Faulkner considered himself free of social constraints—at least when it came to her. It was as if he wanted her to know that the unwritten rules that protected her from other men did not apply to him.

But this was her territory—her brother's house—and she wasn't willing to relinquish any small advantage. Summoning a haughty air, Louisa stared pointedly at Faulkner's grip on her elbow. His hold slackened and she jerked her arm away.

He paused, glancing back at the ballroom. "You are quite the belle of the ball this evening."

Dryly, she said, "You flatter me, sir."

His gaze ran over her, not in a lascivious way, but coldly assessing. "Not at all, not at all. I notice one gentleman in particular has become particular in his attentions. Mr. Radleigh is smitten with your charms."

Smitten with her aristocratic connections, more like. But it was true. No doubt gossips' tongues already wagged about Radleigh's obvious preference for her company. And Millicent would make it her business to fan the flames of speculation. Nothing like societal pressure to help bring a man up to scratch.

Or to make him turn tail and run.

Still, she wasn't prepared to discuss her marital prospects with Faulkner. "Mr. Radleigh has been kind. What of it?"

"I believe he has invited you to spend some time at his estate. A singular honor."

How did Faulkner know that? A cold trickle of unease slipped down her spine.

Slowly, Louisa said, "He has asked me. I have not said yes."

"Oh, but you will say yes," rumbled Faulkner. "You will say, Lady Louisa, enough to encourage his hopes."

She blinked at Faulkner's presumption. "And why on earth should I do any such thing?"

Faulkner didn't answer straightaway. He leaned back on

the wrought-iron rail that guarded the small terrace, bracing his hands on either side of him.

Intrigued, despite herself, Louisa waited, holding very still. Tension tinged with excitement hummed in her veins.

Was he about to draw her further into the dangerous, precarious world Jardine had inhabited for so long?

Why did the idea entice her?

"What do you know about Radleigh?" said Faulkner. With the moon behind him, his face lay in shadow, but she knew she'd read no expression there even if she could see his features. He was a singularly unemotional man.

Louisa searched her memory. "I don't know much about him at all," she said, surprised to find she spoke the truth, even after the many conversations she'd had with him.

She wrinkled her brow in thought. "Radleigh told me his people originally came from the north. He has settled in Derbyshire. He has a sister, Beth, and they both lived abroad until recently. I am to meet her at this party."

Faulkner smiled, a gleam of teeth in the darkness, and she could have kicked herself for speaking as if her attendance was a fait accompli.

"Radleigh is a very wealthy man. Do you know how his fortune was derived?" said Faulkner.

Her eyes widened a little. "Of course not." She paused. "Well, I suppose I assumed he'd inherited it. He told me his parents are dead." Her brows drew together. "Are you saying he came by his fortune dishonestly?"

Faulkner shrugged. "If I could prove anything, Radleigh wouldn't be at liberty today. But make no mistake, Lady Louisa. He's dangerous."

"And you wish me to encourage him? Won't that put me in danger, too?"

"There is a lot riding on your success. More than your safety. More than you could possibly dream."

She licked her lips. "And once I get close to him? What would I have to do?"

"Accept the mission and then I'll tell you." He glanced back to the ballroom. "Now is not the time and here is not the place to talk at length. We must meet again."

Her breathing came a little faster. "And if I say no?"

Faulkner huffed a soft laugh. "Are you expecting me to threaten you with dire consequences? I won't do that. I will always find another way. Besides, I expect that after due consideration you will agree." He eyed her silently for a few moments. "But if it matters to you, there are issues of national security and many lives—the lives of agents like your brother—at stake."

He pushed away from the railing and walked past her. "Think about it. If you want the assignment, send me word."

Reaching into his coat, he extracted a card case and flipped it open. "Here is my direction." He held the neat rectangle of cream stock between his gloved fingertips. Automatically, she took it.

He moved to the window and paused as he opened the door and swept the curtain aside. "Don't delay too long. There is much to arrange."

The brief blaze of the ballroom snuffed as the curtain swung back into place. Louisa blinked dazzled eyes and tried to calm her racing pulse. She ought to throw the card away. She dropped it into her reticule.

She counted slowly to fifty before slipping back into the ballroom.

LOUISA stared, dry-eyed, out the window of her bedchamber while all her hopes shattered around her like the breaking dawn.

He hadn't come.

No word, not a letter nor a token, not even a halfpenny bunch of daisies sent with a grubby messenger boy. Nothing. On her birthday, the one day of the year she'd learned to depend on Jardine, he'd failed her.

When last they'd met, she'd screamed at him, told him he was a murderer, that she never wanted to see him again.

And he'd reminded her that nothing either of them could do or say would change one thing—they were destined to be together.

For years, she'd believed that, carried the hope of him like a small, flickering candle in the shelter of her hand. She'd stayed up all night—in masquerade costume, no less—waiting for him. Despite what had passed between them those months ago, she'd been certain he would come. She hadn't given up, not even after the last stroke of midnight marked the end of her birthday.

Only the lightening sky of a new day finally convinced her. As dawn touched the square outside below, dancing off the windows of the houses opposite, her foolish hope fizzled and died.

It wasn't even that he hadn't come—perhaps he'd good reason to stay away. But the pathetic creature she'd made of herself, sitting up all night waiting for him, longing for some sign he remembered her existence, proved it beyond doubt.

She was nine-and-twenty and she needed to get on with her life.

She wanted a husband, not this dream figure of a man who stormed in and out of her mundane, peaceful world, leaving a trail of destruction and yearning behind him. She wanted a home and children of her own.

Yet, she'd hoped for all these things from Jardine. She'd set such store by his limited constancy. He'd never missed her birthday, not once in eight years.

But this time . . . *Why* hadn't he come? Cold fear swept over her like a blizzard. Her hand flew to her throat. What if he . . .

If he were dead, she would know it. She would feel it. She *would*.

Louisa shot across the room to the clothes press and

rummaged until she found the blue domino and loo mask her maid had put away. She swirled the domino around her shoulders and tied the string, pulled the hood over her distinctive pale hair.

With the mask dangling from her wrist, she eased out her bedchamber door and crept along the dark hall, past the half-moon table with its ornate ormolu clock. No squeaks or creaks betrayed her as she hurried down the stairs, the tread of her soft slippers on the carpet runner the barest whisper in the heavy silence.

The skivvies would already be up, sweeping hearths and laying out fires. She needed to be quick. A bribe in hand, she approached the door, but she didn't need to part with her money this time. The hall boy slept curled up in the deep armchair by the heavy front door.

She let herself out, winced at the slight creak of the hinge. She whipped a glance at the hall boy, but he didn't rouse save for a childish snuffle. Closing the door behind her, Louisa secured her mask, then hurried toward Russell Street.

Her heart beat a frantic tattoo in her chest, and the wet soaked through her thin slippers to chill her feet. Her breath came in sobs. She must know if he was alive and well. She'd forgive him anything, everything, if only he still lived.

Louisa blinked hard, barely seeing where she went through the blur in her eyes. She had the impression of passing traffic even at this early hour, the odd cart rumbling along with deliveries or a cook's maid on her way to market. But Jardine's house was only around the corner. Surely, luck would favor her if she was quick.

Too distraught to think of a stealthy approach, Louisa scurried up the front steps and rapped a sharp summons on the door with the brass knocker. Despite the early hour, the door opened instantly. Jardine's butler, Emerson, looked down at her without apparent surprise. As if masked incognitas visited his master at cockcrow every other day of the week.

Perhaps they did.

She forced down a spurt of unreasonable jealousy and demanded the man's master.

Emerson bowed and conducted her to a sitting room, a darkly opulent parlor filled with crimson velvet and mahogany. "I shall inquire."

Louisa sagged, light-headed with relief. Surely Emerson would have told her if Jardine was dead, or ill, or injured? She drew a deep, shuddery breath. Even contemplated slipping away, now that she'd received the information she sought.

But leaving when she was so close to him would be like changing the course of the planets around the sun. Impossible.

She perched on the edge of a plushly decadent chaise longue, then she stood and paced as she waited. Why was she always waiting for him?

After a long interval, the click of boots on wood made her head jerk up.

Jardine slouched in the doorway, looking every inch the dissolute aristocrat.

Hair black as night sprang back from the suspicion of a widow's peak at his brow. He wore it longer than when she'd seen him last, and it was tied carelessly in a short queue. His skin was dead white, his eyes like gleaming jet under those devilishly drawn brows. He had thick, long lashes, high, slashing cheekbones, and lips that turned down sulkily at the corners when he wasn't curling them into a sneer.

Such unearthly, satanic beauty. Simply looking at him made Louisa's heart stumble and kick and race.

In truth, he belonged to another age, when men dressed in satins and silks and fought duels and damned everyone's eyes as they did. He had all the sleek, lethal elegance of a jungle cat, the stinging sharpness of a rapier's blade.

It never ceased to awe and frighten her that she, plain Louisa Brooke, had somehow caught his interest.

The visceral thrill of seeing him again held her silent, breathless.

And then he opened his mouth.

"WHAT the Devil are you doing here?" Jardine leaned against the doorjamb, felt himself slip a bit, and jerked upright. The woman before him ripped off her mask, but he didn't need to see her face to know who it was.

That mouth. He'd know that mouth anywhere.

"Dammit, Louisa. Get out." His speech slurred only slightly. Though he tried to enunciate the words, his tongue remained damnably heavy and slow. He hoped to God the foul concoction Emerson had given him would work its magic soon so he could think.

The startlingly blue eyes blazed. "You are drunk! I don't believe it."

"Drunk," he muttered. He'd give a lot to exchange the agony of last night for an evening carousing with the brandy bottle. But it was a good explanation for the state she found him in—worse for wear, muzzy with the opiate they'd given him to numb the pain, trembling like a jelly.

Drunk? Yes, it would serve.

He forced his head to nod in agreement. "Three sheets to the wind, m'dear."

Damned if the look on her face wouldn't terrify a man into sobriety, if drunkenness had been what ailed him. Curling his lips into a faint, mocking smile, he watched her beneath half-lowered lids. "To what do I owe this pleasure?"

"You . . ." The tip of her tongue touched her upper lip, before her teeth clamped on it. She threw her shoulders back. "You forgot my birthday."

"Ah." He held up a hand that felt like it weighed a ton. "Now that's where you're wrong. I did remember. Just before I dropped off to sleep, I *knew* there was something . . ."

She gasped, every muscle in her body stiffening in outrage.

To an outsider, her reaction might seem out of proportion to the event. But it wasn't about the birthday. This wasn't the kind of feminine tantrum that one soothed with easy words and hot kisses. He knew that.

He knew her.

And he knew he risked losing her. Risked everything he had on this one, last throw of the dice.

A searing tide of remorse and impotent fury surged through his aching body, enlivening torn muscles, clearing the fog from his brain. His gaze focused on Louisa's untouched features, her skin, pale and flawless as cream, and his hands curled into fists.

If wounding Louisa made her keep her distance, it was worth it. Even though that flare of pain in her eyes seared him like a brand.

"Jardine! Are you *listening* to what I'm saying to you?"

There was a catch in the stoical Louisa's voice that struck him to the soul. No, he hadn't been listening, but he guessed what she'd said.

The need to hold her was an ache in his gut, but instead of taking her in his arms, he gave her his best attempt at a careless shrug. He must enrage her, make her leave him without a backward glance, but he mustn't overdo it. She was smart as a whip and she knew him too well. This would have to be the performance of a lifetime.

He flicked his hand carelessly. "Yes, yes, it was your birthday. I forgot. I apologize. Females set such store by things like that, don't they?"

The murderous look that fell over her features told him

his offhanded apology had the desired effect. Her eyes shot lightning bolts, her cheeks flushed, the lines of her body tightened until they trembled. "They do, do they? You utter *blackguard*, Jardine!"

She launched into an impassioned diatribe, but the effect her fury had on him was the opposite of chastening. Despite his manifold aches, his body roused at the sight of her, standing there tearing strips off him like some avenging Norse goddess.

She wasn't a beauty, his Louisa. She was tall and lean and strong with small, firm breasts that fitted snugly into a man's hands. Her jaw was a little too decided, her nose boldly defined, her straight, black brows an odd contrast with the cold flaxen tone of her hair.

But one look in those fierce warrior-woman eyes and he'd been bowled over, knocked for six. As he hadn't recovered in the many years since, it didn't look like he ever would.

And that mouth. A ripple of lust eddied through him at the thought of Louisa's mouth.

In her lips, she was all woman—contours and soft, ripe sweetness. And she was talking in that low, husky tone again, saying a lot of things about the future, about commitment, about fairy tales and impossible dreams. All he wanted to do was take her to bed, drink from those lips while he made love to her slowly, sink into the blaze of her, burn to ashes in her arms.

He'd missed the chance for such lengthy exploration last night. And now . . . Well, now, she would hate him for what he was going to do to her. What he must do.

At last, he cut through her angry speech.

"Louisa, why are you here? We had an agreement."

"Why do you think I wore this stupid mask?" she flashed. "I thought something had happened to you. I thought you were injured or . . . or dead." Her voice scraped on the last word. He struggled to ignore it.

"Well, I'm not."

At the flippant rejoinder, she visibly ground her teeth. "More's the pity," she muttered.

He knew she didn't mean it, but something in his chest gave a painful twist.

"What would you do if you were free of me?" he said. "Marry one of those vultures you have buzzing around you?" It hadn't escaped him that since her brother had settled a large dowry on the girl, Louisa had become quite the matrimonial prize.

Quietly, she said, "I am nine-and-twenty, Jardine."

"Really?" he drawled. "I'd forgotten." He strolled toward her, suppressing a wince at the pain of every movement. He tamped down the panic, choked off the urge to tell her the truth.

He knew to a minute how old she was. He thought of the night he'd planned for her birthday, the heady anticipation that had made him a trifle less careful than usual, an easy target for the abduction and mild torture that followed.

The *real* torture of knowing she waited for him last night, yet he couldn't go to her.

He reached out and took her chin in his hand, tilting her head so the weak morning sunlight illuminated her remarkable features. Her face was all planes and angles—except for that most sensual pair of lips. So tempting to take that mouth, to lose himself in her, forget what he'd sworn to do.

But if she felt secure enough, safe enough to come here in this reckless fashion, what were the odds she wouldn't make another slip? How could he trust her to stay away from him unless he made it impossible for her to return?

"You have been a lovely diversion, Louisa." Disregarding her cry of fury, he went on. "You were never anything more to me, you know. And now, I find that I've tired of our little game of cat and mouse."

Softly, he said, "The time has come for us to part."

LOUISA jerked back as if his touch burned her, hurt and confusion jumbling her thoughts.

Was this his way of punishing her? What had she done to deserve such treatment? "You always had a strange sense of humor, Jardine." Her throat felt dry, dusty as an unswept hearth. She licked her lips. "It's not a very funny jest."

His gaze fell on her mouth. Then he shrugged, hateful in his careless elegance. "Not a jest at all. I find myself . . . at a crossroads, shall we say? And at this juncture, my dear, our ways must diverge."

He opened the door and flourished a bow, clearly expecting her to precede him through the doorway, out of his house, out of his life.

The realization that he was in earnest crashed through her, blinding her, clutching at her breath. Louisa closed her eyes, braced herself, but the pain didn't come. A cold, numbing wash of unreality slid over her body and mind. It must be a dream. That would make sense. This was too bizarre to be real.

But when she opened her eyes, he still stood there holding the door handle, waiting. As if he expected her to slip away meekly, as if they were nothing to one another, as if the past had never happened.

Just look at him, her inner self said. *How could you believe he'd ever want* you? *Plain, dull, spinsterish Louisa Brooke.*

Jardine could have any woman for the asking. It was an embarrassment, the way ladies of the highest breeding threw themselves at him.

Louisa's heart stamped like a spoiled child, cried that he *had* wanted her once. He *had*!

She might not be his equal in looks and social status, but Jardine had made promises to her. He had committed himself.

Perhaps he'd regretted it later, but no one had held a gun to his head all those years ago. Just because she felt inadequate, undeserving, didn't mean she needed to accept her congé and scuttle back to her hole like a frightened mouse. He'd made promises and he'd broken them.

She summoned all her strength to stop her voice shaking. "Aren't you forgetting something?"

"What?"

Furious, defiant, she lifted her chin, stared straight into those brimstone eyes.

"You utter scoundrel, Jardine. I am your wife."

Three

SILENCE spun between them, and it seemed to Louisa that her heart cringed and cowered, withered just a little, while she waited for his answer.

When Jardine spoke, he seemed to choose his words carefully. "*You* would be wise to forget that circumstance, Louisa."

"Strangely, it is not the sort of thing one forgets."

His lips twisted into a smile that mocked her cruelly. "I will try my utmost to do so, I assure you."

The blow almost felled her spirit entirely. But she couldn't bear to become pitiable in his eyes.

From somewhere, she managed to dredge up a thin thread of pride. "You have denied our connection and I have borne it for years. I kept this marriage a secret because I didn't wish to suffer the humiliation of an abandoned bride and I knew my brother would hunt you down and kill you if he heard how you used me."

She paused, ignoring the insolent lift of an eyebrow that

disputed Max's ability to carry out such a plan. "But that is over now."

She drew herself up so straight that she might shatter from the tension in her spine. "I want a family of my own, Jardine. Acknowledge me as your wife, give me a child, and I will agree to live separately from you."

"And if I don't agree to this?"

What then? she wondered. Remain in this shadowy state for the rest of her life? Divorce was out of the question.

Abruptly, he said, "Is there someone else, Louisa?"

Louisa nearly slapped his face. "No!" How could he ask that?

At her answer, his body relaxed a little. But he remained implacable, his voice taking a harsh note. "Understand this, my dear: You and I never married."

She fell back apace. "What? What are you saying?"

"There is no evidence of our marriage in existence. Even if you told the world you are my wife, you could never prove it."

"But . . ." Inside, she was falling, flailing as if she'd toppled from a cliff. "All these years? Are you saying the ceremony was a sham?"

He seemed to take more interest in inspecting his finger-nails than in their conversation. "Oh no, the wedding was real enough. But you'll never be able to prove it occurred."

"Never? But the parish register . . ."

He spread his hands. "Regrettably, the register was lost in a fire."

"The vicar who married us . . ."

"I believe he moved to America upon receiving an inheritance."

"You paid him to go, you mean." She sucked in a breath. "But there were witnesses. My maid and your valet."

"My valet will deny the marriage ever took place. And who will believe your maid, even if you can find her after all this time?"

Sally had been offered a better position and taken it. Louisa wondered now if Jardine had engineered that defection. He must have, the swine!

But name-calling brought no relief from the corrosive disillusionment that ate at her heart. Clearly, she'd been wrong about many, many things.

She struggled to catch her breath, turned away to hide the pain. Shaking with the need to dam the sobs that flooded her chest, she bent to pick up her mask and her cloak.

He didn't offer to assist her, so she shrouded herself in the voluminous blue domino, tied the strings, and quickly secured her mask. Thus disguised, Louisa raised her gaze to Jardine's face. He swayed slightly, white to the lips.

Anger shot through her despair. Charming! He looked like he might cast up his accounts any minute. Now that would be a perfectly styled finis to their . . . entanglement.

But his eyes . . . Did she imagine a look in them so lonely and lost that her heart squeezed with helpless pity? Despite her crushing disappointment, she had a fierce urge to stay and take care of him, to smooth a gentle hand over his brow.

How could she even consider it? How could she have so little pride? Repressing the sudden impulse, she headed toward the door where he stood, her gaze lowered so as not to meet his eyes. Her farewell was a soft choke in her throat.

"Let my man drive you home," said Jardine, halting her. "He'll take a roundabout way, just in case."

Nodding her acquiescence, she wondered vaguely that he could think of such minor details as her physical safety when her world had fallen apart.

Louisa paused, drew her underlip between her teeth, then let it go. "Jardine—"

She looked up to see his gaze fixed on her mouth. His dark eyes had the Devil in them, hot with intent. He gripped her chin between his long fingers to hold her steady.

Faint inner warnings told her to pull away. It was undignified to crave his kiss when he'd dismissed her so cruelly.

But she stood willing, yearning to have his lips on hers one last time, whatever the cost to her pride. His head dipped lower, his hair falling forward over his brow. She tensed, then softened, her lips ripening with longing for the kind of ravishment his darkened expression promised. If only she could make him want her again.

He was so close, his warm breath caressed her sensitive skin until it tingled. Everything inside her opened, pulsed, rushed with heat and powerful excitement. She didn't want to move or make a sound in case she broke the spell. But she couldn't control her ragged breathing or the small sob that caught in her throat as he hesitated that short distance from her mouth.

At the sound, he blinked, as if he were the prince of a fairy tale suddenly waking from enchantment. Long black lashes swept downward over the dark heat of his eyes and his sensual mouth curved into a sneer. At her or at himself, she didn't know. He drew back, letting cool air rush between them.

"Jardine?"

"Go, Louisa." His harsh voice ripped her in two. "Get out."

With a vicious curse, Jardine turned on his heel and strode away, leaving her to find her own way to the door.

Louisa remained where she was. Her hands were shaking, she realized. The rest of her trembled, too.

Suddenly, she felt weak, hollow with grief. She spent moments in that room gathering the shreds of herself together. Made herself wait until she could summon the appearance of calm. She would not slink out of here like a whipped cur or run like a thwarted child.

"Madam?" The imperturbable Emerson entered quietly. "The carriage awaits."

She managed to steady her thoughts, her voice. "Thank you."

Pressing her mask firmly in place, Louisa picked up her skirts, threw her shoulders back, and swept from the room.

A small, pitiful part of her hoped Jardine would regret his atrocious behavior once he'd slept off his overindulgence.

It wasn't until she stepped into his carriage that she realized.

She hadn't smelled alcohol on his breath.

"HELL and damnation, it's the middle of the night."

Jardine put his hand up to shield his stinging eyes from the light.

Emerson set the candle he carried beside the bed. "Mr. Faulkner's here, my lord. You said I was to let him up."

Jardine grunted, shifting a little against the bank of pillows behind his head, trying to find a cool space. His injuries had resulted in a fever that had simmered for three days. He felt weary to the bone, and irritable as hell, but as soon as he'd regained his wits, he'd sent for Faulkner.

"Bring him in." He scowled down at the nightshirt some idiot with a sorry sense of humor had put on him. The effort of donning a dressing gown seemed beyond him.

When Faulkner entered, Jardine didn't bother with pleasantries, nor did Faulkner ask after his health.

"You were right," said Jardine. "Radleigh is the one putting that list up for sale."

"Ah." Faulkner drew a chair toward the bed and sat, tossing his hat and gloves onto the counterpane. "Who told you that?"

"Never mind who told me. My informant's dead anyway. They killed him and then they started on me." Jardine frowned. "But Radleigh's not the man I want. I hear our friend Smith has been busy running guns all over Europe." He raised his gaze to fix on Faulkner's world-weary eyes.

"But now he's back in England." His hand clenched around the bedclothes. "I want Smith's balls on a platter, Faulkner. This is the opportunity I've been waiting for."

"What have you got?"

Jardine had surprisingly little, in fact. A whisper here, a rumor there. But he had a highly developed intuition where his old nemesis was involved. "A feeling in my gut."

"This feeling wouldn't have been what clouded your judgment that night?"

Jardine's head jerked up. "What?"

Unabashed by Jardine's flat tone, Faulkner cocked his head, considering. "Uncharacteristically careless, weren't you? Getting captured and almost killed? I wonder why."

Louisa. Jardine didn't allow himself to think of her, didn't let the pain of that final meeting show on his face. "Happens to the best of us. I got away, didn't I?"

"Your cover is blown. They delivered you to your own home, Jardine. They know who you are. You're no good to me as an operative anymore."

Jardine repressed a sneer. Faulkner ought to know that it had been many years since Jardine acted for love of Crown and country. He cooperated with Faulkner when it suited him to do so. What was Faulkner up to now?

"I never worked for you, old man." He smiled, showing teeth. "I'm going after Smith."

The older man shrugged. "Oh, by all means. It's your funeral, of course."

"You know you need me to get to the bottom of this," Jardine pursued. "A full list of operatives working for the British secret service . . . If that got into the wrong hands, there'd be hell to pay."

"It already has," said Faulkner heavily.

Jardine frowned. "The question in my mind is how complete is the list and who made it? Heads are going to roll over this if I can't get it back. It might already be too late."

"The list is in code—"

"Yes, and that's what code breakers are for. How did such a document ever come to be made?"

Faulkner cleared his throat. Even in the mellow candlelight, his face appeared pale and strained. "Money. Someone followed the money, traced payments. It must have taken years and a lot of patience to build that list."

Jardine leaped on that detail. "But I'm not paid by the government so I'm not mentioned, correct?"

"Forget it, Jardine. They know who you are. You're finished."

Not by a long shot. But Jardine merely shrugged. If he had to work alone, so be it. He needed to get that list.

The head of operations put on his hat, took up his gloves, and slapped them in his open palm a couple of times. A hint of emotion glimmered in his eyes. "I won't say au revoir. I doubt we'll meet again."

Without waiting for an answer, he turned and walked out of Jardine's life.

"THE date is set!" Millicent all but pirouetted into the drawing room where Louisa sat staring into space and neglecting her embroidery.

"Woolly says we shall be away two months. In Italy and Paris. *Paris!*" Millicent breathed. "Can you imagine?"

Louisa couldn't, actually. She'd never been to Paris because France and England were almost always at war. But now there was peace, and Millicent would travel with her new husband to that glittering city after they married next week. Thank goodness Louisa had finally convinced them not to wait until she was off Millicent's hands before they did the deed.

She smiled. Sir Waldo Felsbrook, "Woolly" to his friends, was exactly the sort of man she would have chosen for her mother. Steady, kind, dependable, rich enough to withstand the depredations on his purse Millicent would surely make, and best of all, dotingly fond of his new wife.

He'd even asked Louisa if she'd like to accompany them on their honeymoon, with the constipated air of someone who had just performed a heroic act of self-sacrifice. Louisa had choked a little on her ratafia cake and managed to reply that she would not be lonely, as she'd be doing the usual circuit of country houses in the months her mother was away.

With visions of her wedding tour dancing in her head, Millicent was easily persuaded Louisa needed no better chaperonage than the presiding matron at each establishment.

A pity Louisa could not prevail upon Kate to go with her, but she and Lyle departed soon for the Scotland estate. Kate's company would have been welcome, Louisa thought now, as her mother's radiance seemed to intensify her own despair.

As the shock of her encounter with Jardine wore off, pained bewilderment took its place. Louisa went about her daily business because what else was there to do, really? One did not lie abed and languish even if one's life had shattered into a thousand pieces. One did not parade one's despair. In any case, showing such excessive emotion would draw attention to her grief and invite questions she had no intention of answering.

Deliberately, she accepted every invitation that came her way, filled her days with all of the gay trivialities of the season. And because Mr. Radleigh called most often and most assiduously cut out the rest of her suitors for the privilege of enjoying her company, she let him. Not that she intended to do as Faulkner asked. Not at all.

But she had to admit the only small frisson of interest she felt in these dark days was in Radleigh and his supposedly evil schemes.

The numbness and confusion slowly dissipated, and in

their place grew anger. Without an outlet, cold, hard fury built and built inside her, layer upon layer like a·glacier forming from compacted snow. Sometimes, she imagined her heart shrinking under the weight of it.

And yet, she went on.

She thought of poor Caro Lamb going after Byron with a fruit knife in the middle of a party. How she had pitied the poor, mad girl when she'd heard of it. Now, she could sympathize with such violent emotion even if she could never bring herself to emulate Byron's erstwhile lover.

In any event, a fruit knife was too good for Jardine. He deserved a horse whip.

·And if that didn't work, she could shoot him through his big, black heart.

JARDINE, brimming with impatience, tapped his long fingers on the desk. Waiting was the worst part of the business. This time, he awaited information that could finally bring Smith within his grasp.

Where the hell were they?

He would have handled the intelligence gathering himself if he hadn't taken so long to recover from the damage done him by those thugs. Fever from his wounds had sunk him in a dark haze of delirium and he'd been weak as a kitten ever since.

Now, Jardine was champing at the bit, ready for action, but he knew better than to underestimate his enemy. He needed to be meticulous, to follow the lead on Smith his colleague had provided, find out everything he could before he formulated a plan.

His strength had always lain in his ability to quickly assimilate information, make connections, strategize. Just because this time the mission was personal didn't mean he'd charge into the fray like a greenhorn. Everything he'd ever wanted was now within his grasp, as long as he played his cards right.

His head jerked up as Emerson opened the door. "Lord Nicholas Morrow and Mr. Ives, my lord." Only by the faint flare of his nostrils did Emerson register his disapproval of the second man who entered Jardine's domain.

Jardine nodded to Nick, then let his gaze run over Ives. Ives was a sneak and a petty crook; he resembled nothing so much as a balding weasel, but he definitely had his uses.

"What have you got?"

Nick took a chair that was pulled up to the desk. Ives remained standing, shifting from foot to foot and turning the brim of his shabby hat around between his fingers. "I followed your Mr. Faulkner, just like you said. Dull work, that was. Nothing out of the ordinary, just the same old routine, back and forth between his home and the office. Until yesterday. Took a little jaunt to the country."

Jardine leaned forward. "Go on."

Ives sidled closer to the desk, head tilted in an ingratiating manner. "There's a cottage, see, in the middle of nowhere. And it's all locked up, like, with two armed guards outside. Dunno how many within."

Interesting. Not quite what he'd expected. He didn't see how he could use it, but it paid to know things. They often came in handy, especially when one dealt with a cold, ruthless bastard like Faulkner.

"Good work, Ives." He rose and walked to the large compendium that held his maps and drew out the relevant one. "Show me where the cottage is."

When they'd pinpointed the place and Ives had left, Jardine saw that Nick was watching him with an added gleam in those impossibly brilliant blue eyes. "Keeping an eye on our esteemed head of operations?"

Jardine grunted. "He's been stirring up discontent in

rural areas, flushing out those who disagree with the status quo, then throwing them in prison for sedition. When someone in his position becomes more concerned with the longevity of the incumbent government than individual liberty, it's time to take action."

Jardine paused. "On that other matter . . . What do we know about Radleigh?"

Lord Nicholas Morrow handed him a slender file. "Not nearly enough. The man doesn't seem to have existed two years ago."

Jardine's eyebrows snapped together. He snatched the file and glanced through it, mastering its contents with the speed born of practice. He'd been in many tight corners that required him to commit a large amount of information to memory before running for his life.

Jardine glanced at his companion. "Your report is concise, yet admirably thorough. Learned that in the army, did you?"

Nick smiled slightly, his gaze clear and tranquil, giving nothing away. There was more to Nick than the reckless ex-cavalry charmer who drove the ladies wild. Jardine sensed the darkness in him—well, only a dullard or an automaton could have failed to be affected by the carnage at Waterloo—but there was some personal trouble there, Jardine was sure.

Jardine had long been friends with Nick's brother, the Marquis of Vane, but lately he'd taken an interest in the younger man, keen to harness both the darkness he sensed and Nick's undoubted skills.

Nick wasn't one of Faulkner's creatures. He had a private income and energy to burn and no loyalty to anyone. Jardine trusted him, as far as he trusted anyone.

He tossed the report aside and leaned back in his chair. "What do you think of Radleigh? Is he our man?"

"Difficult to say. There are faint glimmers of a connection. Certainly, Radleigh has information for sale and he's put it up to the highest bidder."

Jardine gestured to the report. "This is all facts, figures, names, dates. What's your opinion of him, personally?"

Nick took a while to answer. "On the face of it, I'd say he's a mushroom. A wealthy man with social aspirations. He's clever and he wants the best, won't be satisfied with anything less than true acceptance in the ton. And he's smart enough that he's spreading his influence in all directions, not relying on any one sponsor too heavily."

"Astute of him," agreed Jardine, tapping his chin with one finger. "So if he's a mushroom, where did he spring from?"

Nick gestured to the report. "According to the story Radleigh's circulating, he's recently returned from Africa, but it could just as well be India or the Americas, for all the evidence I can find of him. He puts it about that his fortune derives from shipping—I'd say smuggling, more like, but I can't prove it yet."

Nick rubbed his eyelid with his middle finger and continued. "Bought that ghastly place in Derbyshire Lawrence altered to look like a Mogul palace. Thinks himself a canny one because he snaffled it for a song." Nick crossed his legs. "Well, everyone knows the expense of construction quite rolled up poor Lawrence. They say Radleigh has come home to settle down. He's looking for a wife."

Another chink in the armor. This, Jardine could use. "A wife? Set his sights on anyone in particular?"

Here, there was a pause.

Jardine's gaze sharpened. "Well?"

Then Nick's intensely blue eyes met his. "Lady Louisa Brooke."

Stunned, Jardine didn't speak for many moments. Then he recovered himself and snorted. "She wouldn't let him within ten feet of her. She's far too high in the instep to take up with some showy villain like Radleigh."

Nick sighed. "Much as I hate to be a talebearer, you're quite out there, Jardine. It's the talk of the town this week. You'd know if you'd left your sickbed."

Ice-cold fear wrapped around Jardine's chest. His hand clenched into a hard fist. She couldn't. She wouldn't. For God's *sake*, not Radleigh. "What else?"

"They're betting on it in the clubs."

"On *what*, damn you? On what are they betting?"

Quietly, Nick said, "On how soon Radleigh will take Lady Louisa to wife."

REALLY, thought Louisa, it was almost worth accepting Radleigh to put an end to her mother's incessant nagging.

"Only think how comfortable you would be," said Millicent as they dawdled along Bond Street. "Here is a man who is pining for you—*pining*, I say—and you will not give him the slightest encouragement to come to the point. The way you treated him so coolly at Kate's ball quite put me to the blush."

The irony of it made Louisa suppress a pithy retort. Surely *Louisa* had been the one blushing at her mother's blatant attempts at matchmaking.

"Oh, do but look at that hat, Mama," she said, pointing in a milliner's window. "It would be ravishing on you."

Fortunately, almost every hat and bonnet looked ravishing on Millicent, so Louisa's random selection wasn't a complete obfuscation. Her mother's sharp glance told Louisa she wasn't fooled by this attempt at distraction, but how could the relieving properties of a good scold compare with the joy of a truly artistic hat?

Unable to resist the temptation, Millicent leaned forward to scrutinize the bonnet *in quo*, then swept into the shop, setting the little bells at the top of the door jangling.

Louisa took a deep, calming breath and followed.

Someone passing jostled her, knocking her off balance. As she stumbled, a nondescript man in brown fustian caught her hand and supported her under her elbow to right her. He stepped back and swept off his hat, apologizing profusely. Before she could get a good look at his face, the man turned and melted into the crowd.

A little shaken, Louisa entered the shop, her gloved hand making a tight fist. As her mother avidly discussed hat trimmings with the milliner, Louisa turned away, pretending to inspect a display of silk turbans.

Slowly, she uncurled her fingers.

In those few seconds of confusion, the man in brown fustian had pressed a note into her palm. Louisa spread the small, crumpled piece of paper, smoothing it with her thumbs, smudging the ink a little. It read: *Whittaker's Bookshop, tomorrow at one. Don't dawdle.*

Of course, Louisa recognized the bold, slashing hand, and equally, the impatience in that imperious command.

She clenched her hand into a fist again, crushing the message.

Rage licked through her body like a house fire. Confound him! Did he think she'd jump to his bidding now? He'd wanted her out of his life, and yet he expected her to comply with such a terse, rude order?

Jardine crooked his finger without giving her one earthly reason why she should jeopardize her reputation and her safety to come to him. Or had his overabundant caution been a sham all these years?

"Darling, what do you think?" Millicent twirled in front of the looking glass, sporting a frivolous poke bonnet with a fall of dyed ostrich plumes that curled around its brim to tickle her cheek. It probably cost all of thirty guineas.

Louisa plastered a smile on her face. "Oh yes, indeed! Ravishing! Did I not say as much? It might have been made for you, Mama."

THAT night, Louisa didn't sleep. The fragment of a message haunted her, tormented even as it tempted.

She was done with Jardine. Moreover, he'd told her plainly she meant nothing to him. Why couldn't her idiotic heart remember that? Why did that pathetic organ continually overrule her brain when it came to Jardine?

He wanted to meet. Why? In the past, if he'd needed to see her, he'd simply appeared. Perhaps he was being watched and didn't want to lead anyone to her? But if the matter was important, surely he might have sent word to her some other way.

Was it a test? Was he toying with her? Did he risk this meeting to see whether she would still come running, like a dog to heel? She rubbed a hand over her face, pressed her closed eyelids with her fingertips, willing herself not to succumb to useless tears. Ah, she ought to have known a break with Jardine would leave jagged edges.

She sat curled on the window seat for hours, deep into the night. Forced herself to consider the peremptory summons from every angle, calmly, dispassionately.

And couldn't think of a single reason, beyond a nagging curiosity and her unbearable longing to see him, why she should go.

Unfolding her long body from the cushioned embrasure, Louisa took a spill from the mantel, touching it to the fire. Shielding the flame with her hand, she transferred it to her candle and watched the wick flare to life. With a shiver of anticipation, she carried the candle over to her escritoire and set it in the carved holder.

Her mouth firmed in determination, she took out the card Faulkner had given her and drew a piece of writing paper toward her.

Dipping her pen in ink, she composed a short note.

I accept.

Four

BLIND fury possessed Jardine like hell's demons all the way to Lord Vane's exclusive boxing saloon. He stalked into the large, airy apartment full of the smell of sweat and liniment and ripe with curses and the smack of fist on flesh. Sighting steel, he ripped a rapier from the wall and tapped Nick on the shoulder with the button-tipped foil.

The blue blaze of Nick's gaze met his squarely. An eyebrow quirked, then Nick gently moved the blade away from his person with his palm.

"Not swords, Jardine. You know I can't abide the things." He flicked a glance at a couple of meaty pugilists who grunted and danced around one another. "I'll take a few rounds in the ring with you, though."

Jardine's customary mode of hand-to-hand combat would not be welcome in Vane's boxing saloon. He curled his lip. "Peasant."

"A peasant who doesn't happen to wish for an early death, or at least not at your hands, my friend."

The levity didn't make Jardine smile, but it took the edge off his temper. He lowered the foil, tapped the tip lightly on the ground, and paced to the window. The view wasn't enlivening. Vane's establishment was in a shady part of town.

He turned back. "She didn't come."

He'd waited in that damned musty bookshop for two hours before he'd given up hope.

"She's trying to punish me, of course." He wanted to believe it, but the finality of their parting was such that she could not possibly think such tactics would succeed in bringing him to heel.

Besides, Louisa wasn't a woman who played games. She wouldn't take up with another man unless she genuinely wanted him.

The notion shot pain through his chest, tossed fuel on the flames of his simmering rage. If it had been any other man, he'd still want to kill him, but Radleigh!

Jardine couldn't sleep at night for worrying about Louisa in the clutches of that fiend. And at such a crucial time, when Jardine couldn't afford to lay a finger on the bastard. It was exactly the situation he'd striven to avoid all these years.

Perhaps he should simply abduct Louisa and lock her in a tower somewhere. It had worked for Lyle.

Nick sighed. "Do you want me to talk to the lady? Warn her off?"

Slowly, Jardine shook his head, gazing into the distance, as if the four walls surrounding them had vanished.

"No, don't do that." He paused, turning it over in his mind. "Do you know, Nick, I don't believe in coincidences."

"Yes, but how could this association have been orchestrated? To the outside world, you are barely acquainted with her."

That was true, and he'd tried damned hard to keep it that way. But the affair of the Duchess of Lyle's diary had drawn him into the open. If anyone besides Max and Kate had witnessed that scene between him and Louisa, standing over the dead body of a sick young man . . .

No, it was impossible. They'd been in the country, miles from civilization. Who besides the four of them and that hysterical maid of Kate's had known he was there?

Inconceivable. And yet . . .

Icy fear slid down his spine. No. He didn't believe in coincidence.

"Is that all?" Louisa tried not to move her lips as she spoke. She was tense, deflated, annoyed.

To outward appearances, she sat on a bench in the private garden of Berkeley Square, reading a novel.

If a man happened to be sitting at the other end of that same bench, she did not acknowledge him. And if anyone saw Louisa's lips move as she read, they would merely think her the dim sort of female who needed to sound out the big words.

She'd heard nothing from Faulkner for several days after she'd dispatched that terse note. He'd kept her on tenterhooks for so long, she was ready to bite his head off now that he'd finally appeared.

She'd spent the intervening time cultivating Radleigh, against her better judgment. She'd expended time and energy screwing up her courage to accept the arduous mission Faulkner had planned for her. She might not be prepared to give her life for her country, but she'd fully expected to risk a limb at the very least.

It seemed she'd worked herself up over nothing.

Faulkner fished a hunk of bread out of his pocket. "We mustn't run before we can walk, Lady Louisa. All you need do is procure an invitation to Radleigh's forthcoming house party for one Mrs. Burton. She's one of my most experienced agents. She will do the rest."

The word *experienced* seemed heavily laced with irony. Suspicion awakened in Louisa's mind. "And you can't obtain the invitation yourself?"

She stole a glance at him, but his hat sat low on his head and its brim shadowed the craggy bulldog face. Even if she could discern his features, she knew his expression would give nothing away.

Faulkner tore a piece of bread and tossed it into the midst of a flurry of sparrows, who chirped and squabbled over the treat.

"I? A mere civil servant? No, my lady, I certainly cannot. The company is far too high in the instep for one such as I."

A faint undercurrent of sarcasm—bitterness, even—made Louisa pause to wonder about Faulkner's background. He spoke like a man who'd been educated at Oxbridge. But she must remember that Faulkner was in the business of deception, after all.

Who was he? Did he have a family, a wife? For some reason, she thought not. But the man's private affairs were a mystery to her. In all likelihood, they would remain so.

Caution still rode on her shoulder. "I do not know this Mrs. Burton—"

"An introduction will be arranged. You will become very good friends with the lady. She is about your age, I should guess, and moves in genteel circles, though she doesn't have the entrée to the highest society. That is about to change." He paused for a moment. "Thanks to you."

Louisa frowned. It was difficult to keep her eyes trained on her book, to remember to turn the pages. "Is she presentable?"

"Oh yes. She is that." There was a smile in Faulkner's voice, and when she darted a glance at him, she saw one on his face, too.

Misgivings scurried through Louisa's mind, but she quelled them. Perhaps if she performed this small task satisfactorily, he'd trust her with more challenging work later on. At least she'd have something to take her mind off this intolerable impasse she'd reached with Jardine. Married, yet not a wife.

"Introduce us, then, and I'll see what I can do."

"Good." His quick response showed he'd never doubted her compliance. "She will contrive to meet you. You will fall into conversation and be so well pleased with one another that you invite her to tea. From there, you will ask Mrs. Burton to go driving with you in that natty little phaeton of yours."

She grimaced. "Thereby making the friendship as public as possible."

"Exactly. It will come as no surprise to Radleigh when you beg him to include Mrs. Burton in his very exclusive little party. Play your cards right, and he won't be in a position to refuse you." He paused. "I hear you've made some progress in that direction already."

She didn't like the insinuation. "I have allowed him to squire me around, yes. Whether he will agree to invite Mrs. Burton, I cannot promise. . . ."

"Charm him, Lady Louisa. See that he invites her."

She lifted her chin a little. "I am not a honey trap, Mr. Faulkner. I don't excel at flummery."

"Perhaps not. But he is a man, after all."

"Mr. Radleigh merely wishes to align himself with my family, that's all."

"Ah." Faulkner tossed the last piece of bread. "Yes, I expect you're right."

Irrationally, the response irritated her. "Well, if that's all, *sir* . . ." She closed her book and rose.

"Yes, you'd best go." He didn't seem perturbed by her sarcasm. "Oh, and, my lady?"

Louisa stopped herself from turning back to look at him. She paused, her spine stiff and straight, waiting for some kind of benediction, perhaps even an expression of gratitude.

But the gravelly voice simply murmured, "Don't try to contact me again."

LOUISA'S entire body seized with tension. He was here tonight. Oh *God*, he was here.

She hadn't yet seen Jardine when she felt his presence, like warm fingertips caressing the nape of her neck. The heat and shiver of it scintillated down her spine as she moved like an automaton through the steps of the quadrille.

Every instinct told her to flee. But she was in the middle of Mrs. Fanshawe's crowded ballroom and that course was clearly ineligible.

She couldn't stop herself scanning the crowd as she danced, searching for him.

There.

He was not difficult to spot, half a head taller than most other gentlemen in the room. Hair black as his swallow-tailed coat. Sharp cheekbones, circumflex eyebrows, hard, brilliant eyes.

Her heart clutched, gave a sharp pound of excitement.

And then that awful, sick feeling returned.

Blindly, she curtseyed and clasped hands and wound through the rest of the dance.

Seeing him should not come as such a shock. They were bound to keep meeting; they always did in town. She would *not* disgrace herself with tears or by following him with her gaze.

At the end of the set, Kate took mercy on her and swooped on them. She waved Louisa's partner away. "Do be a good fellow and make yourself scarce, Mr. Simpkins. I need to speak with Lady Louisa."

Trust Kate to carry off a summary dismissal with such smiling aplomb. Louisa could have hugged her.

Kate signaled to a waiter, who brought them each a glass of lemonade.

"You are an angel." Louisa sipped and her parched throat was grateful. "But I think I need something stronger."

"Yes. I saw him, too." Kate's face held so much compassion, Louisa had to bite her lip to stop the threatening tears.

"Don't sympathize, Kate. I can't bear it." She took a deep, shaky breath. "Let's talk of something else."

"I'm afraid thàt will be rather difficult," Kate said. "He's coming this way."

"Your Grace." Jardine took Kate's proffered hand and bowed over it.

Louisa's free hand remained fisted at her side.

If Jardine noticed the slight, he gave no indication, merely inclining his head to her as he released Kate's fingertips. "Lady Louisa."

Torrents of words flooded her mind. The pithy retorts she'd thought of too late, the accusations she burned to fling. But all she could force through her stiff lips was "My lord."

Kate's hand found hers. Louisa returned the pressure, then eased free. She needed to face him on her own.

Without taking her eyes from Jardine's, she said, "Kate, I believe your husband is looking for you."

She sensed the concern in her friend's hesitation. Then Kate said, "Yes, I expect you're right." With a soft touch to Louisa's arm, she left them.

Louisa swallowed. Her throat had dried again. She wanted to sip her lemonade but she couldn't seem to move the glass to her lips. Her heart beat fast and hard.

Would her passion for him ever cool to the point where she might meet him calmly, without this violent twist of emotion in her chest?

His gaze ran over her body in flagrant disregard for polite convention. She wished she'd worn a more sober gown than this flimsy white muslin. When he looked at her like that, she felt stripped naked.

And she keenly resented that while she'd lost weight and color, his masculine beauty seemed to have intensified since that horrible morning.

Finally, he spoke. "You had my note."

"Yes."

"Why didn't you meet me?" Jardine's voice barely carried to her over the music and the noise of the crowd. His face was a polite mask, but heat raged in his eyes.

"I have nothing to say to you." She fashioned her lips into a social smile. "Nothing that you would wish to hear."

A brief grimace of frustration disturbed his features. His hand made a swift movement and she could tell he wanted to run it through his hair.

He quelled the impulse. "Dammit, Louisa, I . . . We can't talk here. Tomorrow morning, in the park."

In a low, vehement tone, she said, "I'm not going to meet you anywhere. You've made your feelings abundantly clear. I don't know why you seek to torment me with these games."

"*Games?*" He looked impassive as a wall, but she knew he wanted to shake her. "You stubborn, pigheaded woman," he said softly, vehemently. "This is more important than you and me."

Shock penetrated her fury. He wasn't attempting to reconcile with her or explain his brutal behavior. Her whole world had crashed about her ears that morning. Didn't he know?

How had she been so mistaken about him, about what they meant to one another? What *could* be more important than the two of them?

She stared at Jardine, long and hard. She mustered all of her strength, but still her voice came out low and trembling and harsh. *"Stay away from me."*

Fighting tears, she turned and pushed through the crowd.

"A warm evening," said Radleigh, as they stepped through the long windows onto the terrace that ran alongside the ballroom. "London in summer is almost intolerable."

"Yes, indeed." Louisa was still shaking, sick with misery. How was she supposed to hold a conversation with Radleigh when she wanted to curl into a ball and weep for days?

She searched for a response. "Why do you stay in London if you dislike it so much?"

He looked down at her, and his eyes grew hard. "Business," he said. "Nothing that would interest you, my lady."

Louisa tried to ignore the chill that slipped down her spine like a trickle of cold water. Something about Radleigh repelled her, yet she could not pinpoint the source of her discomfort. He was unfailingly correct in his behavior toward her, yet she sensed a blunt ruthlessness beneath his polished manners.

Something about his eyes . . .

He held out his arm to her. After a brief internal struggle, she placed her gloved hand upon it.

They were not alone. Other couples strolled the terrace, the gentlemen inclining their heads toward their partners, the ladies fanning themselves languidly. Involved with one another, wrapped in the intimacy of the soft, balmy night.

Jardine had left the ball, or she would never have consented to come out here with Radleigh. She shuddered at the thought of a confrontation between the two men.

But now, the task of convincing Radleigh she welcomed his advances seemed overwhelming.

Despite Millicent's matchmaking bent, she'd never forced Louisa to suffer the attentions of a suitor she didn't like. The mere thought of allowing Radleigh to kiss her made her stomach turn over. How could other women bear to bed men they didn't love?

They strolled beneath bobbing paper lanterns, the soft tinted light playing over them. It was a romantic scene, and she wasn't entirely surprised when Radleigh covered her hand with his large one and pressed it.

Panic rippled through her.

Oh, this was not a welcome sign. She would have to decide, here and now, how far she was prepared to go to achieve her mission. Fail to draw the line now and she'd make the fatal error of showing her distrust.

"What will you do when your mother weds, Lady Louisa?" said Radleigh.

She hated that question. It unsettled her, forced her to face the bleakness of her future without Jardine.

She lifted her chin. "Live with my mother and my new stepfather, of course."

Radleigh squeezed her hand. His arm was solid and strong beneath. "You were not made for such a life."

She stiffened. Did he mean to declare himself? "On the contrary, sir. Nothing would please me more."

"No, no, my lady." His voice thickened. He captured her hand and raised it for a kiss.

"Sir!" She snatched her hand away.

He chuckled. "Ah, that offends your maidenly sensibilities, does it? Forgive me. I forgot myself." His smile deepened. "Are you afraid of me, Lady Louisa? Don't be."

She forced a brightness to her tone that she was far from feeling. "Afraid? Of course not! You startled me, merely."

She chose her next words carefully. Better to set the rules from the start. Then there'd be no misunderstanding between them. She knew she'd betray her revulsion if he attempted to further their physical intimacy.

"If I seem startled by your . . . er . . . attentions, it's because I don't . . ." She fluttered a hand as if explanation were rather beyond her. "I am not the sort of lady who appreciates dalliance, Mr. Radleigh. Perhaps it is a certain coldness in my nature, but physical expressions of affection fill me with repugnance." She smiled gently. "Such displays—

if you don't mind my saying so—are rather more suited to the lower orders." Ugh, she sounded insufferable!

He watched her for a moment with a disquieting gleam in his eye. She hoped she hadn't set herself up as a challenge to his masculinity.

But Radleigh made no attempt to change her mind. He turned and led her back toward the drawing room. "I must leave London for a few days, but on my return, I'd like to wait on your brother. Would that be acceptable to you?"

The lantern light glimmered palely on his fair hair. His gaze seemed to deepen, so intense, it captured her, held her fast. The notion that he might kiss her, given the slightest encouragement, passed through her mind. Jardine would have whisked her into the shadows by now.

But although his breathing came a little faster, Radleigh didn't forget himself a second time.

Thank God. An embrace would have tested her commitment to this cause to its limit.

Ought she to continue with this charade? He'd caught her off guard tonight. She hadn't expected him to propose until the house party. If she rejected him now, there'd be no excuse for *her* to attend the party, much less the mysterious Mrs. Burton.

Louisa forced a smile. "I'll tell my brother to expect you."

Five

JARDINE arrived home muddy, wet, exhausted, and savage with frustration. He'd spent the past week on reconnaissance, trying to get a handle on exactly how large a player this Radleigh was in England's seedy world of organized crime.

But it seemed Radleigh was a man without history. Scant intelligence had arrived from Africa, where he claimed to have lived before settling in England a few months previously.

That was only to be expected, of course. British intelligence gatherers tended to concentrate their efforts closer to home. But Jardine had hoped to find out more about Radleigh's operations in London.

The only link he'd been able to discover between the omnipotent Mr. Smith and Radleigh came from an informant who no longer walked among the living. Radleigh possessed a list of government operatives, albeit written in code. Smith wanted that list.

On the night of Louisa's birthday, Jardine had found his informant with his throat cut. Jardine had been set upon himself and then tortured until he'd convinced his assailants he'd simply been passing by the wounded man and tried to help.

But the malice with which they'd wielded their knives, the fact they'd dropped his pain-wracked body at his own door, told him they knew who he was, what he did. And that he needed to be very, very careful.

So damned ironic and typical that Louisa should have chosen that morning to visit his house. That she still lived meant they probably hadn't seen her, or if they had, they hadn't been able to discover who she was.

He couldn't take the chance of them finding out now. He needed to stay away from her until he could find that bastard Smith and put an end to his vendetta, once and for all.

He bathed and dressed and went to his club, where the gossip ran as high as at any gathering of old tabbies at Almack's.

Luck was with him tonight. Louisa's brother, Max, Duke of Lyle, was talking with Nick. Usually, Jardine and Lyle maintained the appearance that they were slight acquaintances, but Nick's presence meant Jardine could join them and discreetly pump Lyle for information about his sister.

"Louisa?" Max's heavy black brows drew together as he looked down at the contents of his glass. "She didn't tell you? Hush-hush for the moment, but she's accepted Radleigh. They're going to tie the knot when my mother gets back from her wedding tour." He grimaced. "Which might not be until next year, the way old Woolly's talking."

Jardine's face froze; the air hissed through his teeth.

Max glanced at him, then returned his gaze to his wine. "I'm sorry," he said shortly, then set down his drink and left them.

Silence. Jardine was shaking. Actually shaking. He leaned forward to set his glass beside Max's in case he disgraced himself and spilled it.

"God, I didn't know," said Nick. His face looked drawn, pale despite his tan, and Jardine knew what he was thinking. *His* Louisa, in the hands of a villain like Radleigh. It didn't bear thinking of. He couldn't allow it. He'd tear the world apart before he'd let that happen.

Jardine launched out of his chair and went after Max, ignoring Nick's sharp warning to wait, think, not act precipitously.

Hell! Dammit, how was he to think when every cell of his body raged to plunge a rusty dagger through that smarmy bastard's heart?

He walked out of White's, into the rain, headed for Mayfair, Lyle's home, hunching his shoulders against the wind, the pelting drops that stung his eyes and soaked his coat.

The only thought beyond murder that ran through his head was to thank Christ the wedding wasn't imminent. He had time.

But the mere notion of Radleigh touching her set his blood steaming. He should have warned Max not to countenance the match, but how could he have guessed it would go this far? One minute, Louisa's blue eyes were drowning in tears, her hands held out, imploring him to keep his wedding vows, the next she was getting leg shackled to someone else.

As he approached a darkened doorway, a breath of vigilance brought him to full alert. There was a dagger in his grip when a hard hand clamped around his upper arm.

Lyle's growl arrested him, stopped the upward sweep of the blade that would have driven up, behind Lyle's rib cage, straight to his heart. "Meet me at the Star and Garter in Seven Dials. Make sure you're not followed."

Jardine gave a curt nod, as the voice added, "And try not to murder some other poor sod on the way."

"WHAT a truly incomparable day," said Kate, turning her face up to the gentle sun that beamed down. "Perfect for a picnic. Was that not an inspired notion of mine? The Martins and the Pendleburys were delighted to accept."

Max glanced back at the carriage behind them, which groaned with hampers and every accoutrement eight people might conceivably need while dining alfresco, including two footmen to serve.

"Inspired," he agreed dryly. "You didn't mention we'd be camping in Richmond Park for a month."

Kate grinned, unconcerned with Max's sarcasm. "Did you hear that, Louisa? Max made a joke."

She allowed her husband to hand her into the open barouche and shifted to make room for Louisa to sit beside her. "I keep telling him he needs to stand upon ceremony every once in a while or people will forget he is a duke. He never pays the least heed."

Max climbed in after them, his weight making the carriage bounce on its springs. He wedged his large form into the forward seat of the barouche. "And I keep telling you, Your Grace, that you need to behave less like a minx."

"I suppose we are not a very ducal pair when it comes down to it," Kate agreed, unrepentant.

"Not a bad thing when you consider the dukes and duchesses of our acquaintance," said Louisa. She put up her parasol as the carriage set off at a spanking pace.

Louisa smiled at her brother with affection. "I, for one, am glad the title hasn't changed you."

"Yes, he is still an absolute savage at heart, aren't you, darling?" said Kate.

Max settled back in his seat, gray eyes glinting. "Come over here and say that."

"See what I mean? A savage," pronounced Kate. "Why, the first time we met, he was dangling a man by his ankles over a balcony."

"You will notice that I haven't done anything of the kind lately," said Max.

"No, but I suspect you'd like to, all the same," said Kate.

"Which reminds me of something I meant to ask you. Why was Faulkner at our ball the other evening?"

Max's brows drew together. "Faulkner? Did you invite him?"

"Is that likely?" Kate's eyes flared. "You mean, you didn't know he was there? I'd assumed you'd sent him a card."

"I leave such arrangements in your capable hands, my dear." Which meant, of course, that Max only endured social functions for Kate's sake, and on the understanding that he wasn't bothered with any of the preparations.

His eyes narrowed. "I wonder why he came."

Thank goodness nothing was farther from their minds than that Faulkner had enlisted Louisa's help. She cleared her throat. "Perhaps he has misplaced confidence in his powers of persuasion."

"Yes, but why choose a ball to make contact?" said Max.

"Well, at a ball, you couldn't refuse to see him, could you?"

"But he didn't seek me out." Max shook his head. "Something smells about this."

Kate scowled. "Don't tell me your curiosity is so piqued you'll go to him to discover the truth. Perhaps that's what he wants."

Sensing a storm brewing ahead, Louisa intervened. "Of course he wouldn't, would you, Max? You know, in all likelihood, Faulkner was looking for someone else entirely. If he didn't even approach Max when there was ample opportunity to do so, perhaps he had other quarry."

Quarry like me.

"Didn't I see him speaking with Mr. Radleigh for an appreciable time?"

"That mushroom! What would Faulkner want with him?"

Kate glanced at Louisa and nudged Max with her foot.

"He is not a mushroom, Max. He's a most respectable gentleman."

"Oh, don't try to defend him on my account, Kate," said Louisa. She tilted her head. "Really, Max? Do you think he is a mushroom?"

"I think he's got more money than sense. More money than taste, as well, if what one hears about that Mogul monstrosity he's bought in Derbyshire is anything to judge by."

"Max!"

"What?" Max looked from Kate to Louisa. "Oh, sorry, old girl." He shook his head. "No accounting for taste, is there?"

Louisa hesitated. It was tempting to tell Max about her conversation with Faulkner. Her brother had many years' experience in the field and knew what Louisa would be up against. But he'd be bound to stop her if he thought she might run into danger on this mission. Besides, she'd signed a certain piece of paper that gave her oath not to reveal anything she learned from Faulkner.

Strange, but wary as she was, the prospect of Radleigh's house party shone like a beacon in the dreary fog of her present existence. She didn't yet know what lay in store for her, but at the very least, her sojourn at Radleigh's house would not be dull.

Jardine had smashed her halcyon dream of the future to pieces, yet she was bound to him, whether she could prove they'd married or not. At least, working for Faulkner, she was doing something that mattered.

But today was designed for pleasure. Even if she couldn't enjoy it with a whole heart, she was glad to spend time with two of the people who were dearest to her in the world. What a pity Kate and Max would be traveling north while Millicent was away. Louisa would have liked their company once this business with Radleigh was done.

As the gentle breeze stirred wisps of hair around her

face, and the sun smiled down, she allowed her mind to drift into a pleasant haze.

She couldn't forget Jardine or reconcile herself to this half-life of being neither fish nor fowl, married, yet not married. But she would endure. There were pleasures to be had in the moment, even if one's future looked decidedly bleak.

"OHH, I could stay here forever," murmured Kate. Replete from a sumptuous meal, the ladies lounged against bolsters set on an enormous checked tablecloth, parasols raised to shield their complexions, while the gentlemen stood a small distance away smoking and talking, the low rumble of their voices carried away by the breeze.

Max detached himself from the group and strolled over to where they sat. "Ladies." He tipped his hat, his eyes a gray gleam beneath the brim. "Thought I'd take some exercise. Anyone care to join me?"

"Splendid idea. I'd love to." Louisa held up her hand and let Max draw her to her feet.

Kate squinted up at her with a lazy smile. "So energetic, Louisa." She patted her pregnant belly. "I and my bump shall stay here, thank you."

The other ladies declined also. Louisa smiled as she took Max's arm. She was glad to be alone with her brother. It seemed a long time since they'd had an opportunity to talk.

Max squeezed her hand in a companionable way and she walked with him, quickening her stride to match his.

"Where are we going?" she asked, as he led her toward a copse of beech trees. Max always walked purposefully, even when taking a stroll, but an air of alertness clung to him that made her uneasy.

"You'll see. There's a pretty glade in the middle of this wood I think you'll like."

The lush grass sprang underfoot, the sun shone, but the copse they entered was shady, silent, and still, save for the twigs and leaves that snapped and crunched underfoot.

It was cooler here, with the thickly wooded forest blocking all but a light dapple of sun.

Louisa gathered her skirts to step over a tree root that cut across the path. She looked up and nearly stumbled.

Standing in a clearing at the heart of the wood was Jardine.

Six

THEY stared at one another for long moments, and under his penetrating, assessing gaze any modicum of peace she'd achieved in the past weeks shattered.

"You." She glanced sideways, but her traitorous brother had already melted away. She threw a fulminating glance over her shoulder.

A sense of betrayal burned tightly in her chest. How could he take Jardine's side over hers?

"You've lost weight," said Jardine softly, prowling toward her.

"Complimentary as ever." Louisa willed herself not to step back, to hold his gaze while he stalked her, circled her like a panther toying with its prey. Forced herself not to turn when he halted behind her, spoke in her ear.

"Well met, Louisa. You always keep a cool head, don't you?"

The heat of his breath, his lips tantalizingly close to her ear made her skin tingle, her body shiver. Panic churned in her stomach. She lifted her chin, swallowed past the lump in her throat.

What did he want with her now?

Part of her slumped with reluctant acceptance. Perhaps he'd been right all those months ago. Perhaps they were destined to be together, to torment each other, for the rest of their lives.

"I don't want to see you. I don't want to speak with you." She spoke through gritted teeth but in a voice that couldn't help a slight tremor.

"Ah, but I have a very great desire to speak with you," purred Jardine in her ear. "What the hell are you doing with Radleigh?"

"You're the clever spy. What do *you* think I'm doing?"

She tried to step away from him, but he caught her arm easily and pulled her into him, one arm clamped around her waist, one hand forcing her chin up so she looked him in the eye.

"Stay away from him, Louisa. He's not what he seems."

She searched his face, noting the faint smudges under his eyes, the deepened lines about his mouth. "Which of us is?" she whispered.

His eyes widened a little, then narrowed. "Are you in love with him?"

"Love!" The word burst from her before she could stop it. Where had that vicious snarl come from?

She lowered her voice. "What do I want with love? Radleigh is rich, he's respectable, and he'll no doubt make an undemanding husband. What more could a woman want?"

Jardine's hot gaze raked her face, settled on her lips. His arms tightened around her. *"This."*

His mouth crushed hers in a kiss that scorched and shook her, picked her up, and flung her to the stars. His tongue stole inside her mouth like a secret agent and she was helpless, plummeting, falling. They were bound so tightly by his strong, leanly muscled arms, she imagined them locked together like this until they turned to stone.

The earth shivered, dissolved beneath her feet until he was her only anchor to the world. She fought to kiss him with every bit as much force, as much passion, as he showed her. They were matched, their souls so intricately entwined as to be one. Sublime. Damned. Destined to rise or fall together, whatever might come.

There could be no other. Not for her.

Hadn't she known that, all along?

His long, deft fingers began working at her clothing while he kissed her. Some part of her registered what he did, craved it, but she was not so lost to the world as to forget what he'd done.

Her brain whirred to life, and with the reawakening of her mind, logical thought popped to the surface like a cork. She gulped back a sob and shoved at his shoulders, wrenching her mouth away.

His hands brushed her breasts as they fell from her bodice, the bodice he'd deftly unpinning as they wrestled passionately in the sun-dappled forest. Jardine was breathing hard; his dark eyes were hazed with desire.

Quickly, she re-pinned her gown. When she looked up from her repairs, that old, cynically indifferent look had already fallen over his sharply handsome features.

How could that be? Surely, he'd been affected by the fiery physicality of their encounter. How could he distance himself so quickly, so easily?

"Break it off with Radleigh, Louisa." He gripped her shoulders. "Tell him you never wish to see him again."

"You expect me to jilt a respectable man on *your* command? That—that kiss was a tactic, I take it, to make me more malleable. I think not, my lord." She struggled against his hard grip. "Let me go."

His mouth tightened. "You don't know what you're doing."

"Oh, I'd say I've a fair idea." And it terrified her, but she refused to show him her fear.

His long fingers bit into her shoulders. "You bloody little fool! Radleigh is corrupt. Dangerous. He'll *hurt* you."

Hurt her? Radleigh? He hadn't laid a finger on her, hadn't even dared to steal a kiss. Would Jardine go to any lengths, tell outrageous lies to stop her marrying him?

Louisa swallowed hard as she searched Jardine's eyes for the truth. If Radleigh posed immediate physical danger to her, it was something Faulkner had neglected to brief her about.

No, she wouldn't let him make her doubt her cause. She would not accede to Jardine's wishes. She'd no intention of going through with the marriage, after all, and what could Radleigh do to her in the midst of a house party?

Even if she believed Jardine, she couldn't let him know it, or she'd have no ostensible reason to continue the engagement, nor to visit Radleigh's home.

Quite apart from the fact she'd given her oath to speak to no one about her role in Faulkner's plans, she couldn't imagine what Jardine would do if he knew why she'd agreed to marry Radleigh. Close those long, white hands around her neck and wring it, most probably.

"I thought you'd tired of our *entanglement*, yet you risked being seen with me to tell me scurrilous lies about my fiancé?"

The last word seemed to inflame him. Air fired through his pinched nostrils.

Suddenly, he released her shoulders. With a strained, muttered curse, he swept her into his arms.

Oh God, not this.

She turned her head to dodge the anticipated kiss, craned her neck to keep her mouth out of his reach.

Her breasts, her body pressed against his hard form in a contact that was delicious torture. On a groan, Jardine bent his head, slowly sliding his lips along her exposed neck.

She didn't fight him; she had enough trouble fighting herself. Despite the call to arms that trumpeted in her head, every cell, every nerve ending in her body urged her to surrender.

Tears of frustration gathered behind her eyes as he drew her fichu aside and kissed the swell of one breast.

She shuddered and forced out on a sobbing breath, "You don't want me. Why do you torment me like this? Let me go, Jardine. The least you can do is let me go."

"Break the engagement," he said roughly. "Break it, or I'll kill him."

She stared up at him. He meant it. He truly meant it. Radleigh might be the worst kind of villain, a traitor, a betrayer of brave men and women, but she wanted him brought to justice. She didn't want his death to be at Jardine's hands.

Jardine's mouth softened a little. "Don't do it, Louisa. Don't settle for him."

Fear whipped into fury. "You are the last person on earth who has any right to tell me whom I should marry. My *God*, Jardine, you have a hide."

"Tell him no."

"I will not!" Louisa's anger hit boiling point at his autocratic tone. She wedged her hands between them and shoved at his chest. "If you want me, just tell me so! Don't come here with threats because you don't know how else to keep me for yourself without actually claiming me as your wife. That's what this is about, isn't it? You're a dog in the manger, Jardine. *You* don't want me, but you can't stand the thought of someone else taking your place."

He let her go, then. Flung away from her to pace, murder written over his features.

Louisa squared her shoulders in determination. She needed to nip this in the bud, before he put himself beyond redemption.

Her voice trembled. She was shaking all over, despite

her stiff posture. "When that boy died last summer, you told me you didn't kill him, that you were no assassin, despite what I'd always believed. Jardine, killing for your country . . . I don't like it, but I've learned to live with it, as a soldier's wife must. But murdering out of jealous spite is something I *will not* forgive."

She swallowed. "I don't know if you care what I think of you. But I will not renounce my betrothal. And I will *never* forgive you if something happens to Radleigh by your hand. You will not win me by eliminating him."

She turned on her heel and left the clearing, blindly seeking the path that Max had brought her down.

WELL, that had gone bloody swimmingly, hadn't it? Jardine dragged hands through his hair in frustration, then stalked off in the other direction, keeping a careful eye out for watchers.

He'd spent hours before this meeting getting rid of two surveillance operatives who had dogged his steps for days. He was certain no one had followed him here, but he'd left Nick to keep vigil, in case he'd been mistaken.

He'd had to take the risk, hadn't he? Needed to warn her what Radleigh was.

A mistake to do it in person, perhaps. He ought to have allowed Nick to speak with her. Nick would not have helped her enact a damned Cheltenham tragedy, nor could she accuse him of telling her lies out of jealousy or spite. *Badly done, Marcus.* But he'd been desperate to see her.

The hell of it was that his threat against her fiancé had been an empty one. He couldn't kill Radleigh. He needed Radleigh to get to that agent list.

He came to the stream where Nick stood with their horses, waiting, silent and alert.

Nick raised his eyebrow and jerked his head in the direction of the copse.

Jardine gave a quick shake of his head. Dammit, even Max would have handled that situation more diplomatically.

But Jardine couldn't regret any time he stole with her. He'd needed to touch her. Kiss her. Remind her how they were together. How they always would be.

He clenched his teeth as the memory of that rising tide of passion swept over him. Despite the years of torment, he couldn't regret a second of knowing her. But it would be so much easier for her if they'd never met.

Did she hate him now? Despise him so much she didn't even trust that he had her safety at heart when he'd warned her against Radleigh?

Without a word to Nick, Jardine headed to his horse, stroking one hand down the mare's soft neck while he struggled against the urge to go back. Unless he told Louisa his true reasons for rejecting her, she would not allow herself to be swayed. But he couldn't give her honesty, not now. If she knew his plans to rid himself of Smith once and for all, she'd want to help. He couldn't afford the distraction.

The agent list was bait. Smith would give anything for that list. Imagine the power a man like Smith would have if he knew every operative employed by the British secret service. Once Jardine retrieved the list from Radleigh, he could lure Smith out into the open and finish him, once and for all.

To acknowledge Louisa as his wife now would be to make her a target of Smith's revenge. And if he failed, if he perished in the attempt, Louisa would be better off believing Jardine had rejected her. She'd be free.

He swung himself into the saddle and urged his horse to a walk, winding along a little-used path until they came to the edge of the copse. Once he and Nick found open ground, Nick spoke.

"I have news from Radleigh's camp."

"News? From the little clerk?" Jardine's instinct bristled. He hadn't been mistaken in Nick, then. He'd turned someone in Radleigh's employ. "Good man."

"He's Radleigh's secretary, actually," said Nick. "Nervous, but there's a good mind there, I think. I ought to qualify this by saying it's entirely possible the man is laying bets on both sides. He informed me that Radleigh's putting up that list of agents to the highest bidder. He's had offers but nothing that tempts him. He's going to drive a hard bargain."

"We need to get our hands on that list."

Nick tilted his head. "Steal it? We have no idea where it might be. He might not even keep it on the premises."

Jardine squinted, as if he could bring Radleigh's estate into focus. "I think he'll keep the document close. Do we know who will be at that party?"

"My source wouldn't divulge that information. The staff have been told to prepare twelve bedchambers."

"They'd better prepare for thirteen."

Nick's head jerked up. "What?"

Jardine returned his gaze coolly. "I'm going to get myself an invitation to this party."

"But if Radleigh has that list, he'll know you're one of us."

"Oh, I don't think so," murmured Jardine. "I'm not employed by the Home Office, or the government, come to that." The corner of his mouth quirked up. "I'm what's known as a private individual with useful connections, old boy. I'm not on any list, anywhere. Besides, the document is in code and Radleigh doesn't have the skill to break it."

"Who has the key?"

"That, I do not know." Without the list, the key didn't matter. But he must obtain that list.

He turned his head to look at Nick. "While I'm at this sterling event, I'd like you to do something for me. There's a house in Lincolnshire that I'd like you to watch."

SHE was sitting by the window, gazing out, when he walked into the villa he'd bought for her under an assumed name. She always sat there when he came. Jardine wondered if she ever moved from that spot, if she even noticed the pretty stand of willows with the stream running through it.

He'd done his best for her. But it wasn't enough.

She must have heard him walk in, but she did not turn her head to look at him or greet him by name. He knew the reason. Even after all these years, he wasn't forgiven.

He'd done his duty by her. By God, he'd given her every comfort money could buy. Staff to see to her needs day and night. A generous allowance to spend however she chose. He'd freed her from her former life. He'd even tried to give her himself, though the attempt had cost him dearly. But she'd spurned his pious, grudging gesture, and rightly so.

"Celeste."

"Yes, Marcus?" She didn't turn her head.

A flash of annoyance quickly fizzled to pity. She didn't want him looking at her face. Vanity had not fled with the passage of time, nor with the ruin of her once-spectacular looks. "I have to go away. I came to see if you needed anything."

Her husky voice, as remote as her gaze, answered him. "No, Marcus. I don't need anything." She paused. "Why should I?"

But she did need something. Many things. All of them beyond his power to give.

And it seemed hard, so very hard, not to resent her.

Because she was the living reminder of all he stood to lose.

SURELY, it was a mean-spirited person who would not take joy in her own mother's delirious happiness. Surely, if she were truly selfless, she wouldn't feel the tiny, poisonous barb of envy pierce her skin every time Millicent extolled the virtues of her prospective husband. Nor would she have to force the words through tight lips when her approval of yet another item in her mother's lavish, endless trousseau was paraded before her.

But misery was a selfish beast, and Louisa couldn't help feeling thin paper cuts of pain every time she remembered that she would never know the joys of a husband and children or a household of her own, even for the first time.

Perhaps she couldn't prove her marriage, but it had happened, all the same. She'd taken those vows and she'd meant every word. She could not cast them off as lightly as a winter cloak.

The memory of Jardine's mouth against hers, his hands on her body returned, an aching torment. It was the height of cruelty, the way he took advantage of her weakness, time and again, despite rejecting her in the most brutal terms. A crime that she could never resist him. She loved him, and that made it so hard to say no.

She despised herself for giving in, but she could never seem to refuse him, even when she'd steeled herself time and again against his wiles.

"You don't think this is too much like mutton dressed up as lamb, darling?" Millicent's light voice broke into her thoughts.

Her mother pirouetted before the cheval glass in her boudoir, clad in a sprigged muslin gown that made her look like a debutante.

"Not at all, Mama. You are a picture to gladden any man's heart."

Millicent's features lit like moon glow. "Do you really think so, Louisa? You have such exquisite taste. I rely on your opinion utterly."

"When you begin to resemble any species of livestock, I assure you, I shall be the first to comment upon it."

Millicent tilted her head, giving her own reflection another doubtful survey. "Are you quite certain? Because I had thought these ribbons might be too fussy."

Louisa took a deep, calming breath.

The air was fragrant with lilac blossoms—overpoweringly so. Thank the good Lord above that her mother's wedding was set for the following week.

Smiling a little, Louisa pictured Woolly relating his plans for Millicent's entertainment abroad. Nothing could have been more calculated to please her mother in every respect. Millicent was more fortunate than she knew.

The door opened and Finch announced, "A Mrs. Burton has sent up her card, ma'am."

Millicent's vigorously plucked brows drew together. "Mrs. Burton, you say? Why didn't you deny me, Finch? I am not receiving visitors today."

"Beg pardon, ma'am, I did mention that you were not at home, but I gather it's Lady Louisa whom Mrs. Burton wishes to see." The glint in Finch's austere eye told Louisa the mysterious Mrs. Burton had given him a handsome douceur for unbending sufficiently to allow her access.

Calmly, Louisa rose and shook out her skirts. "Thank you, Finch. I shall be down directly."

Millicent wrinkled her brow. "Burton? Who is this Mrs. Burton?"

"A very agreeable lady," said Louisa. She hoped so, anyway. "I made Mrs. Burton's acquaintance last week at the British Museum."

If Louisa had mentioned meeting the lady in a brothel house, her mother could not have been more disapproving. "Bluestocking, is she? Honestly, Louisa. I don't know *where* you find these people."

"I told you, Mama, I found her at the museum."

Louisa moved to the door. "I assume you don't wish to meet her. I'll have the phaeton brought 'round, and we'll go for a drive."

Millicent made a little moue of disapproval. "Do as you wish, darling. Only take your wide-brimmed hat. With Mr. Radleigh's house party approaching, I don't want you to develop a freckle."

Refraining from rolling her eyes, Louisa gave the order to Finch about the phaeton, then tidied her hair and hurried downstairs to the drawing room.

As she walked into the cavernous salon, a figure standing at the window turned quickly, an expression of amused surprise sweeping her features.

The woman was no fresh-faced girl, but she was far younger than Louisa had expected an agent of Faulkner's to be—perhaps younger even than Louisa herself.

"Oh, how fortunate I am to find you home, dear Louisa!" The woman started forward, holding out her hands and drawing Louisa in for a kiss on each cheek, in the French fashion.

Louisa had an impression of vivid, cool beauty—blond hair, ice-gray eyes, a delicately provocative mouth—before she became immersed in a cloud of expensive scent, felt the soft press of a rose-leaf cheek against each of her own.

A little overwhelmed at this enthusiastic greeting, Louisa's body stiffened slightly.

Smoky eyes laughed at her with understanding and a hint of friendly derision. It flashed across Louisa's mind that this woman was everything she herself would like to be.

"Won't you sit down, Mrs. Burton? I've ordered my phaeton to be brought around. Would you care to take a drive with me?"

"Oh yes, indeed! I adore going on drives," said Mrs. Burton, managing to convey by her excess of enthusiasm that nothing could have been more calculated to bore her. "Do, please, call me Harriet, darling. None of this stuffy Mrs. Burton!"

Something offhand, almost contemptuous, in this Mrs. Burton's demeanor made Louisa's hackles rise.

Remember what you're doing this for. Remember for whom.

They conversed in vague pleasantries until the carriage was ready, and once they were seated in Louisa's vehicle, they dispensed with the groom and were on their way.

"I suppose you are wishing you'd never been saddled with me," observed Harriet in a tone that told Louisa the notion didn't bother her one bit. "Now, we must settle this before we go any further. How did we meet?"

"I told my mother we met at the British Museum."

"Oh no!" Harriet laughed. "What on earth would someone like Harriet Burton be doing at the British Museum?" She inclined her head towards Louisa's. "Harriet Burton, my dear, is frivolous and charming, with not two thoughts in her head to rub together. Merely adding up the years she has been married to the staid *Mr.* Burton taxes her tiny brain. No one concerns themselves about Mrs. Burton."

Louisa glanced at her companion and Harriet simpered back, her face transformed from the mocking, quick-witted woman who had turned to greet her in the drawing room mere minutes before.

They entered the park, moving at a brisk trot along the carriageway. Thank goodness this Mrs. Burton had turned out to be presentable, at least.

"We are here at the right time," she murmured, scanning the thickening crowds. "Much later and there won't be room to move."

"Let us drive on. We shan't take notice of anybody beyond a polite nod," said Harriet. "You, Lady Louisa, are so enchanted with my company that you don't wish for anyone else. Let us laugh"—Harriet broke off into a trill of mirth that sounded birdlike and sweet—"and appear to be the very best of friends."

Louisa gave a smile that could best be described as perfunctory. "How *did* we meet, if anyone asks?"

Harriet waved an airy hand. "Oh, I daresay we met in a

millinery shop, don't you think? You were there outfitting your mother for her bride visits and I desperately needed someone to advise me on the color of ribbons for my hat."

Her quick eyes took in Louisa's ensemble. "No one will wonder at that, for you are the epitome of elegance, my dear."

"Thank you." Usually, any kind of compliment embarrassed, but the tone of this one was too matter-of-fact to put her to the blush. "Oh, there is Mr. Radleigh. We should stop."

A delicate, gloved hand closed like a vise around Louisa's wrist. "Don't. Drive past and pretend you haven't seen him. You and I find each other too fascinating to be aware of anyone else."

Louisa cast a doubtful glance at Radleigh's tall form astride a showy chestnut gelding. They were almost upon him, but he hadn't seen them yet. He'd paused to reach down and shake hands with a dowager in her open landau.

"But our entire object in doing this is to gain you an invitation. . . ."

"We will, my dear. We will. But one thing you ought learn about men: they value more that which they cannot have. Make him chase you. Lead him a merry dance and when you snap your fingers, he'll come to heel."

"Just like a cocker spaniel," said Louisa dryly.

"Exactly. Men are simple creatures, you know."

The image of Jardine rose in her mind. "I've never found them so."

"Perhaps *you* have not, but I assure you that underneath, they are all the same." Harriet patted her cheek and Louisa's skin tightened in protest. "You are an innocent, my dear. But we can change that."

Ugh. The woman was patronizing her. How would she put up with this sort of thing for the months ahead?

Oblivious of Louisa's reaction, Harriet nodded complacently. "If you are seen in my company often and appear to find more delight in it than in his, Radleigh will be piqued. He'll wonder who I am. Then we'll all meet—accidentally, of course—and you will show how delighted you are with me, and he will be delighted, too. You will bat those remarkably sooty eyelashes and beg your indulgent beau to include me in his house party. He cannot deny you anything, so he'll be forced to say yes."

Seven

LOUISA could only be glad that Radleigh's house party took place so soon after her mother's wedding. Despite Millicent's vagaries, Louisa would miss her in the months ahead.

Now, as Louisa rode in a hired post chaise with the inimitable Mrs. Burton, she did her best to gather her courage. She trusted Harriet would be quick about completing her mission so Louisa could dissolve her false betrothal and leave.

"I am glad you decided to dispense with your maid's services on the journey," observed Harriet. "I wonder how you will manage."

There was a gentle malice in Harriet's tone. Louisa thought of the years she had *managed* without a personal maid, the years she had been housekeeper, maid, and sometimes even cook to keep her mother's household running.

"Yes, how *shall* I survive?" she said dryly. She waved a hand. "Never mind about my domestic arrangements. Just you concentrate on whatever business takes you there and on not getting caught." She paused. "Faulkner said Radleigh is dangerous."

"I wonder, then, that you agreed to do this," said Harriet pensively. She cocked her head, subjecting Louisa to intense scrutiny. "Is it naïveté? No, I don't think so. Foolhardiness? A little, perhaps.

When Louisa curled her lip, Harriet added softly, "Ah, I see. There is some personal imperative, isn't there? I wonder what it could be."

Her lips slowly curved into a smile as she tapped them with her fingertip. "What dirty little secret has Faulkner discovered about you?"

"Surely you know that I am too dull for secrets," Louisa riposted.

Harriet merely raised her brows and waited.

What was it about this woman that always made her edgy and defensive? Louisa carefully smoothed a wrinkle from her skirt. "Mr. Faulkner and I crossed paths on another occasion and I became aware of the work he does. When he asked this favor of me it seemed little enough I had to do."

She paused, then said softly, "You don't think I risk anything from this venture, do you? If you are caught, I will be the innocent dupe. Everyone knows how charming you are. I'll say I met you quite by chance and found you amiable and saw nothing but social ambition in your wish to be invited along to this house party. I don't see that I can be in any danger among so many respectable people."

"You are more naïve than I thought," murmured Harriet. "There are *so* many ways to arrange accidents, you know. Especially on a shoot."

Quietly, Louisa said, "If I am to be in danger, don't you think you owe it to me to explain why? Faulkner mentioned that the lives of many agents are at stake."

Harriet's face registered surprise. "He said that, did he? Well, I can tell you some of it, I suppose. Radleigh has managed to get his hands on a very sensitive document, a document that by rights should not even exist. He's only interested in money and prestige, not politics. We believe he intends to sell that list to the highest bidder."

"The French?"

"Perhaps." Harriet drew a long breath. "There are also possibilities closer to home."

"And what is the nature of this sensitive document?"

"We believe it's a list of agents employed by the secret service, operating both on British soil and abroad. We don't know how the rogue intelligence officer got hold of this information. Usually, operatives work in cells so that we ourselves might know one or two of our fellow agents at the most. A list like this . . . No one but the very high-ups should have that knowledge. We have a traitor in our midst."

There was a hard thrill in Harriet's voice, as if she relished the challenge before her, as if she looked forward to dealing ruthlessly with the miscreant. She added, "I've set up a dead drop with Faulkner in a Hindu temple on the estate."

Louisa hated being so ignorant, but she had to ask. "What's a dead drop?"

"It's a way of communicating with another person without being seen together. If I need to get word to Faulkner, I leave the message in the agreed place and Faulkner picks it up later. The temple is on the edge of the estate, so it will be easy for him to come and go unnoticed."

So, Faulkner would be lurking nearby. Strangely, the thought didn't comfort Louisa at all.

Harriet continued. "If anything happens to me, you can signal to Faulkner to get you out of there. A white ribbon means all is well but you haven't discovered anything yet, blue means you wish to meet. Pink signifies that the mission is compromised and you are getting out."

Louisa marveled at Harriet's composure. Intrigued, she asked, "This temple. How will you recognize it?"

"You can't miss it." Harriet gave a small snort of laughter. "It has erotic images carved all over it."

Louisa's mouth dropped open. What sort of man kept that kind of thing on his grounds, visible to whoever walked past? "The house sounds positively bizarre."

"Yes, it is. I hear Radleigh bought it and completed construction when the previous owner became bankrupt." She shrugged. "I believe he grew up in India. Perhaps the estate reminds him of home."

But Louisa was turning over the information Harriet had given her. That list. How had Radleigh come by such a sensitive document? Did it have Max's name on it? Jardine's? Hers, even? Surely, she wasn't important enough to be named. . . .

She took a deep breath. "I want to help you."

Harriet glanced at her. "You already are."

"No, I mean truly help. I want to do something worthwhile."

Harriet's face shuttered, and her voice grew hard. "If you want to do something worthwhile, give veils to the poor, Lady Louisa. Don't interfere with me."

THEY were only five miles from Radleigh's house, but Harriet insisted they stop for the night at an inn in the nearby village. "It's late. We'd do better to arrive in the morning," she said, unpinning her hat.

Louisa thought this reasoning a little odd but she made no comment. The establishment was clean and comfortably furnished, accustomed to housing the gentry. The landlady showed them to a private dining parlor, making no comment about the absence of ladies' maids.

For such a petite woman, Harriet's appetite was voracious. Louisa eyed her in awe as she popped the last sweetmeat into her bow-shaped mouth, having already consumed a hearty dinner of sole, oxtail soup, roast partridge and asparagus, green beans, and several removes.

Did Harriet's rich clothes hide straightened circumstances, or had a recent mission involved severe deprivation? Perhaps all that subterfuge simply sharpened the appetite. The only thing she took in moderation was the light table claret she'd ordered to go with their repast.

There was nothing wrong with Harriet's manners, however. She touched a napkin to her lips and rose gracefully. "I must leave you now, my dear. I have an errand to run. Don't stay up waiting for me. You need your rest."

Shivering, Louisa glanced out the window to the deep darkness beyond. "Do you think you ought to go alone? It's not safe for any woman, but for you . . ."

"Oh, aren't you sweet? But I can look after myself, darling." She tapped Louisa lightly on the cheek. "Never you mind about me."

She left with a swish of her cloak and a slight toss of her blond head. Louisa narrowed her eyes. She would dearly like to put Harriet Burton in her place.

The door closed behind Harriet. Louisa counted slowly to twenty. Then she flew up to her chamber and made her own preparations, secreting a tiny muff pistol in her reticule. She watched from the window for a few moments, until the shadowy figure of a cloaked and hooded woman crossed the busy courtyard to the stables.

In short order, one of the ostlers led a horse from the stables, saddled and ready. Louisa expelled a frustrated breath. Harriet would be long gone before she could even reach the yard. No hope of following her.

What was she up to?

Frustrated with herself for letting Harriet give her the slip so effortlessly, Louisa sat down to wait.

LOUISA woke to the sun streaming through the window and a killing ache in her neck. She blinked, squinted, and realized she still sat upright in her bedchamber chair. She must have fallen asleep waiting for Harriet's return.

She groaned a little. The side she'd slept on swarmed with the hot prick and tingle of numbness. She stretched and rubbed her arm until sensation returned, then sighed and rubbed her eyes, drawing slowly to her feet.

The inn maids had unpacked her things and her toiletries were laid out neatly on the dresser. She rang for hot water and a maid to help her dress. Soon, she felt much more the thing, alert enough to deal with Harriet, at least. She tapped quietly on Harriet's door.

No answer. Perhaps Harriet was still abed after her late night doing goodness knew what. For a few moments, Louisa stood there, undecided. Should she check to make certain Harriet had returned last night? But if she were in her room, asleep, Harriet would not thank her for waking her at this hour.

Louisa ordered breakfast for an hour hence and decided to go for a walk.

As she left the inn, one of the ostlers started toward her. In an urgent undertone, he said, "Ma'am, your friend did not return last night. The horse she took came back to the stables this morning without a rider. I think something has happened to her."

Louisa froze. Her fears had been justified. When Harriet so casually mentioned her errand, Louisa should have questioned her further, but she obviously hadn't been meant to know about Harriet's secret mission.

"Do you know where she went?"

The fellow shook his head with a frown. "I saddled the horse, that was all. I didn't even see which way she took."

Louisa scanned the yard, trying to make sense of the situation. Fear twisted in her belly.

She thanked the ostler and turned back into the inn to inquire if any messages had been left for her.

The flustered landlady quickly wiped her hands on her apron and turned to scan the pigeonholes behind the desk. "Ah, yes, m'lady. I do apologize. There is a message here, to be given to you on your departure this morning."

She handed over a note that had been twisted into a screw. Louisa opened it, aware that anyone could have come along and read the missive while the front desk lay unattended.

Harriet's note was short, obviously written in haste and in the knowledge that it might be read by eyes other than Louisa's.

Do not be alarmed. I am safe and unharmed, but find I cannot go with you. Forgive me.

The note was unsigned.

What?

The bottom fell out of Louisa's stomach. Harriet had left her to carry on the mission alone!

Louisa shivered in the sunshine. She wanted to turn around and retreat to the safety of London, let Faulkner deal with all of this. But she couldn't, not with so many lives at stake.

Not with Jardine's life at stake.

At the least, she ought to get word to Faulkner . . . Wait. No, she couldn't do that. He'd forbidden all direct communication after that initial meeting. Harriet was to have been the one to get word to him. What had Harriet called it? A dead drop, yes, that was it. Louisa, not Harriet, would have to seek out that shocking temple.

In a state of heightened awareness, Louisa jumped at every wayward sound as she took a light breakfast in the private parlor she and Harriet had hired. Her nerves thrummed. Her neck muscles ached with tension. She did her best to eat, though her stomach protested and squirmed.

She returned to her bedchamber and washed her hands and face and saw to the packing of her trunks in readiness for the remainder of her journey. Her movements were slow and deliberate. She couldn't stop her hands shaking, no matter how hard she tried.

What a poltroon she was! Harriet had been quite right to scoff at her nebulous wish to help. Lady Louisa Brooke had no skills, no training. When Faulkner discovered how matters stood, he would find another way to infiltrate the party rather than gamble the mission's success on her.

Was it cowardly to experience such a flood of relief? A day, at most, and she'd be finished with this dreadful engagement. She'd be free.

Eight

As Louisa's carriage swept around a bend in the long graveled drive, the full magnificence of Radleigh's home burst into view. She had the impression of pearl-white stone fashioned into a fantasy of minarets and arches, with one low-set crescent wing that swept outward like an arm ready to embrace all comers. Halfway down, the drive was flanked by a pair of stone elephants with their trunks raised, as if in welcome.

Louisa grinned in appreciation of the phantasmagoria before her, the copper onion-shaped dome that bloomed from the classical structure of the main house.

She stepped down from the carriage and supervised the footmen unloading her baggage. Did she imagine it, or did a faint whiff of spice lend the air an exotic tang?

The soft blue chamber allotted to her was on the small side, unremarkably furnished in the current English mode. But the view from the wide bay windows more than compensated for the unexpectedly mundane interior.

Acres of manicured green lawn were dotted with fountains and trees and grottoes like any other gentleman's estate. But the follies were Hindu temples and shrines, the formal gardens delicate and twisted and spare, like an Oriental painting. Farther from the house, however, the woods were wholly English. The juxtaposition intrigued her.

Her mother had unwittingly done her a favor, prevaricating about Louisa's love for the East. She'd have no need to explain her wish to explore the grounds while she looked for the temple Harriet had described.

Louisa removed her hat and gloves and washed her hands and face.

"If you please, my lady, would you like me to press something for you to wear this evening?"

Louisa started. Heavens, but she'd forgotten the girl was in the room. "Yes, the celestial blue tonight, I think. What is your name?"

The girl dimpled. "It's Merry, ma'am. I'll see to it right away. Will you require anything else, my lady?"

"No, thank you. But will you come back later and help me dress for dinner, please? My maid took ill on the road and I've no one to do for me, I'm afraid."

"Yes, my lady." The girl curtseyed. "You will find the rest of the guests in the drawing room, ma'am."

As Merry curtseyed and withdrew, it was on the tip of Louisa's tongue to ask the way to the drawing room, but she stopped herself. What better opportunity to reconnoiter a little?

She tidied her hair, took one last look at the view to get her bearings, then went in search of the drawing room.

Or, at least, in search of information.

By the time Louisa joined the other guests, she had a fairly good sketch of the second floor in her head. Despite its exotic embellishments, the house was laid out in a format common to houses of classical design. She was reasonably certain she could also predict the series of rooms she'd find on the first floor.

Of course, the focus of any search must be Radleigh's book room and perhaps his private apartments, as well.

She stopped, stock-still, in the cavernous hall. Was she mad? What had she been thinking, to plan a search for this sensitive document? She had no skills, no training, and not the least clue what the list of agents even looked like. She needed to get that message to Faulkner, abort the mission, break her uncomfortable betrothal, and leave.

She scanned the faces of Radleigh's other guests, looking for an acquaintance, or at the very least a slightly welcoming expression. No. No one she knew.

"Ah, there you are, my dear," Radleigh's pleasant tenor sounded behind her.

She turned on a gasp, her poise slipping like an ill-fitting mask. Recovering, she smiled back at him and curtseyed.

Radleigh bowed. "How do you do?" He took out his snuffbox and tapped it with a fingernail. "Mrs. Burton is not with you, I take it?"

"Mrs. Burton is indisposed and asked me to send her regrets," said Louisa.

He raised a pinch to his nose and sniffed, then blinked his muddy hazel eyes a few times. "How unfortunate. I do trust she will recover sufficiently to join us. Later in the week, perhaps."

"Yes, it is to be hoped she will." No one hoped that quite as much as Louisa. She feared, however, that she had seen the last of Harriet Burton.

Returning his snuffbox to his pocket, Radleigh took Louisa's arm and introduced her to his guests. She was relieved to see he didn't claim her as his fiancée, though his proprietary air left them in little doubt that such an announcement was imminent.

"And here, Louisa, I've saved the best for last," said Radleigh, leading her to a sofa on which two ladies sat.

The younger female was plump, curvaceous, and dimpled, with brown hair and green eyes and healthy roses in her round cheeks. The other lady bore all the hallmarks of a poor relation—shabby dark clothes, dark hair scraped back from her brow in a no-nonsense knot, and a certain gauntness about her neck and shoulders that made Louisa wonder if they kept the poor woman on half rations.

Louisa smiled impartially on them both. She glanced up at Radleigh and found herself arrested by the tender expression on his face. Clearly, he adored this girl.

"Lady Louisa Brooke, may I present my sister, Miss Radleigh?"

The young lady curtseyed, large eyes round with excitement and curiosity. Louisa suppressed a grimace. Lying to Radleigh was one thing. She didn't relish misleading an innocent girl.

"How do you do?" she murmured. "I'm so pleased to make your acquaintance, Miss Radleigh." Louisa spared an inquiring glance at the companion, but the poor woman went unnoticed.

"Oh, you must call me Beth, for we're to be sisters, aren't we?" The girl made an impatient shooing gesture at her companion. "Do go away, Honoria, so that Lady Louisa may sit beside me."

Unruffled, the diminutive companion turned to gather up her embroidery. When she turned back, Louisa held out her hand. "How do you do, Miss . . . ?" She sent Beth an inquiring look.

Far from abashed, Beth said carelessly, "Oh, that is Honoria Beauchamp, my companion. A dreary soul! Don't mind her." She offered Radleigh a saucy smile. "I never do."

The companion bowed her head and murmured a greeting, apparently eager to get away. Louisa allowed her to pass, but she blushed for Beth's rudeness. The glance she slid at Radleigh showed he'd no more notion of how bad such behavior appeared than Beth herself.

Seeing no alternative, Louisa sat in the space Miss Beauchamp had vacated. Radleigh made his excuses and drifted in search of other guests.

Louisa barely repressed a sigh of relief.

"I've wanted to meet you ever since I heard of my brother's betrothal," gushed Beth. "It must have been so romantic!"

"Oh, er, um. Yes. Yes, I suppose it was. We are keeping it secret for the moment, however. Just in the family, you know."

"Oh, you may rely on me. I'm *very* discreet."

Beth clasped her hands together and gave a little bounce. "Lady Louisa, I am *tremendously* glad you're here, for you will enter into my feelings *completely*."

The girl had an emphatic way of speaking that set Louisa's teeth on edge. But she smiled. "Are you in love, Miss Radleigh?"

She doubted Beth knew the meaning of the word.

Beth nodded, her eyes shining with puppylike devotion. "How did you guess?"

The sour spinster inside Louisa recoiled at the thought of listening to romantic outpourings. But her better self knew what was expected of her, and nobly, she rose to the occasion. "Tell me all."

"I have known him a bare week, yet it seems like an eternity."

Oh dear. This tale would not end well, she knew it in her bones. An ache for another young, passionately deluded girl echoed in her chest.

"I expect he's very handsome," said Louisa.

"Yes. How did you guess? I have never seen such a man before."

He is like a wicked god in human form. And he makes

you feel as if you are the most beautiful, most desirable woman in the world. . . .

Inwardly, Louisa shook herself, wrenched her mind away from that path. Instead, she looked about her, lending only half an ear to Beth's ravings about her lover. This would be the perfect time to assess Radleigh's guests.

It was a relatively small party, unless there were more guests yet to arrive. Foreign diplomats, a banker, minor European royalty. Did they all know why they'd been gathered here? It seemed a strange way to conduct the covert sale of a piece of intelligence.

But perhaps the eccentricity of it appealed to Radleigh. Perhaps he liked having them all here, dancing to his tune.

The half ear that was listening to Beth registered a word here and there. Only met . . . know someone in a week . . . feel as if I *do* know him . . .

Yes, it sounded all too familiar.

Suddenly, conversation halted. Beside her, Beth gasped, tensed, then seemed to quiver.

With a tingle at her nape, a sense almost of inevitability, Louisa turned her head.

There, in the doorway, stood Jardine.

For once, he appeared perfectly groomed, his unruly black locks trimmed and tamed to a recognizable style, his shirt points precise, the tailoring of his black coat so exquisite it was certain to make Radleigh swoon with envy.

Beth's hand squeezed her wrist so hard, Louisa winced. "There he is!"

Beth shot out of her chair and pelted across the drawing room. For one bewildered, crazed moment, Louisa thought the girl would leap into Jardine's arms.

Jardine's gaze locked with Louisa's over Beth's head. An instant of searing heat passed between them in that look, and then his gaze passed over her and he was smiling—*smiling*—down at Beth.

She couldn't remember seeing him smile in quite

that way for a very long time. Perhaps not since their courtship.

Pain squeezed her heart. Had Jardine thrown her over for *this*?

Why else would he have given her such a final farewell?

Cold washed over Louisa, wave after shocking wave. Why hadn't she thought of it before? Jardine wanted to marry someone else. That was why he'd given her those marching orders, told her she couldn't prove their marriage had taken place.

He sauntered toward her with Beth clinging to his arm. She simpered up at him as if he were her only reason to live.

Had she, Louisa, ever looked at him like that? Not lately. Perhaps not since the wedding that had never actually taken place.

She pinched the meat of her palm, sank her teeth into the inside of her lip, willed herself to preserve her composure.

When they stood before her, she wanted more than anything to bow her head and rush from the room. But she forced herself to meet his devilish eyes with a glaze of indifference in her own.

"Lady Louisa, may I present the Marquis of Jardine?"

Louisa inclined her head, as regal as Kate at her haughtiest. She raised her brows a little, the question in them clear—to him, at least: *How well do we know one another today?*

For an instant, Jardine's eyes glittered with a passing emotion she couldn't interpret.

He bowed. "We've met. How do you do, my lady?"

Beth looked from him to her and back again. "You know one another? Oh, now you have spoiled my surprise. I made sure to be the first to give you the news, my lord. Lady Louisa has consented to marry my brother. We shall be sisters! Isn't that altogether delightful?"

Wretched girl! Discreet, indeed! At this rate, the whole of England would know of Louisa's sham betrothal.

"I wouldn't know," murmured Jardine. "I never had a sister."

"Nor have I, but I'm persuaded it must be a very fine thing, indeed," said Beth, tucking her hand into the crook of Jardine's arm.

Louisa's gaze fixed on that comfortable intimacy. She couldn't seem to drag her eyes away.

With an effort, she cleared her throat. "Will you not sit down?"

Her stomach churned with the need to escape Jardine and his new inamorata's presence, but she couldn't let him see how greatly he hurt her.

With his usual elegance, Jardine disposed his long limbs in the chair she'd indicated while Beth plumped herself down beside Louisa.

"Tell me, Lord Jardine—" Was that her voice, all husky and strained? Louisa cleared her throat again and strove to modulate her tone. "Do you make an extended stay or are you merely a dinner guest?"

"Miss Radleigh has invited me spend the summer," said Jardine with a feline smile. "I shan't trespass on her excellent hospitality for quite that long, however. I have duties that will take me back to my estate in Wiltshire before the month is out."

"How pleasant," said Louisa, nearly choking on the words. Was she to endure Jardine's presence for the rest of her stay?

She caught herself. She *was* putting an end to this charade of an engagement and leaving as soon as may be. She'd made up her mind about that.

Someone else would have to infiltrate the party, find this errant list, and bring Radleigh to justice.

"We have such plans for your entertainment, you will be

amazed!" said Beth, wriggling in her seat like an excited child.

"I can hardly wait," murmured Jardine.

Louisa looked up at him sharply. There was a lazy glint in his eye. Was he up to something?

As Beth went on, enumerating the arrangements she'd made for her guests, Louisa's grip on her own hand turned brutal. But the more Beth talked, the less inclined Louisa was to believe that Jardine had fallen in love with the chit or had any serious intentions toward such a rattlepate. Besides, it was all too coincidental to ring true.

What was Jardine's real reason for being here? Had he merely used Beth to get an invitation to this party?

Perhaps he'd come to put a spoke in the wheel of Louisa's betrothal. If so, what did he plan to do? Even Jardine wouldn't accept a man's hospitality and then turn around and kill him.

Surely not.

Could he be here for the same reason as she was?

She frowned. That didn't seem right. If Jardine were here to find that list, why would Faulkner send her and Harriet to the house party at all?

Regardless, Jardine clearly enjoyed her discomfiture. Which of course made her determined to be excruciatingly polite.

"What a fascinating house this is, Miss Radleigh. I'm intrigued by the Indian influence I've seen."

Beth made a moue. "Not our doing, but Radleigh likes it. He was smitten as soon as he saw the place. I suppose it reminds him of our childhood."

She lowered her voice. "Some of it is quite . . ." She leaned forward to whisper. ". . . *Shocking*. Not at all the thing."

Was she referring to the erotically decorated temple Harriet had mentioned?

Jardine's lip curled. "Great art is often not at all the thing, Miss Radleigh."

Beth's face dropped ludicrously at the mild setdown.

With a slight smile, Jardine added, "Perhaps you ought to show me these despised creations. Then I can offer you my opinion."

The silly girl melted into a puddle of shining gratitude and hurried away to get her hat. Obviously, she'd missed the implications of Jardine's ploy to get her alone.

"Like shooting fish in a barrel, isn't it?" Louisa narrowed her eyes at him. "Jardine, she's a child."

"I find her . . . refreshing," he said. "I'm hardly in my dotage, either, you know."

"Using her to punish me is just about the most despicable thing you've done," she hissed. "Do you have an understanding with her?"

"Who said I was using her to punish you?" He threw his arms along the back of his chair. "The planets and all their moons do not revolve around you, strange as it might seem. *My lady.*"

Anger flared at the rebuke. Was she really nothing to him anymore? No matter how she suffered at his hands, she couldn't believe it. What about that desperate kiss in Richmond Park?

Oh, she knew better than to set store by the physical affection a man might show. But he'd kissed her as if they were the last mortals left in the world, as if his life would be nothing without her. Folly to believe it, and yet inside, in her *soul*, there was no doubt. They belonged together.

Her voice grew husky again. "How long have you known her?"

Shrugging, Jardine spread his elegant white hands. "A day? An hour? What does it matter?"

This bit of whimsy would have drawn a scathing reply if they hadn't been sitting in the midst of the other houseguests. His lips curved into a smile that held a hint of understanding and a healthy dose of challenge.

The ache in her chest flared to a knifing pain. Not jealousy, no. She knew he was shamming it. But this parody of courtship playing out between him and Beth cut her to the quick.

She looked away.

Beth returned, bonneted and flushed with happy anticipation. Louisa studied her, took in the sparkling green eyes, the warm honey tone of her hair, the lush curves of her well-developed figure. The adoration in Beth's gaze as she lifted it shyly to Jardine's reminded Louisa of another besotted girl, many years ago.

Jardine rose and offered Beth his arm.

Raw with pain, Louisa watched them go.

Nine

JARDINE escaped to the card room that evening in time to see Louisa denude her slender arm of a glinting bracelet and toss it on the table between her and Radleigh. It landed with a chink against its mate.

His jaw tightened. The intimacy of that little tableau made his blood simmer with rage. But he forced himself to hold back and wait for them to play out the hand.

If Radleigh had been any kind of gentleman, he wouldn't allow Louisa to stake personal valuables, but Radleigh was no kind of gentleman at all, was he?

Jardine watched as Louisa lost both her pretty pieces to the blackguard. Radleigh pocketed his winnings without a qualm.

Louisa gave a small shrug, as if the matter was of no consequence, but her eyes shot daggers. And for once, the daggers weren't for Jardine.

Not for him. He ought to be glad, but something inside

him reared up in protest. He wanted her glaring looks—all her looks—to be for him alone.

He slid into the chair Radleigh had just vacated.

"Fleeced you, did he, my little lamb?" He reached for the deck of cards, shuffling them between his long fingers.

He suspected Radleigh had cheated. The fierce storm of emotion in those blue eyes confirmed it. Her expression shuttered. Then, with a long, cool look, she answered. "Apparently so."

"Never mind. I'll send you another pair of bracelets. Prettier than those baubles you lost." He hesitated. "If you'd told me you were short of funds, I could have franked you."

"I'm not short," she snapped. "I just don't have the ready with me. And thank you for the offer but I'm quite capable of buying my own baubles."

Slowly, he nodded. "Your brother is generous."

"Absurdly so."

"He owes it to you, I should think."

Louisa bowed her head, refusing to reply. He gazed at the complicated arrangement of her pale blond hair, remembering how it streamed between his fingers like quicksilver, like moonlight.

He slapped the stack of cards on the table. "Will you cut?"

She complied and he shuffled, then dealt the cards.

"What stakes shall we play for?" she said.

"I don't want to take your money. Let's play for something else."

His gaze flickered over her suggestively. One hand crept to the diamond at her throat. Did he make her nervous?

Good.

He tilted his head. "Let us play for truth."

"Truth?" Her brow furrowed, and the tiny line across the bridge of her nose deepened. "What do you mean, truth?"

He leaned forward a little. "If I win, you tell me why

you are here, what you are doing with a jumped-up toad-stool like Radleigh."

She shrugged. "You already know the truth about that." She hesitated, her expression turning speculative. "And if I win?"

"You're not going to win."

She ignored the interjection. "*When* I win, you must tell me why *you're* here. What you are doing with Radleigh's sister."

"Done." There were many reasons for his presence. He could give her at least one true one. But he didn't intend to let her beat him, so it was a moot point.

The hands passed with little comment beyond the play. They were so evenly matched in skill it surprised him. There were large gaps in his knowledge of Louisa Brooke. The notion didn't sit well with him.

He was reckless, brilliant; she, more cautious, counted cards and calculated the odds. Luck remained firmly with the wicked, however, and Louisa was down by the final hand.

"These cards have been marked," said Jardine conversationally, running his fingertip over the slight scratch in the corner of an ace. "We ought to have called for a new pack."

He'd intended to rattle her and he succeeded. She played a card she should have kept. "I hope you're not accusing *me* of cheating."

He swooped on her mistake. "Hardly. What would you do if I were? Call me out?"

"At least admit I am as good a shot as you."

"Oh, undoubtedly. How do you fare with a smallsword?"

Her mouth twitched slightly, as if it wanted to smile. As if she imagined how satisfying it would be to run him through. The idea made his blood race, and most of that blood seemed to collect in his groin.

What did that say about him?

He let his gaze wander over what he could see of her, the low-cut neckline making the most of her sweet, small breasts. The single diamond nestled between them as if to symbolize the treasures that awaited a man bold enough to explore. That slender throat and angular, intelligent face, the cold fire of her eyes.

His.

If he lunged across the table, picked her up, and dragged her away with him, would anyone notice?

Hissing through his teeth, he forced himself to bide his time. If he showed more than a passing interest in her at this party, all he'd worked so hard to achieve would be lost. Almost as an afterthought, he played the winning card.

At her look of chagrin, he smiled. "This will be most interesting."

Apprehension spiked her gaze. Louisa had a secret. Important enough to keep from him despite the implied promise of honesty. But he was skilled in the gentle art of interrogation. He'd have the truth from her this night.

"And now, I shall claim my prize," he said softly. "Come." He rose and held out his hand to her. "There are too many eyes on us here."

Slowly, she rose and placed her hand in his, her gaze never leaving his face. How could she contemplate for a bare second becoming betrothed to another man?

As they left the room, a harsh voice spoke behind them. "Lady Louisa? Going so soon?"

Louisa didn't know whether to be relieved or sorry that Radleigh had stopped them. She'd been too intent on the play to spare a thought to what she'd say to Jardine if she lost. How did she tell the truth and still withhold the information she'd sworn to divulge to no one?

But never mind that now. She stood like a bone between two snarling dogs.

She directed a quelling look at Jardine. "Will you excuse me, gentlemen? I'd like to return to the music room."

"Of course." Radleigh bowed and held out his arm, which she ignored.

Jardine's lip curled. "Debts of honor must be paid at once, my lady."

"The debt will be satisfied tomorrow," she said stiffly. "I assure you, Lord Jardine, *I* don't forget my obligations."

She curtseyed to them both and slipped away.

Louisa returned to the music room to find that the opera singer had already made her triumphant finale. The room was abuzz, mostly with gossip over the flamboyant singer's latest aristocratic lover rather than her musical excellence. Beth's little companion was serving tea.

Beth pounced almost as soon as Louisa took her cup.

"Oh! I thought you'd never return. Honoria won't let me play cards for money, so I had to stay and speak to all the old ladies."

Taking her hand, Beth drew her to a sofa. "I'm so glad you're here. We can have a comfortable coze."

Listening to girlish confidences about Beth's current infatuation scarcely appealed. Louisa wanted to take the chit by the shoulders and shake some sense into her. But quite apart from the impropriety of such a course, if Beth was half as besotted with Jardine as Louisa had been at her age, nothing Louisa could say would sway her.

Louisa herself had never had the luxury of disclosing her feelings for Jardine to anyone. When they'd first met, Max had forbidden her to entertain the dashing Marquis's advances. He was dangerous, Max had said. Dangerous, reckless, and the most unrepentant rake to grace a London ballroom.

None of that had mattered to Louisa. The danger that clung to him excited her. The other women mattered not a whit when his dark eyes burned into hers.

But she'd been forced to keep her love for him to herself. They'd wed secretly. She'd been treading on air and rose petals.

And then, even before the sun set on their wedding day, he'd abandoned her, told her they must pretend they were strangers, that they'd barely met. That they'd never shared more than polite conversation, much less shared marriage vows and a bed.

She'd no choice but to accept his edict, despite the fact he'd never told her more than that her safety was jeopardized by her association with him. She could hardly compel him to stay with her without causing a scandal or involving Max. The two men had already come to blows over her. She'd been terrified that the outcome of their next fight would be the death of one of them, or both.

Perhaps she might have confided in her mother, or her other brother, Alistair. But she hadn't. She'd never dreamed the estrangement would drag on for years.

By the time she'd finished her tea, she'd heard far more than she wanted to know about Beth's youthful passion.

"I'm afraid I long for my bed," she confessed. "The fatigue of the journey, you know. An early night will set me up nicely for all the activities you have planned tomorrow."

Louisa slept fitfully, her mind too full of the day's events, her heart too sore to rest. The clock chimed two before she decided something must be done.

She would never sleep like this, so full of pent-up anxiety. She sat up, wishing she'd thought to bring a novel. Reading always helped when she had trouble getting to sleep.

She lit a candle and found her wrapper laid over a chair. With only the light of a single candle to see by, she stole down to the first floor and eventually found the library.

She searched the shelves that lined each wall.

Hmm. No novels. The books were all in pristine condition, as if they were never taken down from the shelf.

Had Radleigh collected all these volumes? He didn't

strike her as someone who valued philosophy and knowledge. Perhaps the books had come with the house.

There were many tomes on India, some in English, some in a language native to the country. There were books on natural history, Greek and Latin primers. . . . Ah, at last! Shakespeare's sonnets were old friends.

She eased the slim volume from the shelf and turned to go. Her eye caught on the massive mahogany desk that hulked in front of a large picture window.

Could the list be in that desk?

No, Radleigh would be a fool to hide a valuable document in such an obvious place.

But . . .

Perhaps a quick search would yield something worth knowing, some kind of clue.

She set the book down within reach, in case anyone disturbed her.

The desk drawers yielded nothing of interest. She ran her fingers over carved decoration on the desk, searched for hidden springs, false drawer bottoms, anything that might conceal the prize.

She pressed her fingernail into one innocuous curlicue, and what looked like part of the paneling shot from its home to reveal a small concealed drawer.

Louisa pounced, but all she found was a packet full of locks of hair, each tied with a thin ribbon, each a different shade and texture.

Well, well. Who was a naughty boy, then? Looked like Radleigh had his fair share of lovers strewn around England. Good Lord, there must be at least twenty of them—

A creak of floorboards made her gasp and drop the packet on the desk. Her hand flew to her breast. "Oh! How you startled me."

Ten

THE figure moved toward her, barely discernable from the gloom beyond the glow of her candle. The hairs began to stand on the back of her neck.

After a heart-stopping moment, the man approached close enough for her to discern his features. She didn't recognize him as one of the guests. He was of no more than medium height, neatly dressed. He had a balding head edged with a tonsure of short black hair, a mobile mouth, and the most brilliant black eyes she'd ever seen.

The expression in those eyes was understanding, even faintly sympathetic. "I am Saunders, Mr. Radleigh's secretary, ma'am. And you are Lady Louisa, I believe? Might I be of service?"

Then he saw what she held in her hand and his thick black brows drew together.

"Forgive me, I came to get a book, but then I . . ." She gestured to the desk.

Think! *Think . . .*

"I—It was wrong of me, but I wanted to know everything about him." She swallowed past her fear, and let her face crumple a little. "I'm well served for my curiosity, aren't I? It appears I have a rival. Several of them, in fact."

She did not need to feign trembling fingers as she held up the packet of mementos for him to see. Thank goodness Saunders had found her with nothing more incriminating in her hand.

The man drew closer. "It is not my place to say it, but you would do well to disregard what you found, my lady." Gently, he removed the packet of love tokens from her grasp. "Youthful peccadilloes, nothing more." Behind his spectacles, the obsidian eyes warmed. "I assure you."

If she'd had a handkerchief, she'd have put it to good use. Instead, she set back her shoulders and lifted her chin in a show of courage. "Thank you. I expect you're right."

She licked her lips. "You will not tell him I've been here? I'd be mortified if he found out, but I couldn't help myself." She shrugged, gave him what she hoped was a tremulous smile. "A woman in love."

A little startled and perhaps embarrassed at this gushing disclosure, Saunders inclined his head. "Of course, my lady. There is nothing to tell."

LOUISA retired to her bedchamber, shaken by the encounter, yet strangely exhilarated. She'd managed to keep a cool head in a potentially dangerous situation. If Radleigh had discovered her there, rummaging through his possessions . . . She shivered. Thank goodness it had only been his mild-mannered secretary.

The secretary seemed to wish for this alliance between her and his employer. She trusted he wouldn't jeopardize that by telling Radleigh about her little foray into his private papers.

She'd been convincing, though, hadn't she? Even if the

secretary did inform on her, he'd merely be reporting a piece of ill-mannered curiosity, rather than the ill-conceived bit of investigative work it had been.

She remembered something Harriet had said in the days leading up to the house party.

Always be on the lookout for someone close to the individual you're investigating who might help you. They will have more hope than you of getting the information you want.

As Radleigh's personal secretary, and one who lived in the same house, Saunders would be the most likely to know where Radleigh kept important papers. Perhaps he was privy to his master's secrets, as well.

Turning a loyal employee into an informant was a skill she doubted she possessed. She considered it from a few angles and decided it couldn't hurt to at least try to get to know the secretary better. One never knew . . .

And why was she concerned with converting Saunders to the cause? Why did she keep forgetting that she was out of this business now? She'd send word to Faulkner that the mission had failed, that Harriet had gone missing.

Tomorrow, Lady Louisa Brooke would break her false engagement, pack her bags, and leave.

Wouldn't she?

DESPITE her late night, the habit of a lifetime couldn't be broken and Louisa woke early to go for a ride.

"There you are, lovely," she murmured as her gray mare nuzzled her hand, nostrils quivering as she sniffed for the usual offering of an apple or a lump of sugar.

"Nothing today, I'm afraid, but I'll make sure I have a present for you tomorrow."

The groom saddled Miniver and led her out of the stall, assisting Louisa to mount.

She arranged her legs and her skirts, keeping a firm,

light hand on the reins as the gray danced and frisked beneath her.

"She's fresh, ma'am." The groom looked ready to catch at her bridle.

Louisa laughed with delight at the feel of horseflesh beneath her. "Oh yes, but we understand each other very well, never fear!"

Easily, she brought Miniver under control. "Is there a particular ride you recommend?"

The groom gave her directions. Apparently, he remained unconvinced of her horsemanship and offered to accompany her.

"No, thank you. I assure you, I'm accustomed to riding alone."

"But if there's an accident, ma'am—"

"Then I shall be well served for my arrogance, shan't I?" Louisa smiled. "No blame will fall on you. I promise."

She clicked her tongue and guided Miniver out of the stable yard. The gray yearned to gallop, but Louisa had a purpose and she kept the pace to a walk and stayed on the designated bridle paths rather than seeking open fields.

She was here to explore.

The reconnaissance was an interesting one, full of surprises. She passed strangely decorated grottoes and fountains, a thornery full of exotic plants, and wondered a little at Radleigh's choice of abode.

She'd gained an impression of a man who was all correctness and polish on the surface. Beneath, he seemed all too aware that his background didn't hold up to scrutiny. There was a hint of desperation in him, a craving for acceptance.

Why else would he want to marry her?

She shook her head. The ton might tolerate him for his money and political connections; it would never take him to its heart. Not even if he married a duke's sister.

With a sigh, she urged Miniver up a small rise, one that had been artistically arranged to afford a view of the extraordinary house.

Where was the temple that Harriet had described?

It wasn't as if she could ask for directions. Even if it hadn't been the site for the dead drop, the temple was full of erotic imagery. She shuddered at the gossip a maiden lady's interest would cause.

The morning was warm and sunny, with the faintest breeze ruffling the leaves, stirring the lush, green grass around her. Water hushed somewhere nearby.

She guided Miniver toward the sound and eventually came out at a small glade, a secluded spot surrounded on all sides with dense foliage.

Louisa dismounted, tethering the horse where she could lip at the grass on the edge of the clearing.

Water cascaded down a graded stone wall behind what appeared to be some sort of Eastern shrine. Hindu? She didn't know.

A female icon, perhaps a goddess, towered over the small glade. Her tongue protruded from her wide, ugly mouth. Her expression was fierce, grotesque, and while she otherwise had the body of a normal woman, as many as eight arms fanned out from her body.

One hand held a sword, one a ball-shaped object Louisa realized was a human head. Around her neck was a long rope made of skulls, and from her belt dangled a row of human arms. One of her bare feet rested on a man.

But it wasn't so much the strangeness of the figure, it was the skill of the carving that made Louisa catch her breath in wonder. There was life in that statue, fire in the goddess's eyes, a suggestion of movement in the arms and in the male figure who writhed at her feet.

A short flight of steps led to a raised platform in front of the figure.

Louisa tilted her head as she circled around the shrine. "Where did you come from?" she murmured. "What wonders have you seen?"

She wanted to touch it. Stripping off her gloves, she was about to climb up to the platform when Miniver whickered.

Louisa's head jerked around. Scanning the wood with narrowed eyes, she said, "Who's there?"

Jardine emerged from the shadows on foot.

Her eyes narrowed. "*You*. Have you been following me?"

He shrugged, let his gaze wander over her. "I didn't need to think too hard to guess where you'd be at this hour."

Was she so predictable? "I'm surprised you are not dancing attendance on Miss Radleigh."

The beautiful mouth sneered. "I've no interest in that chit."

The arrogance of him! "Well, she certainly has a lot of interest in you. Have a care there, or you might end up in parson's mousetrap."

His smile took on a hint of irony. "Oh, I'm quite adept at eluding snares. As you've cause to know."

She flushed and bit back an angry reply.

He lifted a hand toward her, then let it drop, his lips twisted in a grimace. "Ah, that was not well done of me, was it, Louisa? I should at least have the grace to admit our passion was mutual, while it lasted, should I not?"

He held out a hand to touch her face, but she jerked back. "Don't toy with me, Jardine. Mr. Radleigh—"

"You will not mention that bastard to me unless you want to see a bullet through his heart."

"Your threats won't change facts." Louisa fumbled with her gloves, tugging them back over shaking hands and fingers.

A seam ripped in her haste and awkwardness. She let out a frustrated exclamation. "Oh, why can't you leave me alone? Why did you have to come here?"

"I'm here on business that has nothing to do with you,"

said Jardine brusquely. "The girl was the easiest means of securing an invitation."

"I'm sure she'd be most happy to have been of service," said Louisa bitterly, giving her ragged glove up for lost. "She's more than half in love with you."

He shrugged. "Calf love. She'll recover. This is more important than some silly moonling's hurt feelings. Tell me what business brings *you* here, Louisa. Tell me what you're doing with him. Good Christ, of all men, why did it have to be Radleigh?"

There was something in his face, an earnestness, a desperation that stopped her breath. Ruthlessly, she suppressed the urge to assure him that he was the only man she would ever want. That the sooner her sham engagement was at an end, the better she would like it.

But she and Jardine—that torrid chapter of her life was over now. Why did he seek to prolong her agony?

"You lost the card game, Louisa," he reminded her. "I won the truth from you. Are you going to pay your debt?" He moved closer, his gaze dipping to her breasts and back to her face. "Or shall I collect a forfeit?"

Her eager, foolish heart urged her to accept the offer of a forfeit, regardless of her wounded pride.

But the memory of her weakness in Richmond Park rushed back. Despite all she'd felt, all she'd tried to convey in that passionate embrace, he'd left her with no assurances, and a little less pride than before.

That stupid card game! She couldn't tell him about Faulkner and the mission Harriet had passed on to her. She'd given her oath.

Louisa took a deep breath. "I—I was angry. I encouraged Radleigh to spite you."

That was the truth—partly. She'd accepted Faulkner's commission because Jardine had left her furious and bereft. Of course, she'd scorn to use another man to make Jardine jealous; but it *had* been a side benefit, she admitted that.

His black eyebrows drew together. "Spite? That's not like you."

Oh yes, the ever-compliant, obliging Louisa. Ready to subordinate her needs and desires to everyone else's, to make the best of a very bad lot.

Not this time.

Tightly, she said, "A woman scorned? How could you doubt it? I was in a temper at your callous dismissal, so I took up with Radleigh to make you jealous. But . . ."

Louisa licked her lips, then cursed herself for the betraying gesture. She shifted as Jardine's gaze focused on her mouth. "But as I came to know him, I discovered that Radleigh has many fine qualities."

Ignoring his incredulous snort, she went on, "This is my last chance for a family and a home of my own, Jardine. You're a man; you don't know what it's like to live as I've done for the past eight years."

"How did you and Radleigh meet? Who introduced you?"

Louisa hesitated. Did he suspect Faulkner's involvement? "I don't recall. Why do you ask?"

Pacing the bright green turf, he ignored her question, his gaze becoming distant as he pursued his own line of thought. "There *must* be a connection," he muttered. "But who . . . ?"

"I don't know what you're trying to get at."

"Let's just say I don't believe in coincidence."

"Coincidence?" She shrugged and began to turn away. "Jardine, if you're going to turn cryptic, I'm afraid I can't—"

He gripped her wrist and drew her back to face him. "There are things going on at this house that you don't understand."

She arched her brows. "Really? Well, perhaps you'd care to enlighten me."

She could hear Jardine's teeth grind at her impertinence.

"You slipped out to meet Radleigh last night, didn't you?" She opened her mouth to reply, but he cut through her denial. "Don't lie to me. I saw you."

Much as it rankled, she accepted his reading of her nighttime exploration. "And what if I did?" she said breathlessly, lifting her chin. "What business is it of yours?"

His face darkened with fury. "Did you let him touch you?"

At his expression, her courage dipped. All very well to poke a stick at a sleeping tiger, but she didn't want him murdering Radleigh in a jealous rage.

That he *was* jealous made no sense. Yet there could be no other explanation for his behavior.

She swallowed hard before answering. "Radleigh's a gentleman. He wouldn't press me to physical relations before we are married."

The derisive bark of laughter Jardine gave told her his opinion of her naïveté.

Jardine had always been deluded into thinking every man who looked at her twice must want to bed her. The idea used to tickle her sense of the ridiculous. Now, it seemed an attitude fraught with danger.

His voice turned silky. "If I catch you wandering the corridors at night again, I'll show you exactly what can happen to a lone female who's as trusting as you."

A thrill burned a path down her spine. "You wouldn't dare."

But she wanted him to dare, didn't she? That's how pathetic she was. She wanted him, even if he didn't care the snap of his fingers for her.

Jardine dashed a hand through his hair. "You need to leave this place, before you get yourself into trouble."

"Well, I'm not going," said Louisa, surprised to find that in that moment, she meant it. "How do you expect me to bow to your wishes when you won't even tell me why? What's all this about, Jardine?"

He seemed to struggle with himself. "For God's sake, can't you just trust me?"

For a full, incredulous minute, she couldn't speak.

Something flared in his dark eyes as knowledge settled over his face. His intent gaze faltered, flickered away.

"Trust?" she whispered. "Trust *you?*"

He took a ragged breath, gave a quick shake of his head. In a voice so subdued she barely heard it, he said, "Of course not. Why should you?"

Once, she would have trusted him with her life, her dreams, her future. Was that man still inside him, or had he become dead to all finer feeling? Despite the evidence of his recent conduct, she couldn't believe it.

Instinctively, she reached out to him, but he'd turned away from her and the moment was lost.

Fortunate that he hadn't registered that moment of weakness. If he had, he'd exploit it to the full.

Jardine's head jerked up, as if startled at a sound. She heard it a second later, a horse's hooves crunching on the bridle path, a murmured "Whoa there."

"Someone's coming." Louisa turned to scan the woods, trying to pinpoint where the noise originated, her brain already formulating an explanation for her presence here, alone, with a man who was supposedly a bare acquaintance.

"Jar—" She turned back, but he was gone.

Eleven

———— ✦ ————

"THERE you are, my dear." Radleigh dismounted and tipped his hat to her. "Ah, admiring the heathen idolatry, I see."

He took her arm in that possessive way he had, and she struggled not to pull from his hold. He handed her up the stone steps that led to the shrine she'd been about to examine more closely when Jardine had arrived.

The goddess was even more impressive up close. "A fearsome creature," Louisa murmured.

"Yes, it's the Hindu goddess Kali." He gave a faint smile. "You, being a good Christian lady, are probably shocked."

She tilted her head. "Not at all. The carving is beautiful." She reached out and trailed her fingertips along its ridges and curves.

"Isn't it?" Pleasure rang in Radleigh's voice. "Her purpose in this guise is to fight evil and fear. There's a legend about her. Would you like to hear it?"

With a glance at him, Louisa nodded.

"Kali was called forth to do battle with a demon that was terrorizing humans. The demon had the special power that for every drop of blood he spilled, another demon was made. The goddess saved the people by drinking the demon's blood and swallowing the spawned demons whole. She was so ecstatic with the taste of blood that she danced on the battlefield over the bodies of the slain."

"Charming!" Louisa said dryly.

A slight smile acknowledged her sally. "To calm her down, her consort, Shiva, was sent in the form of a crying baby. Kali finally quieted and put the infant to her breast."

Louisa gazed at this powerful warrior goddess. "She looks evil, but she's not, is she? I suppose one must be fierce, ruthless to fight true evil."

Perhaps, one must even sacrifice one's own principles. Was that what Jardine had done in his career?

There are things going on at this house that you don't understand.

She understood more than Jardine knew, but not as much as she wanted. Who was Radleigh beneath all that surface polish?

There was little room to move on the platform where they stood. She became acutely aware of how alone and intimate they were, in this secluded place.

Moreover, as her fiancé, Radleigh might expect her to show some affection toward him. She repressed a shudder. Not even for King and country could she feign pleasure at Radleigh's touch.

Though he didn't touch her, she felt the presence of his body all down her back, his hot breath stir the tendrils at her ear. She wanted to step away, but that would mean moving off the small ledge that gave the best vantage from which to view the statue. Then, it would be obvious she wanted to distance herself from him. Odd behavior in a future wife.

But she had told him she was cold, hadn't she?

Vignettes of her interactions with Jardine flashed

through her mind. She wished she could be cold when the occasion clearly demanded it. She'd never been able to resist Jardine.

Radleigh's hand cupped her elbow, making her start and turn her head. "Shall we go? I'll show you some of the prettier rides."

His thick mouth quivered. He'd made a double entendre that he hadn't expected her to understand. Louisa frowned a little and walked with him, doing her best not to jerk free of his hold. "No, thank you. I am a little fatigued and I'd like to return to the house."

At the bottom of the stairs, he did not release her.

Louisa repressed the impulse to jerk free. Did he mean to kiss her now?

Radleigh observed her reaction with the expectant, slightly malicious gaze of a cat waiting for its prey to recover from a swipe of its paw so it could bat the poor thing again.

"My dear," Radleigh's voice deepened, as if with emotion. "Much as I respect the finer feelings that lead you to wait, I'm impatient to have you as my wife. When can we set a date to marry?"

"Oh." Louisa hoped her face didn't betray the revulsion that clutched at her belly at the mere thought of being tied to Radleigh for the rest of her days.

"Indeed, I look forward to it, too, Mr. Radleigh, but—"

He held up a hand. "Please, not this formal 'Mr. Radleigh.' Call me Duncan."

She sucked in a breath. "Well, Duncan . . . I am impatient, also, but my mother would be inconsolable to miss my wedding. She will not be back from her own bride tour for two months, at least. I hate to, ah, prolong your suffering, but we must wait until she returns so she can celebrate the, er, happy day with us."

She forced her lips to smile. "I'm sure you understand."

That look of chagrin on his face couldn't possibly be from any personal yearning he felt for her, could it? He stepped closer, air shooting from his nostrils like a blown horse. Despite her resolve to appear accepting of any advances he might make, she shrank back.

Radleigh's entire aspect changed. His expression lightened and his body relaxed. "Are you afraid, my little dove?" He chuckled, prepared to be indulgent. "I won't hurt you."

She lifted her chin. "Not at all, but it would be more fitting to save *that* sort of thing for after we're married, don't you agree?"

She'd explained to him that she didn't seek intimacy. She hoped he'd take her reluctance as maidenly modesty rather than the fear and revulsion it was.

He stared at her for some time, as if watching for an outward sign that would permit him to disregard her verbal denial. She tried not to hold her breath. Instinctively, she knew she must not show him fear.

All at once, her vulnerability struck home. They were alone, more than a mile from the house. He could throw her down and rape her, and no one would be the wiser.

And why she should think that way, she couldn't fathom. He unsettled her greatly.

She made herself break the connection of their gazes and walk over to her horse. The mare snorted and pawed the ground, still restless.

She stroked the mare's flank. *Sorry, old girl, no gallop for you today.*

"Let me help you."

His voice startled her so much that she jumped. She hadn't heard him approach so close.

She wanted to refuse but that would sound churlish. "Thank you, sir." She lifted her foot for him to give her a boost up, but he disconcerted her further by gripping her waist and lifting her clear off the ground.

The sensation of utter helplessness made her give a

choke of distress. Her eyes met his, and she couldn't hide
her momentary panic. His smile broadening, he deposited
her carefully in the saddle as if she weighed no more than
a little girl.

She fussed with her skirts in an effort to regain composure. The only means she had of keeping him at bay was to
affect an aristocratic hauteur. "Thank you." She gave him
the kind of dismissive nod that she'd give a groom. "I'll see
you back at the house."

In an ironic gesture of farewell, Radleigh touched his
hat, hard eyes glittering beneath its brim.

AFTER a light nuncheon, Louisa escaped for another
exploratory foray. The day was brisk with breeze and
sunshine. The ribbons of her chip straw hat fluttered and
her walking gown flirted around her kid half boots as she
made her way down the terrace steps.

This time, she knew which direction to take, having
carefully and, she hoped, subtly elicited the information
from Beth.

Mercy, but the house party would be even more intolerable if Beth sought to commandeer every minute of her
guests' time. A hostess made available any number of activities for her guests' enjoyment, then left them to their
own devices. It was the height of gaucheness to schedule
and choreograph their movements as if it were a military
exercise.

The girl would soon be worn to the bone, at this rate, or
else her guests would soon recall sudden pressing engagements elsewhere.

A pity that companion of hers didn't drop a word in her
ear, but perhaps bumptious Beth wouldn't have listened
anyway.

Cool, water-spritzed air met Louisa as she passed a
fountain surrounded by lily pads in an interesting geo-

metrical design. The rush of water was such a soothing sound, she could have stopped there, but she had a mission to accomplish.

"Halloo there!" A voice rose above the cascade of water. *Oh no.* Louisa's shoulders tensed. She stopped and turned around.

Beth hurried toward her, waving her handkerchief madly and puffing a little. "Oh! I'm so glad I caught up with you, Lady Louisa." Without asking permission, she linked arms with Louisa and walked with her in the direction Louisa had been heading.

No hope for it, then. Louisa plastered a smile on her face. "Beth! How kind of you to join me."

She heartily wished she could extract herself, but she couldn't think how to manage it without giving offense. Repressing a sigh, Louisa slowed her steps to match Beth's.

"I saw you walking all alone and thought you might need company."

Beth smiled engagingly up at her. She was a full head shorter, which made Louisa feel like a gangling giraffe.

Oh dear. Not more confidences about Jardine. She couldn't bear it.

"What a pretty day," she said quickly, glancing about her as if only noticing the weather for the first time. "The men took their guns out this morning, I believe."

Louisa would have gone with them, if not for the need to find this temple. At least on the moor she'd have been free of her garrulous hostess.

Beth's dawdling pace was getting on her nerves. "I have an ambition to see if I can walk to the top of that rise over there."

She couldn't afford to take too much interest in the temple while Beth accompanied her, but she could at least judge how far it was from the house and any escape routes in case of trouble.

Always look for the exit, Harriet had told her. *Map out in your mind how you'd get away.*

Amazing how many small pieces of wisdom Harriet had imparted over the course of their time together. Had she guessed this situation might come to pass?

Beth was rambling on about meeting Louisa's family. Thankfully, she excelled at making a lot of suppositions that required no response from Louisa. Thank heaven Louisa would be at liberty within the next day or so, if she chose. She'd never have to meet Beth again.

Loathsome to have to play the jilt, of course, even to such a character as Radleigh. He'd pinned his hopes of advancement on this marriage. She felt a twinge of remorse, but suppressed it. If Radleigh was caught committing treason, a broken engagement would be the least of his worries.

Beth rattled on. "I suppose your people are very grand. I should be quite terrified to meet them."

Louisa smiled and shook her head. "Oh, not at all. Quite the contrary. My father is no longer with us, but my mother is like a pretty butterfly, even tempered and sweet. She recently remarried, you know, and my new stepfather is all that is amiable."

Louisa stopped, searching inwardly for that stab of regret and envy that had been with her throughout her mother's courtship.

Nothing.

Strange.

"What about your brother, the duke?" Beth asked, as they wound through a shady wooded stretch.

"My brother never expected to come into the title, so he was not bred to the role. He is the best of men. Straight to the point. No nonsense or flummery about him, no puffed-up conceit. He is, perhaps, the least likely duke you might come across, but also the very best kind."

"Oh." Beth seemed a little disappointed not to hear tales of pomp and ceremony. "And his wife?"

"Ah, Kate is pure delight and she leads him a merry dance, which is wonderful to see." Louisa grinned, thinking of her friend. "There is nothing better than a strong man felled by love, is there?"

And wouldn't Kate have relished the adventure into which Louisa had stumbled? There'd be no question in Kate's mind about whether to stay or go. She'd pursue this mystery and fight anyone who tried to stop her.

If only Kate were here . . . But no, much as she loved her sister-in-law, she didn't want Kate's or anyone else's help.

Suddenly, Louisa felt alone as she'd never felt before.

No, not alone. *Independent.*

As they rounded a bend, the wood fell away and the infamous temple came into view.

Louisa started toward it, barely conscious of shaking off Beth's hold.

"Oh, pray, Lady Louisa. Do not go up there." Beth panted as she struggled to keep up, muttering, "Oh, how unfortunate!"

"Fascinating!" Louisa called back, her heart suddenly light. "What do you call it?"

"Oh no. Oh *dear*! This is most indelicate. Indeed, I don't call it anything. It is not a subject that one should mention in polite company."

And yet, Beth had mentioned it obliquely, hadn't she? Louisa couldn't help teasing a little.

"Well, let us pretend we are not polite and satisfy our curiosity, shall we? The carvings look marvelous at this distance. Goodness, it's like one of those dripping castles one made as a child out of wet sand."

As they neared the temple, she saw the cause of Beth's consternation.

Louisa's lips trembled in shocked enjoyment. Oh, what she'd give to have shown this temple to prudish Kate!

Tier upon tier of figures in all kinds of improbable na-
kedness filled her vision. She glanced at Beth, who was
blushing furiously and averting her own gaze.

"Oh, don't be such a ninny," said Louisa, though heat
had risen to her own cheeks, she was sure. "Come on."

She went inside, where it was degrees cooler and the
decoration was slightly less detailed but even more outra-
geously wicked than outside.

The people depicting every kind of sexual act were
obviously Indian, and remarkably flexible, if their antics
were any indication. The women's bodies were rounded
and lush, making Louisa acutely aware of her own lack of
endowments.

Speaking of endowments . . . Louisa's eyes widened
a little. Surely, those figures weren't carved in accurate
proportion.

"Oh, Lady Louisa, do come out of there! I am so mortified, I . . ." Louisa shut out Beth's wailing and stifled her
own prurient curiosity to glance about her.

The interior of the temple was roughly the same size
as a parlor, with cushioned benches lining the walls and a
table in the center. Obviously, the structure was used for
some kind of entertainment, rather than worship. She'd
prefer not to guess the nature of that entertainment, but she
had a fair idea.

Louisa mulled over what Harriet had told her. A blue
ribbon to request a meeting, white for all is well but nothing discovered. Pink was the distress signal, the one that
meant she wanted to get out.

There were any number of places she might leave the
signal for Faulkner to find. But she needed somewhere he
would think to look, yet would not be immediately obvious
to a casual observer.

The fringed Oriental rug that covered the central table
seemed like a good choice. She might tie a ribbon around
one of the tassels at the corner. To a casual observer, it

would look as if it were meant to be there, yet someone searching for a ribbon would not miss it.

She left the temple feeling rather smug and slipped her arm through her gibbering companion's. "Please stop that, Beth, or I shall be obliged to slap you," she said pleasantly, turning and drawing Beth back down the hill.

Beth gulped and sniffed and shuddered, her eyes very wide and fawnlike. She looked as if no one had ever spoken to her in such a way before.

Louisa fished out her handkerchief and handed it to Beth. "There you are. Truly, there is no need to cry. I won't tell anyone where we've been."

Beth nodded and gulped and blew her small nose with an inelegant snuffle. Her face was blotchy, her eyes red. Goodness, how could Jardine even contemplate making up to such a wet fish?

But she'd calmed down enough to fold Louisa's handkerchief into a neat square and offer it back.

"No, er, you keep it, dear."

Beth raised her watery gaze to Louisa's face and gave a tremulous smile.

Louisa nodded as she stepped out at a brisker pace. "That's the barber. Now, do tell me. How far is it to the village? I have ribbons to buy."

Twelve

THEY gathered in the drawing room before dinner with the rest of the guests. The men were boring on endlessly about the grouse they'd shot that day. Louisa found the masculine drone comforting and wished she might join in.

But of course, she sat with Beth, sipping ratafia, which she loathed. Jardine sauntered over to them, the ever-present challenge in his eye, with a hint of animosity mixed in.

That look energized her, made the blood course hotly through her veins. In the past eight years, she'd been almost dead to excitement, moving through the days like an automaton, except on those rare occasions when he came to her. Now, she felt as if her body had reawakened, and it wasn't only his presence that did that to her, made excitement clench in her belly.

It was the danger, the uncertainty, the heady feeling that what she did here was important, vital.

In that instant, she knew she would not leave a pink ribbon at the temple tonight.

"May I?" He indicated a chair next to Beth's. So polite! The consummate gentleman.

"Of course!" Beth's attention was all on Jardine.

He disposed his long limbs in the chair, crossing his legs in a negligent way he had, swinging one foot as though he hadn't a care in the world.

Beth looked as if she longed to climb into his lap.

Jardine's attention swung back to Louisa. Forestalling whatever acid comment he seemed about to make, Louisa said, "We were just discussing hunting and so forth. Have you taken your gun out yet, Lord Jardine?"

Those mobile eyebrows climbed a little. "I beg your pardon?"

"Mr. Radleigh told me he bagged a brace of partridges this morning." She widened her eyes a little. "Have you taken out your gun?"

The corner of his mouth twitched. "I must confess I am a little out of practice. But I hear you are proficient in the art, Lady Louisa." His smile grew wicked. "Perhaps I might persuade you to help me fire my piece."

If she'd been given to blushing, she would be as red as sealing wax, but fortunately, that wasn't one of her weaknesses. "By all means. I'd be happy to lend you the benefit of my . . . advice."

"Oh, shooting!" Beth shuddered dramatically. "Honestly, just hearing the awful bang makes me scream and put my hands over my ears."

"You get used to it," said Louisa, never taking her eyes from Jardine's. "The sport can be most . . . satisfying. Don't you agree, my lord?"

His eyes burned into hers. "Yes," he said softly. "If one has the skill and the patience to do it correctly. And one needs the right teacher, of course."

"Naturally." Louisa smiled, holding his gaze. "It's so easy to rush things, and go off half-cocked."

Jardine's foot stopped swinging. His fingers tightened their grip on the armrest of his chair.

Interesting.

At least she hadn't been mistaken about the heat between them. It survived, powerful and volatile as ever.

She'd have to watch herself. While they sat in a room full of people, she was safe. Heaven help her if he got her alone after she'd taunted him like that.

Louisa turned her attention to Beth, whose elegant brows knitted in puzzlement, as if she sensed some underlying meaning to the conversation but couldn't fathom what it was.

Thank goodness for small mercies. Louisa could tell the girl was innocent, if a little too obvious in her affections. Jardine was altogether too much for Beth to handle, that was certain. It would be like pairing a wolf with a spaniel pup.

Louisa took a long sip of her ratafia and suppressed a grimace.

Jardine reached forward, his long fingers closing around hers, which were curled around her glass stem. "May I refill your glass for you, Lady Louisa?"

The heat of his fingers pressing against hers sent her senses reeling. Before she knew what she did, she nodded.

Jardine went to the sideboard with the beginnings of a cock-stand in his trousers and a burning desire to carry the sly minx upstairs to show her exactly how he could use his weapon to best effect.

The bawdy innuendo in her banter had taken him by surprise. He trusted he was the only one to receive the benefit of such wit. If that was how she flirted with all those suitors of hers, she'd soon find herself somewhere with her skirts up around her ears.

The image that thought pulled up made him swallow hard.

He poured ratafia, smiling grimly. At least he could torture her a little, too.

A drop of ratafia spilled on his hand. He set down the decanter, raised his hand to his mouth, and sucked. He tasted the almond-laced sweetness, imagined tasting that same flavor on her mouth . . .

His fingers tightened around the glass. Damn her, she had him tying himself in knots. What game was she playing now?

He returned to hand Louisa her drink. Again, their fingers made fleeting contact. A jolt of pure lust pounded through his body, as if he were a schoolboy who'd never known a woman's touch.

He recovered, but not soon enough, for when he met her gaze, he detected a sensual knowing in those ice-maiden eyes. An awareness, a confidence he'd never seen in her before.

What had brought about this change?

The idea that leaped to his mind made his blood burn. He glanced to where Radleigh stood, his golden head bowed a little as he listened to a garrulous dowager whose turban only reached his shoulder.

Had Louisa been intimate with him last night? Something in her demeanor when he'd questioned her had told Jardine that wasn't so. But now, the knowing in those eyes gave him pause.

When they moved in to dinner, he offered his arm to Louisa. They were the highest-ranking guests, so it would not seem odd that he'd done so.

But he'd moved toward her as if no one else existed, as if she were a magnet and he a hapless iron filing that lay in her path.

She laid her fingertips on his arm and his whole body tensed. As she moved at his side, her skirts hushed around her, brushed his legs with a gentle, whispered caress that tingled down his spine and wrapped loving fingers around his genitals.

Oh Christ. This was exactly what he didn't need.

He handed Louisa to the chair beside him and waited for the footman to seat her. The brief connection ended abruptly, left him frustrated and shaken.

Shaken? His body vibrated like a bloody tuning fork.

God help him, but his resolve to stay away from her seemed flimsy as spun sugar. He didn't know how he'd get through the house party without strangling her or having her.

Either way, he was heading straight for disaster.

According to Harriet, the best time to prowl a house was at about four o'clock in the morning, when most people slept the deepest.

Louisa eased open one of the long windows in the orangery and stepped over the sill.

The gibbous moon shed baleful light on the landscape. Enough to see where she was going, at least. She didn't dare unshutter her lantern until she was well clear of the house. If anyone saw her, she would lose her reputation. If Radleigh saw her, she wasn't sure what he'd do.

She passed the fountain, which had been turned off for the night. The still water limpidly reflected the night sky. She avoided the path that crossed the open garden and instead skirted close to the house, melting into a stand of trees as soon as she cleared the building. This way was longer than the path she and Beth had taken earlier, but she was less likely to be seen from the house.

Nervous despite her newfound resolve, Louisa glanced over her shoulder as she moved deeper into the wood. Night creatures rustled, and the sudden flap of bats' wings made her jump and let out a breathy cry.

Ninny. What sort of secret agent was she, to start at every stray sound?

She firmed her grip on the lantern. Should she open the shutters now? It seemed safer not to, even while screened by forest. She forged on, thankful for her walking boots on the uneven terrain and for the moonlight that shafted through gaps in the tree canopy to pick out her path.

Judging herself to be far enough from the house to circle back toward the temple, she turned down a narrow trail.

Her heart pounded and her breathing quickened. The night was cool and mercifully fine. A stiff breeze ruffled the leaves on the stand of copper beeches, a steady rustle and hush that seemed to whisper a warning.

Louisa reached the clearing at the foot of the temple hill. A warm spurt of triumph rose in her. She'd judged correctly where this route came out.

She skirted the hillock on which the temple stood. If she angled up toward the back of the building, the hill itself and its backdrop of foliage would conceal her from the house.

As she approached the temple, her heart stepped up its hammering. Air sawed through her lungs. Deliberately, she stopped. Drew a long, deep breath and let it out. Then she put her head down and continued the climb.

There was only one entrance to the temple. She scanned the surrounding landscape, her eyes accustomed by now to the darkness. Nothing, as far as she could tell. She listened, but no foreign sound disturbed the night.

Louisa ducked around the small building and flattened her back against the wall. After assuring herself there was no one lurking inside, she slipped within.

She was reasonably certain no one had followed her here. If they had, she'd settled on an explanation for her conduct. She'd say she came to look at the fantastically erotic carvings. It would be a mortifying admission of prurient curiosity, but more believable than that Lady Louisa Brooke had turned spy. Safer, too.

Always assume you're being watched. Harriet's crisp accents popped into her head.

Following that advice, Louisa forced herself not to dispose of her ribbon straight away. She opened the shutters on her lantern and made a show of inspecting the scenery.

A cursory examination earlier that day in Beth's company had given her the impression of a series of writhing bodies and impossibly dimensioned body parts in a tangle of limbs and strange positions.

As she peered at the figures more closely, Louisa realized that not only were there figures of one man and one woman copulating but sometimes three or more people were depicted, doing unspeakable things to one another.

She gasped, angled her head a little. Did men and women really . . . ? It looked virtually impossible to achieve that kind of balance, but she'd heard that people in the East were capable of incredible feats that boggled the Western mind.

Blood pounded in her cheeks. She tore her gaze away. *Mind on the job, Louisa!*

What now?

Always assume you're being watched.

She turned and craned her neck, as if inspecting the figures on the wall opposite. As she moved toward the table in the center of the room, she pretended to stumble.

With a low exclamation, she set the lantern on the table and bent as if to tie her bootlace. Using her body to shield what her hands did from the wide opening to the temple, she tied the blue ribbon onto the tassel of the rug and quickly rose.

As calmly as she could, Louisa made another show of inspecting the carvings, just to be on the safe side.

"Well, well. If it isn't Lady Louisa."

Thirteen

"Damn, damn, damn."

Louisa muttered under her breath as she turned around.

A faint smile curved Jardine's lips. Brows raised, he sauntered farther into the temple.

She decided to go on the offensive. "What are you doing here?"

"You thought I wouldn't follow you?"

Thank God she'd masked her movements when she'd tied that ribbon. Perhaps he'd been fooled. Perhaps she might deceive this master of deceit.

He wore only shirtsleeves and breeches and his black hair was rumpled as if he'd risen from bed to follow her.

How had he known when she'd make her escape?

He took a long, considering look around, and the significance of their surroundings hit her with the force of a cannonball. She cringed as those sharp, dark eyes took in all the luridly displayed couples copulating with flexible abandon.

Jardine's gaze returned to her, glittering with heat. Slowly, he walked toward her. With each step, the tension in her body wound tighter. Her heart thudded in her throat. Her mouth abruptly went dry.

Her mouth. His gaze latched onto it, then traveled lower, down her body, and she felt it like a hot liquid caress inside.

"I—" Her voice came in a husky whisper. Determined, she cleared her throat. "I must go. We cannot afford to be seen together like this."

She tried to sidle around him, but he caught her arm in a firm, inescapable grip.

He didn't hurt her, but she winced anyway. His touch was torture. It was bliss.

"Why did you come here, Louisa?"

She bowed her head, swallowed, then lifted her chin. "I was curious."

"You are not meeting someone?"

"What? No! Is it likely I'd arrange to meet anyone, much less in this locale?"

Jardine let go of her and shrugged. "I'm not altogether certain I know what is likely that you would do anymore, Louisa. I'm not sure I know you."

She remained silent.

"Your betrothal to Radleigh." He spread his hands. "That, I did not expect. And somehow, I still can't believe you did it."

"Believe it," she snapped.

If only she'd never got herself caught up in this tangle. But the blue ribbon on that rug committed her even further to the cause. She couldn't tell Jardine about her mission, or he'd whisk her away from the estate quicker than she could blink.

"Then what are you doing here, among these orgiastic delights, Louisa? Isn't your future husband satisfying you?"

Before she could stop herself, her hand flew up to slap his face. But his reflexes were dagger sharp. He easily deflected the move, brushed her hand aside as if it were a fly. Moved closer with purposeful intent etched over his patrician features.

Those devilish eyebrows deepened in a frown.

Louisa started backward, a hand on the table to steady herself. He followed, and she retreated, until her back flattened against the wall.

The bumps and rough edges of the carvings dug into her back as she pressed into them. She swallowed, but it was as if a huge ball of stone wedged in her throat.

Jardine's beautiful mouth formed a sneer at the way she'd so stupidly worked herself into a corner. There was nowhere to run. She had to stand and fight.

"If it becomes known that you and I were here like this, there'll be a scandal. You'd have to take me as your wife."

"It won't become known." He raised one hand, bare of a glove. His fingertips feathered her cheek. The gentleness of his touch lay in odd contrast to his harsh expression.

She shivered. Anticipation coiled tightly in her chest. "Don't. I don't want you to—"

He lowered his head to capture her earlobe in his teeth.

Ohh. He knew that always drove her to madness.

Briefly, he bit into the fleshy lobe, sending hot chills through her body, then released.

"No?" Warm air caressed her neck, made her melt inside.

His lips slid down her throat and more tingles cascaded through her. Her body flourished and opened like an orchid in the tropical heat.

"No," she whispered. "Please don't." But she was already ripening, drinking him in like the sun.

He lifted his head to look into her eyes, pressed two fingers to her mouth to stop her protest. She was breathing rapidly, her mouth parted to suck in air.

He dipped his fingers into the moisture, running them

over her tongue. Gently, he dragged his fingertips downward, drawing her lower lip into a sensual pout. Releasing it, he smeared her moisture over her upper lip, circling again to the lower.

She felt his gaze, intent on her mouth as he did this, slowly, carefully, over and over. By the time he bent his head to taste, her lips tingled with sensitivity.

The leisurely caress of his mouth on hers made her knees buckle. He caught her around the waist, pulled her against him.

She gave a shuddering sigh at all that masculine heat and hardness pressed against her. He deepened the kiss, tantalized her with slow strokes of his tongue. And she was his, as she always would be his to take.

How she'd missed this. She'd almost forgotten that wild sensuality he awoke in her, the need to give him everything, to do unspeakable things with pleasure and wholehearted trust.

Trust.

Could she bear to trust him again? He'd rejected her. He'd refused to acknowledge her as his wife.

His hands molded her hips, traveled up her waist to cover her breasts, teasing her aching nipples.

In spite of her growing unease, the place between her legs grew damp and needy. He seemed to know it, because his hand bunched up her skirts, reached beneath.

"Ah, Louisa. It's been too long."

Her heart twisted. How could he speak that way, with a voice so full of raw emotion? Yet he'd still discard her like a used mistress when he was done.

"No."

He didn't hear her. His hand skimmed up her thigh.

"Jardine, I want you to stop."

She shoved at his chest, suddenly frantic. "Jardine!"

She said it sharply enough to penetrate. His head jerked up. He was breathing hard, his lips a little swollen, his eyes glittering with passion.

Gasping for air, she rested her head against the wall. "I can't let you do this."

"Let me? You were begging me a moment ago."

He closed in, as if to resume his assault, but she held him off. "You don't want me."

His incredulous look made her say, "I mean you don't want me as your wife."

He continued to stare at her as if he didn't understand plain English. A small dart of satisfaction that he didn't seem quite as knife-witted as usual sang through her.

She raised her brows, silent, though her blood still pounded through her veins, though she wanted to take his stupid, stubborn head between her hands and dash some sense into it, then pull it down to her for a kiss.

She sucked in a breath. "I believe there is an expression about cows and giving their milk away that, though crude, is apt in this case."

Men don't buy the cow when she gives her milk for free. Where had she heard it? From one of the maids, probably.

He ran a hand through his hair. "That old chestnut," he muttered. But he didn't meet her eyes.

With a stab of pain, she noted he didn't argue the point. How could she be alone in this, every time? Their passion had been so all-consuming, so right, she'd hoped he'd be swept up in it, as she had. That he'd beg her to come to him and be his wife.

Wife. Radleigh. Oh, confound it! A fine time to recall she had a more obvious reason not to allow further intimacy.

The deepening look of the satyr on Jardine's face told her that the thought had struck him, too.

A slow smile spread over his face. "Well, well. At least I stand reassured on one point. Radleigh hasn't laid a finger on you, has he?"

She wondered at his reasoning but didn't ask, merely turned to pick up her lantern.

"You would have remembered him sooner if he had."

Jardine's voice grew tight. "When's this farce of a wedding supposed to take place?"

She didn't owe him an answer, but she said, "Not until my mother returns." She tried to steady her pulse, her breathing. "But he is impatient."

"Don't let him touch you. I *will* kill him if he does."

She gave a broken laugh. "Oh, pray, be my guest. And what about the next man?" Raising her gaze to his again, she whispered, "I don't want to be alone anymore, Jardine. Can't you see that?"

She turned to go.

"What were you really doing here, Louisa? What are you doing with Radleigh?"

She tensed. "It's obvious, isn't it?"

"Not to me."

"Then you are being willfully obtuse. Good night." Before he could say more, she hurried from the temple.

JARDINE watched until the glimmering lantern light vanished, swallowed up by the forest.

His deception was like a vise around his chest. Should he have told her the truth? But if he did that, she would expect some sort of commitment, and he couldn't give her one. Not until he'd finished off Smith for good.

It was also possible that she'd want to help. His gut gave a sick twist at the thought of Louisa running headlong into that danger. He'd worked so hard to keep her safe all these years. Now that Smith was back, a threat to everything Jardine held dear, he couldn't possibly confide the real reason for his abandonment of her.

He couldn't blame her for trying to make a life for herself when he'd so unequivocally cut her out of his.

And yet . . .

The sheer coincidence of her choice made it impossible for him to let the matter rest. Why had she come up here at such an hour? Prurient curiosity? His gaze alighted on the wall before him. This particular piece of frieze depicted a woman being serviced by two men. Slowly, he shook his head.

No. Not Louisa. She was up to something.

He held his lantern aloft and shone it slowly around the small room, his eyes searching every crevice for the reason Louisa had come.

Nothing. Bare walls, bare floor. The place must be tended regularly, as there was very little dust. Pity. If there were, it would be easier to see where the dust had been disturbed.

The only item of interest in the room was the table, covered in a brightly patterned rug.

Then he remembered Louisa's pose as he'd seen her when he arrived at the temple. She'd been crouching, hadn't she? Next to the table.

He emulated her pose, went down on one knee, holding his own lantern up to examine the cloth.

Suddenly, a detail leaped out at him. He stared at it, his brows knitted.

Then he swore viciously and long.

RADLEIGH hovered on the threshold of his father's bedchamber, listening intently. The old man had to be asleep by now.

His enormous mahogany bed was set on a high dais, with ornate draperies hanging from a gold-tasseled canopy. It was a bed for a nobleman, a king. A sour taste pervaded Radleigh's mouth. His sire had always enjoyed an inflated sense of his own importance.

Wealth, power. Those had come easily. He'd come by them dishonestly, it was true, but that didn't diminish the old man's insufferable sense of self-importance.

The once-fearsome criminal was now an invalid, confined to his bed, but he still held the purse strings, still wielded his power like a warlord.

Radleigh moved toward the bed, shielding the candle flame with a cupped hand.

He mounted the steps to the dais and set down his candle on the table at the bedside.

Careful not to make a sound, he drew back the curtain that shielded his father from stray draughts.

The candlelight barely illuminated that heavily lined face, now relaxed in sleep. The big chest rose and fell in a steady motion. A bank of pillows clouded beneath the old man's head.

His hand trembling a little, Radleigh reached out toward his father, then snatched back his hand. With a deep breath, he tried again. This time, his fingers sank into a loose pillow. He eased it free.

Radleigh stood there, clutching the pillow for a long time, heart pounding, chest aching, his mouth parched and sore. Vignettes of his childhood flashed through his mind. The air, scented with spice, his flesh raw and aching from another beating.

The rage built and built until he shook with it, until his head was so suffused with fury, he thought it might explode. He reached a kind of tipping point, then. His arms unlocked and the pillow seemed to float over the old man's slumbering face.

"You spineless little bastard." The voice, deep and calm, came from the supposedly slumbering figure.

Radleigh staggered back, cold shock sliding through his body. The pillow dropped from his grasp. He nearly toppled down the carpeted stairs, but managed to regain his balance just in time.

Heavily hooded eyes stared fearlessly into Radleigh's. "You can't even kill me."

God, the man was totally helpless, yet he was unafraid of the son who hated him.

"Have you married that wench yet?"

Radleigh's body slumped. He didn't know why he couldn't simply kill the old man, release himself from the prison of his father's overweening ambition. "Not yet."

"Well, you'd better snap to it, boy. I'm not dying until I see you wed."

Fourteen

JARDINE stood silently among the dense foliage that skirted the Hindu temple. Cold fear gripped his heart, shivered down his spine.

It was a boy. A boy had come for the message that blue ribbon contained. Stuffing something in his pocket, the small figure darted out of the entrance, keeping to the shadows. He headed for the village, if Jardine judged correctly.

However, he couldn't be sure, so he followed, silently, swiftly, tamping down the fury, the fear. He needed a clear head to deal with whatever lay beyond this wood.

The boy had been taught a few tricks, it seemed, but then, so had Jardine. He simply melted into the night when the boy doubled back on his path, or stopped to take a piss and glanced around casually to check for pursuit.

Finally, the boy approached the busy village inn. This was the week of the Glorious Twelfth, of course, the opening of the hunting season, and the place was packed to the rafters.

The boy slipped into the Bird in Hand's noisy taproom. Jardine hesitated. He didn't want whoever was in that taproom to know he'd been found out.

He went around to the side of the inn, where the diamond-paned windows were too smeared with soot and goodness knew what to see inside. He took out his knife and soon had one casement open a fraction, enough to see inside.

The boy was nowhere to be seen. Damn!

The time he'd lost while he tried to find a way in had meant he'd lost the boy, too. He scanned the patrons who sat around tables with foaming tankards in their hands, but there was no one he recognized. Certainly, the man he'd expected to see wasn't there.

He searched the faces again. Perhaps . . . A bent old man rose from his table and walked slowly, a little unsteadily, to the door. Some helpful lad put a hand under his elbow to support him, and when the old man turned his head to thank the lad, Jardine suffered a shock.

Yet, he'd known it had to be. He'd known from the moment he'd seen that bloody ribbon.

Faulkner.

Hell.

Jardine set his jaw. He wanted to storm into that inn and knock Faulkner's teeth down his conniving throat.

The rotten swine was using Louisa.

Now her betrothal made some sort of sense, didn't it? For some reason known only to that Machiavellian mind, Faulkner wanted her to get close to Radleigh.

Bastard! One did not force civilians into such dangerous and sensitive work.

Jardine strode away, thinking furiously. Louisa had fallen into Faulkner's orbit because of that damned business with the Duchess of Lyle's diary. Bloody Max! Why had he seen fit to involve his sister, even peripherally, in something like that? Max knew what Faulkner was. How could he let the old man get his manipulative and very grubby hands on her?

Max ought to be horsewhipped . . . But no, that wasn't fair, was it? Who could have foreseen that Faulkner would grasp an opportunity to recruit a new operative? Jardine hadn't dreamed of it, that was certain.

Why? The question pounded through his brain as he strode back to the house.

Why would Faulkner want Louisa at this party? What did he have to gain by sending someone so inexperienced . . . *Was* she inexperienced, though? She'd planted that ribbon with the aplomb of a seasoned professional. Too bad for her that he was by nature the most suspicious of men. Any casual observer would not have given her movements a second thought.

He frowned. Had Faulkner trained Louisa in secret for this work? Was she here for the same reason Jardine was? And if Faulkner had known she'd be here and the reason for her presence, why hadn't he briefed Jardine accordingly?

Too many questions. And he'd be damned if he'd go to Faulkner for answers, or at least, not immediately. Might as well keep the element of surprise up his sleeve. He had bugger-all else to his advantage, it seemed.

When he cooled down, he'd be sure to think this through logically, but he was too unsettled by this new discovery—not to mention his recent round with Louisa—to think with any semblance of clarity.

What did that blue ribbon mean?

He'd been striding along without consciously thinking of where he was going and almost left the screen of the wood without dousing his lantern. Grimly, he extinguished the light. He'd send Ives to sniff around the inn, report on Faulkner's movements.

As for Louisa . . . Oh, *Louisa* he'd handle personally.

DESPITE not gaining her bed until almost dawn, Louisa rose early, ready to start the day.

She never missed her morning ride. It was an ingrained habit, one that her darling Miniver depended on. They always went out, even on the most dismal day, even when Louisa had danced the night away at some ball or other. For some reason, it had become a point of honor never to miss.

She shook her head as a thought occurred. That she never missed a day showed exactly how dull and predictable her life had been to this point.

As a girl, how often she'd longed to give her pony his head and gallop from her family home, through the fields of the home farm, far beyond the estate's boundaries, and out into the world. She wouldn't stop until she reached Scotland—or had an adventure—whichever came first.

And then her father had died. Well, why wrap it in clean linen? Tobias Brooke had killed himself. She'd known all along his fall on the hunting field had been due to uncharacteristically reckless riding. No, not simply reckless. Wantonly dangerous. Max knew it, too, though they'd never spoken the truth to one another.

Their beloved father had left them, and from that moment, Louisa had been terrified. Desperate to keep her home and her family intact. Holding everything together while Max went out to work and her mother collapsed with grief and self-pity.

Today, with a wistful glance toward the stables, Louisa broke her habit and instead donned a dark blue walking dress and a becoming chip straw hat for her stroll to the village. She hoped Miniver wouldn't fret. The dear would have an extra lump of sugar today as an apology for Louisa's missing their regular appointment.

She had an appointment with a far different character. Or, at least, it was to be hoped she did.

She still hadn't decided what she'd say to him.

The two-mile walk to the village passed in mental debate. She barely registered the scent of heather and sun-drenched grasses mingled in the air. The Derbyshire countryside, with its peaks and rocky moors, would have to be explored some other time. Her focus remained fixed.

The distant crack of guns made her start. Oh, of course, the shooting would be under way. The beaters would be out, sending flurries of grouse skyward. She shaded her eyes from the strengthening sun and looked up into a near cloudless sky.

There. A flock of birds arrowed upward. One, two, three halted, arrested mid-flight, then plummeted to earth, their eventual resting places swallowed by the thick wood that stood between the moor and the road that led into town.

Now, the dogs would fetch the kill, holding the limp, feathered bodies tenderly in their mouths so as not to maul them.

She walked on, glad of an excuse to stay away. She preferred inanimate targets to birds these days.

The road eventually wound into the village, a single row of buildings and cottages on either side. A pretty, picturesque place, as so many English villages were, culminating in the church at the end of a lane, and opposite that, a green with an enormous horse chestnut tree.

The shops had opened and some displayed a selection of their wares in barrows outside.

And there was the Bird in Hand. She'd reasoned that if Faulkner were in the vicinity, he would most probably put up at the village's only inn.

Of course, she knew better than to walk into the establishment and inquire after the head of the secret service. Quite apart from the damage asking for a man would do to a spinster's reputation, Faulkner might not use his own name here.

She wondered, for the first time, why he lurked in the vicinity rather than remaining in his headquarters in London.

She'd always assumed he was the puppet master that set all his agent marionettes dancing. Now, here he was, "in the field," as Max termed it, waiting for word.

If finding that list were so important that he'd become personally involved, why would he entrust such a matter to her?

Only, he hadn't, had he? He'd entrusted the mission to Harriet.

And Harriet had abandoned her post.

The notion still rankled. What had taken Harriet away? Had she discovered something important? Had that note even been in her hand? Louisa couldn't recall ever seeing an example of Harriet's writing.

Oh.

"Oh God!" she whispered, furiously replaying the events of that morning in her mind.

What if Harriet had been taken? What if Radleigh already knew that she, Louisa, was involved in a scheme to recover the list of names?

Cold panic swept over her in waves. Her gaze darted right and left. She felt an overwhelming need to be *with* people. Not alone and vulnerable like this.

Blindly, she entered a shop, a haberdasher's. The abrupt tinkle of the bell overhead as she opened the door made her start.

She sent a quick, nervous look over her shoulder, but outside it seemed as if everyone went normally about their business. Had someone followed her? They might have done, quite easily. How would she know?

Suddenly, she was afraid. More afraid than she'd been last night. Then, all this cloak-and-dagger business had still seemed like a game.

How would she get back to the house if she had to walk alone?

She realized she'd been standing stock-still at the entrance, and that the lady proprietor had called a cheerful greeting.

Louisa made herself respond pleasantly, calmly. In her ordinary life, she might spend an hour in such a place, poring over ribbons and trimmings and bolts of fabric.

She had little patience for her mother's extravagant frivolity, but back in a time when they'd been obliged to make over gowns and hats instead of buying new ones, it had become a point of honor to strive for fashionable elegance despite their pinched purses.

She possessed a talent for it, she discovered, or perhaps it had been sheer bloody-mindedness that had produced such inspiring results. She had not wanted to look like the charity case she was. And though connoisseurs of the London ton would have easily descried the chasm between her wardrobe and the latest mode, in her and Millicent's very small sphere during those lean years, people had always complimented them on their style.

And why did her mind run after such inanities when she needed to plan and think?

She fingered a length of scarlet ribbon. Her native caution told her to end this charade, immediately. She had no real hope of finding the paper in question. She ought to report what she knew to Faulkner and leave, whatever he might protest to the contrary. In fact, the safest course might be to hire a post chaise from the inn and not even return to the house.

But . . .

The bell clanged and Louisa's head jerked up. Lord, she was jumping at shadows! It was only a plump matron with her daughter. But when the pair moved away from the door, Louisa saw him. Faulkner. Standing across the street.

The panic she'd suffered gave way to utter relief. She had to suppress the urge to burst from the shop and call out to him.

She forced herself to be circumspect. She asked to see several bolts of cloth and rubbed them between her fingers, eventually settling on two different types of heavy serge and a frivolous length of ribbon. When her package was safely stowed in her basket, it occurred to her she'd no idea what she'd purchased.

When she emerged from the haberdasher, Faulkner had vanished.

She nearly cried out, the disappointment was so acute.

But of course. She and Faulkner needed to avoid having anyone see them meet. Otherwise, why go through all that rigmarole with the ribbons and the dead drop?

Louisa made her way along the street by degrees, pausing now and then to stare in shop windows while her brain worked furiously. Where might Faulkner think it safe to approach her? Harriet had told her she must always assume she was watched. If a man followed her now, she would need to shake him off before Faulkner would make contact with her.

She completed the length of the street, arriving at last at the green, where it looked as if the villagers were planning to host some sort of festivity, perhaps in honor of the hunting season?

She didn't know, but she sent thanks to heaven, for the crowd assembled there would make it easier for her to accomplish her plan.

Louisa looked for a place to conceal herself. Finally, she found it. An enormous, hollow oak tree with enough space inside to hold a bench, perfect for lovers' trysts.

She drew out the two lengths of fabric she'd bought at the haberdashers and folded both into rough triangles, tying the smaller one over her head like a kerchief. Hopefully, that would hide her distinctive pale hair.

The second, she wrapped around her shoulders like a shawl.

She waited in that hollow for what seemed like hours,

until a distraction came. One of the massive beer barrels two burly men had been rolling along the green must have hit something—a stump, perhaps. It bounced and sailed through the air. Somehow, during the commotion, the tap on the barrel broke off and dark, yeasty ale burst forth.

The villagers were delighted and ran to collect what they might of the spillage.

Louisa joined the throng that surged toward the spewing barrel, walking with a stoop and a slight hobble to add to her disguise. She edged through the crowd, eventually skirting it until she might slip away. While all eyes watched the beer catastrophe, Louisa, transformed into a middle-aged woman, entered St. David's Anglican church and settled in a back pew. She could only hope that Faulkner, and no one else, would penetrate her disguise.

She was shaking.

In the still, cool quiet of the cavernous church, she made her mind slow, forced her hands to still.

She thought of what she knew and what she might infer from those bare facts. Who could she trust? The sad reality was that she had no logical reason to trust Faulkner. The head of the secret service would have no qualms about sacrificing her to his cause if it became necessary.

Would he come? Had Faulkner followed her, as she'd hoped?

She bent her head, as if in prayer.

If Faulkner was as wily as he was reputed to be, he'd be here any minute.

"I told you not to contact me." The gravelly voice sounded to her left, breaking the contemplative quiet.

She kept her head bowed. "Things have changed," she whispered, as if in prayer. "Mrs. Burton disappeared the night before we arrived. I've not heard from her since. She left me a message."

A faint hush as a prayer book slid toward her. Louisa slipped the short note into the prayer book, then laid it between them on the seat.

Silence.

"What should I do?" She paused, her heart drumming in her throat. "Can *I* do anything to get that list back? I searched Radleigh's desk but came up with nothing."

A faint snort told her what he thought of that ruse.

Should she mention that Jardine was there? But she wasn't supposed to know about Jardine's work for the service, was she?

Faulkner took his time answering. "There might be a safe. Try to find out if Radleigh has one in his private apartments. Report back on Thursday morning here, at midday. By then I might have more information for you."

She hesitated, then gave a quick nod. "And what if I'm caught?"

Her only answer was the click of his footsteps as he walked away.

Fifteen

LOUISA left the church. Instead of retracing her steps to the high street, she skirted the Gothic edifice and wandered through the adjacent graveyard, hoping to find another way out.

A high stone wall enclosed the graveyard. Clutching her headscarf beneath her chin, she forced herself to dodder like an old woman along the path that cut through the higgledy-piggledy sea of headstones. Resisting the urge to look over her shoulder, she let herself out the lych-gate into a narrow lane.

Ah, just as she'd hoped, this lane ran along the back of the shops she'd passed on her way to the church. She'd follow this less-frequented path, slip along the length of the high street unseen.

Louisa fished out her hat from her basket, then took off her kerchief and shawl and stuffed the material back in. The hat was a little the worse for her harsh treatment, but with a few judicious tweaks, the straw resumed its former shape.

She looked up from her task, directly into a male chest. She gasped and fell back a step.

"Don't creep up on me like that," she snapped, jamming the hat on her head and making to push past him.

But Jardine was having none of that. He gripped her arm and bent so that their faces were bare inches apart. "So this is what you've been up to."

She didn't quite know how to answer that. She assumed he knew everything, for he was tiresomely perceptive, but she couldn't work out how. Unless . . .

Had he seen her with Faulkner? But she'd been so careful!

The heat from his body, his breath, his closeness made her senses swim. She was tired and afraid, and she wanted to sink into him, beg him to hold her, but what a craven, humiliating act that would be.

"You are leaving. Now." He shifted his grip to her elbow and hustled her along with him.

She stumbled, but his hand held her up. "I shall do nothing of the kind!"

"I've hired you a post chaise and you'll go straight back to town." He halted them both. "What were you *thinking*, you little idiot! Prowling around in the middle of the night. Leaving clandestine messages for Faulkner. My God, you could have been killed."

Coolly, she said, "Don't be dense, Jardine. Why would Radleigh kill me when he could have me to wife?"

The way his nostrils flared and his lips tightened when she said the word *wife* made her recoil.

But it gave her hope, too. A hard kernel of it lodged in her breast, threatened to flourish and grow.

The menace in Jardine's voice was unmistakable. "He will never have you, do you hear me?"

She stared up at him. What was going through his mind?

Was it pure, sexual possessiveness that motivated this fury, or something more?

He was breathing hard. They both were.

And suddenly, she was in his arms, held fast, and he was kissing her closed eyelids, her temple, her cheek, her lips. The contrast between the lung-crushing tightness with which he held her and the gentleness of his kisses nearly undid her.

With a dull kind of ache, she felt her heart uncurling itself, like the fingers of a long-clenched fist, opening, reaching out to him.

She needed him. *He* needed *her*. She would not let him push her away again.

"We ought not to be seen together," she said breathlessly, as he nuzzled her neck. "It is dangerous for us both."

He lifted his head, his eyes dark and glazed. Suddenly, those eyes seemed to snap into focus, as if he'd only just registered what she'd said. "Yes, you must go. I've hired a carriage under the name Mrs. Foster at the inn."

He slid his hands down her arms and took her hands. Placed a soft kiss on her brow.

"Go now, and Godspeed."

Eyes downcast, she nodded, and moved past him, toward the Bird in Hand. She did not turn to look at him, not once, but she felt his burning gaze following her.

As she turned the corner, she glimpsed him still standing where she'd left him, a tall, solitary figure. He had always stood alone. She must remember that.

Louisa slipped up a side lane between shops and walked out onto the high street. She entered the bustling inn yard and looked about her for an ostler.

She had never been so afraid.

JARDINE watched her go with a heady surge of relief. That had been surprisingly easy. He'd rather expected Louisa to put up more of a fight when he'd told her to go.

She'd never been a foolish woman, though, and she knew that she was in over her head on this occasion. She was intelligent enough to take him at his word that the situation was dangerous.

Perversely, he would miss her. He could admit it to himself, now she was gone.

Ives materialized at his elbow, shaking his greasy head. "Kissin' and nuzzlin' in a public place," he muttered. "'T ain't right."

It had *felt* perfect.

He sneered down at Ives from his superior height. "When I want your opinion on my conduct, I'll ask for it. And then I'll get my head examined. Go and see to the horses. I'll meet you at the crossroads in half an hour."

"You lying, unscrupulous bastard." Only the recollection that Faulkner must have about fifty years in his dish stopped Jardine from bunching his hands in the man's shirt and slamming him against the wall. "You knew I was after that list. You knew I'd get it, too. Why send Louisa Brooke to do your dirty work?"

Faulkner said, "I don't see what concern it is of yours if I send Lady Louisa Brooke or the Queen of Sheba. *You* don't work for me, as you've stressed repeatedly."

There was a smug light in those hard gray eyes. Why wasn't Faulkner scared? He ought to be. But that bulldog tenacity shouldn't be underestimated. Faulkner was an old hand at this game.

"I would have delivered the list to you, nevertheless," Jardine answered. "And you know it, so why this charade?"

Faulkner grunted. "All Lady Louisa was supposed to do was get another operative of mine an invitation to this party. She did, and they were to travel together to Radleigh's house." He paused. "My agent did not arrive."

There was no emotion in his voice as he said it, but Jardine knew he must fear the worst.

Faulkner shrugged. "Perhaps you and Lady Louisa can work together. You are acquainted, I presume?"

Jardine set his teeth. "She's Lyle's sister. I am, perforce, acquainted with her." Thank God she was already on her way back to London. "She is a gently bred lady. You had no right embroiling her in this."

"No right?" Faulkner raised his shaggy brows, his eyes widened a little. "We do what is necessary, Jardine. You know that. I saw the interest flourishing between Radleigh and the lady. I had some previous acquaintance with her and asked her—quite mildly, you understand—for a favor. Her role was insignificant, hardly likely to get her into trouble."

"You didn't warn her about the dangers—"

"As a matter of fact, I did. Lady Louisa is a determined young woman. In fact, she wanted more responsibility than I was prepared to bestow."

Faulkner's brows knitted slightly. "There is something about her. A core of strength and steadfastness, and a deep, cold rage. She would be a perfect operative, given time and training. But we didn't have the time, so I sent someone else. Someone who seems to have vanished between here and London."

"So this betrothal *is* a sham." Elation shot through Jardine, a profound satisfaction that he hadn't been wrong about her motives. A drastic step to take. What a nerve the woman had!

"As to that, I could not say." Faulkner spread his hands. "I certainly did not urge such a thing. I told Lady Louisa that Radleigh was dangerous."

Faulkner fingered his chin. "Sometimes, danger makes a man so much more attractive to a woman. Don't you think?"

The words clanged in Jardine's head as he and Ives rode back to the house. This was no longer a scouting mission. He needed to find Smith and do it now. And the only way to do that would be to draw him out of hiding. Dangle some juicy bait.

He had thought his presence might be enough to draw his old enemy out, but no such luck.

The next step was to get hold of that document, the list of operatives that Smith would kill to have, the one that Radleigh was offering up for sale.

Jardine smiled grimly. There was no need for thievery or subterfuge, after all. He'd simply buy the list himself.

LOUISA drove back to Radleigh's house at a spanking pace, causing the groom standing behind her to give a startled grunt. "Never fear. I shan't overturn you," she threw over her shoulder.

They came to a straight stretch of road and she dropped her hands, shooting them forward at an even faster clip. If Jardine overtook her before she arrived at the house, she was sure to be kidnapped and bundled into a coach headed for London.

High-handed, pigheaded man. Had he seriously expected her to meekly do his bidding?

She shook her head, but she smiled, too, because in those kisses, in that embrace, in his concern for her safety, Jardine showed more than arrogance. He showed he still cared.

Why had he sent her away so cruelly on the morning after her birthday? There must have been a reason, one that seemed cogent and compelling to him.

She doubted she would find it so.

The smoldering coal of anger in her heart flared. Why did men always think they knew best? Why must they always try to shoulder everything alone, thrust their women aside when things became difficult?

Her father had been the same. If only he'd shared his problems instead of keeping them locked inside, he might still be alive today.

Radleigh's fantastical house burst into view, artfully framed by copper beech and cedar and oak. If she could reach the house before Jardine discovered she hadn't meekly followed orders, she'd make sure he had no other opportunity to eject her from the party without creating an undesirable scene.

Exhilaration and fear made a choke of laughter catch in her throat as she pulled into the stable yard. She'd arrived without incident, and with the gruffly expressed admiration of the groom, who took over the ribbons.

She tipped him and alighted with her basket. Grinning a little and swinging the basket to and fro, she turned to leave the stable yard.

"My dear."

The smile fell from her face. She stopped, feeling as if two fingers pinched the back of her neck.

Somehow, she managed to find her smile and paste it back on. Turning, she said, "Mr. Radleigh. Duncan. How do you do?"

He was an imposing figure in buckskin breeches and a bottle green coat. He carried a crop that he tapped against his boot in a rhythmic way that seemed to string her nerves tighter with every stroke. "You have been to the village this morning?"

"Yes, I always like to take exercise in the morning but I found my basket became heavy with all my purchases and I decided to take a hired conveyance back. It's a pretty village, is it not?"

She was babbling. She needed to calm herself.

He nodded. "I had it moved there when I landscaped the park so it wouldn't spoil the view from the house."

"Oh." There didn't seem to be much to say in reply to that. She knew it was done all the time. The practice had always seemed to be a little hard on the villagers, however.

She lifted her brows. "And you, sir. Have you been riding?"

"Just about to. Care to join me?"

She looked down at herself. "I'm so sorry. I'm not dressed for riding. Perhaps tomorrow?"

His hazel eyes glinted. With anger? Frustration? "Yes. Tomorrow, then."

"I shall look forward to it." Something about his expression sent chills creeping over her flesh. Every fiber within her seized with the need to get away from him.

"You won't escape me forever, you know, Lady Louisa," he said softly, as if reading her thoughts.

Despite the hairs that pricked at her nape, she forced a light laugh. "Why, Mr. Radleigh. What nonsense you speak! We are betrothed. Why should I desire to escape you?"

"I don't know." He tilted his head. "It's a question, isn't it?"

Before she could think of a reply, he bowed over her hand, turned on his heel, and strode away.

Louisa looked after him, watching sunlight glint on his fair hair. He jammed his hat on his head and cracked his crop against his top boot.

Radleigh grew impatient. It was scarcely to be wondered at, but she hoped his impatience was for the alignment of their two houses and not for their wedding night.

Until now, she'd managed to hold him off. His assumption about the coldness of her nature, her prudishness, had been one she'd wholeheartedly encouraged.

But an engaged man was entitled to some liberties with his fiancée, wasn't he? She didn't know how much longer she could elude him.

JARDINE rode in as Radleigh came trotting out of the stables on a raw-boned stallion.

"Ah. Just the man." Dismissing Ives, he wheeled his mount and accompanied his host. "Mind if I join you?"

Radleigh could hardly refuse. He narrowed his eyes, giving Jardine a quick survey. "Why not?"

They rode in silence for a way. Then Radleigh said, "I know who you are." He spoke in a pleasant tone, but with an unmistakable edge. "I don't know why you should be making up to my sister. . . ."

"Don't you?" Jardine's mouth lifted at the corner. "Then you are not as acute as I'd imagined."

They cleared a high hedge, and Jardine leaned forward to pat his mare's neck while he waited for Radleigh to catch up. "I hear that you have an interesting piece of merchandise for sale. I want it."

The time for groping in the dark was done. The matter lay open between them. Jardine was prepared to match any price to save his colleagues—and to secure the bait that would draw Smith into the open. What Smith could do with that list of agents . . .

"Who do you work for?" Radleigh rapped out.

Jardine curled his lip. "My dear fellow. I haven't done a day's work in my life."

Radleigh cracked a laugh. "You want me to sell you what I have? A lone individual? Jardine, I have nations vying for this, offering me untold wealth and power."

Slowly, Jardine shook his head in a pitying gesture. "They won't keep their bargains. Think about it. Why should they leave you alive, once they have the list? Alive, you are an expense and a liability. Dead . . ." Jardine shrugged. "A problem solved."

Radleigh was silent. They rode on while he considered, weighed the pros and cons.

"And don't forget that I know what you're up to, which means I can go to the powers that be and tell them their entire network of spies is compromised. They'll take action to dismantle their operations, and your information will be worthless."

He let Radleigh digest this information. Eventually, the other man said, "Why do you want the list if you're not working for them?"

Jardine snorted. "You really think I'd tell you that? You might as well ask what's the highest price I'm willing to pay."

They circled one another now, their horses catching the mood, snorting and tossing their heads.

Turning away from Radleigh, Jardine squinted up at the sun. "Some can give you money, true. But you are already an extraordinarily wealthy man. What I can give you is beyond any foreign ambassador's power, for I have the ear of the Regent."

He caught the moment Radleigh's eyes sharpened. "A knighthood?"

"Perhaps. But . . . let us not be ungenerous. Every East India man and his boot boy has a knighthood these days." Jardine smiled. "How does 'Lord Radleigh' sound?"

The bastard couldn't hide his shock.

"Think of it," purred Jardine. "I could turn you into a hero, Radleigh. Not the sniveling petty villain who somehow came by a sensitive piece of government information he managed to sell the highest bidder. But the great man who discovered such a plot and foiled it single-handedly."

He watched Radleigh absorbing the grandiose picture he'd painted. The man was far too cool a customer to show elation, but Jardine could tell the notion warmed the cockles of his corrupt, black heart.

In every man, there is at least one weakness, and one deep-seated desire. Sometimes, the two are the same.

Faulkner had said that to him once, and Jardine had never forgotten. Let criminals and soldiers use force to achieve their aims. Jardine was a master at turning the key that unlocks a man's brain, his heart, his soul.

He opened them wide, turned them inside out. And then manipulated them until they yielded exactly the result he most desired.

"Think about it," he said with a hard smile. "I'll expect your answer tomorrow morning, before I leave."

RADLEIGH stood in the small cabinet room next to Lady Louisa's bedchamber with the hot satisfaction of the forbidden scintillating through his veins.

The peephole was discreet and effective, and no one knew it was there. Except him.

In retrospect, he was glad Louisa had been so very reluctant to allow him any premarital shenanigans. She was a lady, after all, with no pretensions to a sensual nature. He wondered if she even knew what her reproductive organs were for. He stifled a snort of laughter.

Mustn't let her hear . . .

Her reluctance, her aloof, untouchable quality made it all the more fascinating to watch her undress. How shamed, how utterly violated she would feel if she knew.

He would tell her, eventually, and enjoy her response.

Radleigh bent to the peephole again, but she had finished dressing now and dismissed her maid. She crossed to the window, elegant and erect in her carriage even when alone. She sat in the window seat, looking strangely pensive.

Radleigh sighed and straightened. The curtain was down on that show for the moment.

Oh, but she was cold. He hadn't sought sexual satisfaction from this union but nor had he expected this delicious, almost delicate anticipation.

Her resistance, the flare of fear he'd glimpsed occasionally in her eyes excited him, but he was determined to keep himself under control, at least until their wedding night.

He thought of the proposal Jardine had laid out that afternoon and knew he would take it. In view of Radleigh's own imminent rise to nobility, to some men of limited vision, it might seem unnecessary to marry Lady Louisa.

But he knew a little of the world which he hoped to enter. A title would open many doors, but for the very elite, a recent title would make him only marginally more acceptable than he already was. For assured entrée into the ton, he needed an insider to pave the way. He needed Louisa.

And he found that he anticipated their union more and more.

The door opened. Saunders walked in. "Mr. Radleigh."

Radleigh jerked his hand away from the peephole and quickly hung the miniature that covered it back in its place.

The secretary's brows lifted fractionally, but he didn't comment on what he'd seen.

Radleigh sighed. "She's making me wait, Saunders. It is . . . difficult to wait."

He would not tell Saunders about Jardine's proposals. Not yet. He wasn't ready to bring the game to a close.

"Why wait?" murmured the secretary. "Ladies like grand romantic gestures. Why not marry her out of hand? Do it tomorrow."

"Tomorrow?"

"You have the special license, have you not?"

Radleigh nodded.

Saunders spread his hands. "Well, then."

The notion exploded in Radleigh's mind like a sunburst.

He could do it. She would be reluctant, but he'd impress her with his masterfulness, sweep her off her feet.

It would set the tone for their marriage, too. He'd show her he'd no intention of brooking disagreement or resistance once she was his wife. Desperate not to frighten her off, he'd been all compliance until now, but this pussyfooting about irked him. The sooner he made Lady Louisa aware of her place, the better.

Beneath him.

A pleasurable frisson stole through him at the double entendre. He smiled.

"If you'll pardon, sir. It would be beneficial if you could show that the strength of your feelings overcame you. Indeed, a show of passion tonight would not be inappropriate."

"Compromise her?" He liked the sound of that. His mind flew back to the image of her that he'd glimpsed through the peephole. Her spare, elegant body, the silvery blond hair. He imagined running his fingers through all that silken loveliness, cutting the small trophy at the end.

But he knew himself, and he knew he'd go too far if he had her tonight.

If that happened, she might run rather than wed him. Once the knot was tied, however, she wouldn't be going anywhere.

Saunders shook his head. "Compromise her? Oh no, Mr. Radleigh. That would never do. You don't wish any scandal to attach to Lady Louisa's name. I was thinking of a kiss, merely. An embrace. You don't want to queer your pitch."

The gentle chiding note made Radleigh set his shoulders. Coldly, he said, "You forget yourself, Saunders."

The dark eyes gleamed. "Oh no, sir. I do not forget a thing."

Sixteen

REFRESHMENTS had been laid out on the terrace and Beth was pouring tea for her guests. Louisa smiled and greeted them. How civilized and calm they all were. And how hungry she was.

She hadn't taken breakfast in her haste to get to the village. It was an effort to eat daintily and not gobble her Bakewell tart.

Beth handed her a cup of tea and sat down beside her. "Honoria can do the rest," she said carelessly.

Louisa had noticed that about Beth. She liked the idea of playing hostess but soon grew bored of the manifold duties the role entailed. She would make some poor man a very inconsistent, indolent wife.

Thank goodness there was no real danger of Jardine succumbing to the temptation of that lush figure.

The pang Louisa usually suffered when she compared herself to a better endowed female was absent today. How petty such concerns seemed now.

Jardine cared for her. Whatever his motives for that shocking and hurtful display when she'd visited his house, the tenderness of his kisses behind the village shops spoke the truth.

The knowledge lifted a weight from her heart, made happiness sing through her body.

How to get him to admit to his feelings was the next step. After he'd calmed down from his rage at finding her still here, of course.

Or perhaps she might use his inflamed passions to ignite a passion of a different sort.

She dabbed her lips with her napkin and looked up, to see Beth watching her expectantly. Clearly, she awaited an answer. Louisa had no idea what the girl had said.

"Do forgive me," she murmured. "I was lost in a brown study, I'm afraid. How terribly rude."

But she was destined not to hear Beth's words repeated because at that moment, Jardine came striding toward them.

His expression was a careful blank, but there was banked fury in his eyes. That he found her in company where he couldn't speak his mind clearly made him even more livid than he already was.

She smiled. It was, perhaps, the first genuine smile she'd given him since he arrived.

"Ah, there you are, my lord!" Beth held out her hand to him, which he ignored. "Do sit down."

With his gaze fixed on Louisa, Jardine took the indicated chair. His eyes sizzled like caramel over a flame.

She lifted her chin. *I'm not afraid of you. You've already done your worst.*

There was liberation in that thought.

Jardine transferred his attention to Beth, who'd been yapping at him like an excited puppy all this while, never noticing the dangerous undercurrent between her swain and the woman next to her.

Unlike Louisa, however, he seemed to have kept track of the girl's prattle, for he gave an easy, glib answer when she paused, a questioning tilt to her head.

How could Jardine even pretend to be enamored of such a forward, excitable chit?

The same way she could become engaged to a man like Radleigh, presumably.

She hadn't given Jardine the truth about her reason for accepting Radleigh's proposal. She hadn't become engaged to Radleigh to make Jardine jealous. She would scorn to behave in such a fashion.

But she didn't need Kate to tell her that jealousy might just be the key to unlock Jardine's feelings. She knew now that she hadn't been mistaken. He did care for her, perhaps even love her still.

Why had he turned her away?

"Penny for your thoughts, Lady Louisa," said Beth, giggling. "Upon my honor, you looked excessively grim just now."

Louisa raised her brows. "Did I? Forgive me. I have a touch of the migraine, which often lays me low."

As an excuse, it was a lame one, but Beth wasn't to know Louisa had the constitution of an ox.

Jardine wasn't similarly ignorant, however. The corner of his mouth twitched.

"Oh, *poor* Lady Louisa," said Beth. "How dreadful for you. Perhaps a touch of the sun?"

Jardine interposed, "Ah, the infirmities of age." In a soothing tone, he said, "Perhaps, my lady, you ought to go upstairs and rest."

"Yes, that sounds like just the ticket," agreed Beth, jumping up. "I shall come and help you up the stairs. Should I have a tisane prepared, do you think? Our housekeeper makes excellent remedies."

Louisa gripped the arms of her chair. "Thank you, but I

believe I might manage to totter my way to my room without assistance."

She rose to leave, her eyes snapping at Jardine.

Wait till I get my hands on you.

It was a prospect she looked forward to with some relish.

WHAT a bloody interminable evening. Jardine took a deep pull of Burgundy and rolled its richness around his mouth. You could say this for Radleigh: he had good taste in wine.

Women, too, he supposed. Jardine scowled. Louisa had capitalized on the excuse of a migraine to avoid coming down to dinner. Clever of her. He'd have feigned a little *mal à la tête* himself if he'd thought that would get him out of one of the most tedious evenings of his career.

What was she doing up there? Searching the house, probably. He'd made it his business to keep watch on Radleigh tonight, but that didn't mean she was safe. There were always servants to inform on her.

Stubborn little fool! He ought to have known she wouldn't meekly do his bidding. If he wasn't so furious at her, he'd smile to think how utterly she'd rolled him up back there at the village.

He ought to have deposited her in that carriage and driven her back to London himself.

The gentlemen of the party had sat drinking and exchanging war stories in Radleigh's library until the early hours. Jardine wished they'd all go to bed. He was determined to keep an eye on Radleigh, though, so he was obliged to remain until the bitter end. He'd give the man no chance to importune Louisa tonight.

Ah. Finally, Radleigh made a move. After a few moments, Jardine rose to follow.

When he arrived in the corridor, he caught a glimpse of Radleigh heading toward the central staircase.

Jardine followed, trusting Louisa could talk herself out of trouble if she were found doing whatever she'd stayed away from dinner to do, ready to act if she could not.

Jardine's hands clenched into fists as Radleigh made a beeline for Louisa's bedchamber.

Quietly, Radleigh knocked on the door.

No answer came to his knock. Louisa either wasn't there or she was feigning sleep. Either way, Radleigh surely wouldn't persist.

He knocked again but didn't wait too long for an answer. He turned the door handle and Jardine took a reflexive step forward.

The door was locked.

Good girl.

Relief swept through Jardine. By God, he must put an end to this charade of hers. If he lost her now . . .

Radleigh gave a small shrug and paused. Then he let himself into the room next to Louisa's and closed the door behind him.

What was he up to?

That room was a curiosity cabinet, wasn't it? Perhaps Radleigh had gone in there to retrieve something he meant to show his guests.

But in minutes, he came out, empty-handed. Jardine ducked into an empty doorway and watched him walk past.

The second he was clear, Jardine moved swiftly. He found the curiosity cabinet as he'd remembered it from earlier reconnaissance. A small branch of candles on a table illuminated all kinds of interesting objects—foreign, exotic, priceless.

What had Radleigh been doing in here? Had he listened at the wall? Jardine pressed his own ear to the space but heard nothing.

The room was called a cabinet for the very reason that it was so small, about the size of a dressing room, purpose-built to hold all a man's treasures from his Grand Tour. The wall that backed onto Louisa's room was lined with two sets of shelves, with a small space in the middle for a couple of framed miniatures.

Jardine's skin prickled with unease. He chose the miniature at eye level and moved it aside.

A noise made Louisa glance over her shoulder as she searched the sitting room next to Radleigh's bedchamber. God help her if he caught her in here. She'd searched every other likely place and concluded that if Radleigh owned a safe, as Faulkner suggested, it must be in his private apartments.

Though it was after dinner, Radleigh would not retire for several hours yet. There was no reason for his valet to be there, but she listened at the door for some time before she opened it.

Radleigh's private rooms were opulent, all gilt furnishings and heavy brocade. She scanned the anteroom, but the delicate, spindle-legged furniture could hold no surprises. There was not a desk nor any similar receptacle in the place.

Perhaps a safe lurked behind one of those oils on the wall. Quietly, she checked behind each painting and found nothing. Two of the paintings were so large, she didn't dare move them in case she made too much noise.

She couldn't open a safe. Did Faulkner intend to send someone else to do that work?

Why hadn't Faulkner asked Jardine to do it? He seemed proficient in any number of nefarious activities—breaking and entering her bedchamber, most commonly. Had he already searched here? Was she wasting her time?

Nothing. She moved into Radleigh's bedchamber, swiftly

checking the walls there. Radleigh must attend to all his correspondence in the library, for there wasn't even an escritoire in this room. Just an ornate canopied bed surmounted with snarling gryphons, a rather elegant Adam fireplace with two wing chairs on either side of it, and a Chippendale table by the window.

Another door presumably led to his dressing room.

From that room, she heard noises. She froze, then slowly, silently backed out of the room. She turned and hurried to her own chamber, fishing the key out of her pocket as she went.

She inserted the key into the lock, but the tumblers didn't seem to want to move. Panicked, she darted a glance up the corridor. No one. She tried the handle, and the door opened easily.

Strange. Had she omitted to lock the door, after all? Or . . .

She hesitated on the threshold, her heart beating hard. Bustling footsteps sounded down the corridor, coming toward her. With a quick huff, she blew out her candle. Having retired with a headache, she couldn't afford to be caught outside her room. She had no time to consider but made the choice, whisking herself into her chamber, closing the door softly behind her.

A hand clapped over her mouth from behind and an arm stole around her waist. She was clamped to some man's body, her head forced back against his shoulder.

Fear spiked inside her, rushed through her body, drummed in her ears. She tried to bite the hand that covered her mouth, struggled in a frenzy to get free, kicked backward, but her slippered heel made no impression on the man.

Her captor spun her around, pushed her against the wall. Her cry was cut off by his mouth, hard, demanding, plundering hers.

Jardine. She knew his kiss, his scent.

Fear turned instantly to hunger, anger, longing, as his lips dragged from her mouth, his sharp teeth bit her ear, her throat.

"Yes, yes," she whispered.

His body pressed against her, flattened her between him and the wall. She wore only her night rail, a flimsy defense. The loose wrapper she'd thrown on for respectability lay discarded on the floor somewhere, ripped off in their struggle.

She felt the hardness of him—his chest, his hands, his length pressed against her.

"Yes," she said again, kneading his back with her hands, undulating her hips against him, tempting him, hoping beyond reason that this meant something, that this was real.

He still hadn't spoken a word. She let her hands wander lower, gasped when he captured them and swiftly pinned them to the wall above her head. With his other hand, he pulled down the gathered bodice of her night rail, exposing her.

The fabric caught beneath her breasts, lifting them as if to offer them up to his pleasure. Jardine bent his dark head and took full advantage of the offer, suckling her strongly, licking, kneading one nipple while he pinched and rolled the other between his long fingers.

With a pleasured sigh, Louisa laid her head against the wall and succumbed.

After that leisurely foray, he made his way back to her mouth by degrees, trailing kisses and nips along the small mounds of her breasts, the hollow of her throat, behind her ear.

His tongue traced her lips and she opened to him. He kissed her deeply, released her so that he could explore.

His hands roamed her body, setting off fireworks across her skin. Against her lips, he panted. "Ah, God, Louisa. You make me insane."

She clung to him, and her loins throbbed, cried out for him. "Love me, Jardine."

Panting, he set his forehead against hers.

Their harsh breathing mingled. He kissed her, closed his arms around her, and held her tightly.

Tenderness, agonizing and poignant, swept over her.

"Take me to bed, Jardine," she whispered. *Let's forget everything but us.*

"Dammit, I can't." His arms fell to his side. He pulled and tweaked her bodice so that it covered her once more and bent to pick up her wrapper.

Suddenly cold at his unequivocal rejection, she took the wrapper and held it tightly around her. She made as if to move away, but he trapped her again with his body. "Don't move." The words were a breath in her ear. "He might be watching."

"What? Who?"

"Hush." He rested a finger against her lips, tilted his head to listen.

His lips brushed her ear as he all but breathed the words. "Radleigh has a peephole in that wall. He's been watching you."

Louisa was dazed, uncomprehending. It took moments for his words to sink in.

Radleigh had seen her in the supposed privacy of her bedchamber? She gave a ragged gasp, buried her face in Jardine's coat.

"Louisa?"

Horror held her speechless. She'd been naked in this room. He'd seen her undress. Embarrassment crawled over her skin.

"Louisa? Do you understand? Nod if you understand."

Mutely, she nodded, squeezing her eyes shut against angry, humiliated tears.

"He is not there now, but I can't take chances. This is a blind spot, right here, where we stand."

She just nodded again. How many times had she revealed herself to that lecherous swine's avid gaze?

Jardine rubbed his hands up and down her arms, as if to warm her, and she realized she was shivering.

"This has gone far enough, Louisa. You must leave here, you understand? Get dressed. Meet me in the orangery in twenty minutes. We'll work out a plan."

He waited for her to give another wordless nod. Then he slipped from the room like a shadow.

Louisa hugged herself tightly and slowly slid down the wall to huddle on the floor.

Seventeen

By the time Louisa arrived in the orangery—rather more than twenty minutes later, Jardine noted—she was clearly furious.

"Hanging is too good for him," she hissed as she stalked through the door. "I'll cut off his privates and feed them to the dogs."

Jardine exhaled the breath he seemed to have been holding since he'd seen that peephole.

"Bravo, Louisa." He took her hand and guided her down a long row of orange trees. The air was redolent of citrus, sharp and sweet. "I thought you were going to turn maudlin back there."

"Well, it was a shock," she admitted. "But how dare he spy on me like that?"

"You were here to spy on him," said Jardine mildly.

"That is beside the point. He is doing the wrong thing. I am acting for altruistic reasons."

God, how he'd missed her! "He will see you without

your clothes on every day once you're wed, you know. It's part of the contract."

"Is it?" she answered dryly. "I hadn't noticed." Her gaze ran over him with bold speculation that heated his blood and sent it due south.

"Jardine, you know very well that betrothal was a sham."

He had guessed, of course, but to hear her say it made his insides turn over with relief. "A risky one. The entire venture was most ill-conceived. How on earth did you come to be working for Faulkner?"

She shrugged. "He made me take an oath of secrecy when there was all that fuss over Kate's diary. I did a few small favors for him. And then he asked me to get one of his operatives an invitation to this house party."

Jardine frowned. Her story certainly tallied with Faulkner's. "Faulkner said the operative disappeared before she even reached Radleigh's house. Who was it?"

Louisa shrugged. "She called herself Harriet Burton. Whether that was her real name, I have no idea."

Jardine frowned. He didn't know her, but that meant nothing. Faulkner had plenty of agents on the payroll and commonly, they weren't acquainted. It was safer that way.

"So it was never your brief to get hold of this list yourself."

"No, of course not. Why should they trust me with an important mission?" She gave a huff of exasperation. "And they were right. I've made no progress whatsoever."

She told him all she knew and he let her, seeing that it was a relief to unburden herself. She wasn't cut out for this game, she was too softhearted, but he couldn't help but admire her resourcefulness as her story unfolded.

Her courage, her utter, foolish courage in hunting for that safe tonight. "There's no need to keep searching. I've made Radleigh an offer he can't refuse. I hope to have that list in my hands by tomorrow morning."

She tensed, and he guessed how chagrined she must be that her efforts had come to naught. "I can help you."

He took her hand. "You were very brave, darling. But now it's time to go."

"Don't patronize me, Jardine!" She snatched her hand away. "How will you get him to sell the list to you? He must have other offers."

"Yes, but you see there's something I can give him that no one else can. Or that's what I've led him to believe."

"And what is that, exactly?"

"What our friend Radleigh desires more than anything is an entrée into our world. Thus, his betrothal to you. He is already wealthy beyond most men's comprehension. He doesn't need more money, and what would he do with the foreign honors those other nations wish to bestow? But a peerage . . ." He shrugged. "I'll have that paper in my hands by lunchtime."

He jabbed a finger at her. "So, there is no need for you to continue this dangerous charade. Make your excuses and leave as soon as breakfast is over."

Her chin came up. "I'm not going anywhere. I'll see this through to the end."

Did the woman never learn? "What is there for you to do save get yourself into trouble? Good God, what more evidence do you need of Radleigh's character than that damned peephole?"

He turned to face her, gripped her shoulders, and shook her. "He will do worse than merely look at you, Louisa. You know that!"

"What can he do in the middle of a house party?"

He didn't know. He didn't know how far Radleigh was prepared to go to achieve his aims. The one saving grace was that he wanted Louisa as his wife. That should keep her alive, but . . .

"Promise me you won't let him touch you."

She gave an exasperated sigh. "Jardine—"

"You will not be alone with him. You will say he can have nothing without the ring on your finger. Is that clear?"

"You don't think I want him to touch me, do you?" She shuddered.

"Are you afraid of him?"

She turned her head at that, pierced him with those cool blue eyes. "Jardine, why did you send me away?"

And thus, she caught him unprepared. Unwilling to continue that cruel pretense, but with no logical reason to give her the truth.

Nothing had changed. He still hunted in the darkness for Smith, the ruthless villain who would balk at nothing, not even torturing an innocent woman, to wreak revenge on Jardine.

In a strained voice, he said, "I told you why. I've tired of you. I'm thinking of looking about me for a real wife."

She didn't even flinch. Steadily, she gazed into his eyes as if she could read all his secrets. "I don't believe you."

She enunciated the words clearly, crisply, as if he was a foreigner with very little English, or a half-wit.

He stared at her, and there was a new strength, a new vitality to her that he hadn't noticed until now. She'd always been a determined woman, with that fire beneath the ice that had caught him from the first.

Now, those qualities seemed to have intensified, found focus and purpose. The revelation made him half crazed with the desire to put his mouth on her, to take her and stoke that blaze until it raged beyond her control.

When had she become so dangerous?

"I'm not going to go meekly this time, Jardine. I'm going to fight for you. I'm going to fight with you."

"You will be damnably in the way." *I can't think, much less fight, with a permanent cock-stand in my trousers.*

A queer little smile lit her features, as if she read his thoughts. "No, darling. I'm going to help you. You'll see."

She reached up and hooked an arm around his neck, pulling him down to her. She brushed her lips over his, once, twice, then slid her tongue along the seam of his mouth in the most lascivious, unladylike gesture imaginable.

His breathing came heavy and hot. He wanted to take her there, under the stars, ravish her until she begged for mercy—and considering her ferocity, that might take a good long while.

But the risk was too great.

He put her away from him, gently. "Be careful." It seemed an inadequate thing to say. But he'd stand guard over her until he'd done the deal, then he'd kidnap her, take her away from this place bound and gagged if necessary.

He stroked the soft, flawless skin of her cheek and felt a shiver of longing ripple through his body. "Good night."

A twig cracked. They both spun around in the direction of the sound.

But Jardine's keen eyes detected only darkness. "Go now," he said. "We can't be seen together."

And for once, she obeyed him. Moved swiftly away from him and back toward the orangery.

LOUISA had barely gained the stairs when a male voice accosted her.

"Lady Louisa." The hushed tones of Saunders, Radleigh's secretary, reached her.

She jumped, turned, and tried to appear natural. Her mind worked furiously, searching for an excuse for being here in the early hours of the morning.

But the secretary was apparently too agitated to demand an explanation. "Oh, thank goodness, it is you!"

"Whatever is the matter, Mr. Saunders?" Louisa whispered.

He wrung his hands a little, as if reluctant to proceed. "It is . . . I fear there has been an accident."

Her heart gave a hard pound. Jardine? But she'd only just left him. She shouldn't have left him. Oh God!

"A female. In the Indian temple."

Relief gushed through her, quickly followed by shame. How awful to be glad it was some unknown woman who had been hurt and not Jardine!

Saunders hadn't mentioned her by name. "Not one of the guests? Do you not know her?"

The secretary shook his head. Despite the cool night, he fished a handkerchief out of his pocket and mopped his brow. "In such circumstances, I believe a woman prefers a lady to, er, minister . . ."

"Calm down, Mr. Saunders. How is the lady hurt?"

"I could not tell the details. She will not let me examine her. I have a medicine chest with me, if you would be so good . . ."

"Of course."

She followed Saunders. Who could this unknown female be?

She wasn't dressed for the terrain. They kept to the pathways, rather than taking the more circuitous way through the woods, but her feet began to protest as stones and tree roots played havoc through her thin slippers.

Saunders didn't speak another word as they moved through the night, guided by the strong light of his lantern. He seemed such a gentle man, this woman must either be ridiculously coy or in a very bad state to refuse his help.

By the time they reached the temple, Louisa was panting a little. She stopped in the doorway to catch her breath, her hand resting lightly on the door frame. Saunders swung his lantern in a circle.

Louisa gave a cry and crossed the hard floor, swiftly going to her knees. The battered, bruised face of Harriet Burton stared up at her.

There was no recognition in Harriet's silvery eyes. She shrank back as Louisa reached out a hand to touch her.

"Oh no!" What had he done to her? Logic told her she couldn't be certain, but in her bones, she knew this was Radleigh's work.

Panic threatened to rise in Louisa's throat, but she ruthlessly thrust it away. She needed to keep a clear head to help Harriet.

Why was Harriet here? Had she been taken that night at the inn? Had she been in Radleigh's power for all that time?

Ah, dear God, what had he done to turn the fearless, flippant Harriet Burton into this cowering, bloody mess?

Louisa put out her hand very slowly, murmuring soft assurances. She touched Harriet's hand, which was gloveless, its fingernails torn. That featherlight touch made Harriet's ragged breathing hitch, her eyes flare in panic.

But she allowed it. "Yes, my dear, that's right. I'm not going to hurt you. You're safe now."

She didn't know how true that was. She didn't know where Radleigh might be, or whether he would be back, or why he'd let Harriet go. Had she managed to escape?

Faulkner was in the village, staying at the inn. If Louisa could deliver Harriet to him, she'd be safe.

She couldn't afford to wait for a doctor, if one could be persuaded to come at this hour. She needed to get Harriet away from the estate and under Faulkner's protection.

Louisa turned her head a little to address Saunders. "I think she needs a doctor. Do you have some kind of transport? We must take her to the village without delay."

"Yes, of course. I'll arrange it." Saunders left her with the lantern and hurried away.

She waited until she judged him out of earshot. "Harriet!" she whispered. "Harriet, don't be afraid. I won't hurt you. I'm here to help."

The blue eyes were glazed with horror. A large purple contusion swelled around her left eye. Her lips were mashed and bloody, as if someone had stomped on them.

Or, as if she'd bitten through them in an effort to withstand excruciating pain.

God only knew what injuries hid beneath that cloak. Had he broken bones? Louisa needed to persuade Harriet to let her touch her. She took Harriet's hand, laid it gently on her own, palm to palm.

"I'm here to help you, Harriet. Will you let me help?"

Louisa waited, and then set Harriet's hand down gently. With light, slow movements, she peeled away the man's cloak that, presumably, Saunders had covered Harriet with.

Louisa's senses reeled at what she saw beneath. There was blood, lots of it. The strong, coppery smell filled her head, made her stomach churn.

Whoever had done this to Harriet liked to use a knife. Deep slashes crisscrossed the swells of her breasts.

With a hard swallow, Louisa suppressed a whimper of sympathetic horror. She turned to open the small medical chest Saunders had set down next to her.

Painstakingly, carefully, she cleaned Harriet's wounds, driving herself to continue, even though her heart hurt with every cry of agony Harriet gave.

Gently, thoroughly, she tested joints and limbs for breakage, murmuring reassurances, wishing she could fold Harriet in her embrace and rock her and tell her all would be well.

But it was clear that Harriet could barely stand the most necessary touch. This examination was pushing her beyond endurance.

Finally, Louisa sat back wiping her hands on a piece of gauze. She was no expert, but she didn't think any bones were broken. It looked as though whoever had done this confined themselves to the knife. The bruise on Harriet's face and the livid chafing around her wrists and ankles appeared to be the only exceptions.

It was enough. Far more than enough. Harriet stared straight ahead, and there was blind terror in those eyes, as if she was trapped in her own mind, reliving her experience, as if she didn't know she was safe.

"Oh, my dear. Who did this to you?" Louisa murmured.

She was very much afraid she knew the answer.

Eighteen

JARDINE unwrapped his fingers from Ives's throat.

"What the hell did you sneak up on me like that for? I could have killed you."

A strained wheeze was Ives's only reply. He was bent double, panting, his bald pate glinting in the moonlight.

Jardine experienced a faint tinge of remorse, but he suppressed it. He waited a good few minutes for the fellow to recover, wondering a little that Louisa hadn't defied him and followed, after all. Perhaps, at last, she was learning obedience.

His mouth twisted in a reluctant grin. Bloody unlikely, but one might always hope.

He addressed Ives. "Well, you dirty little sneak. What do you have for me?"

"Haven't seen hide nor hair of any document, guv. Radleigh's been going about his usual routine, far as I can tell. No furtive forays of any kind. He does spend a bit of time in that curiosity cabinet of his—"

Jardine ground his teeth. Radleigh would die for that.

Ives watched him, black eyes gleaming. "—But I dessay you know all about that, guv."

He hesitated. "The only other out of the ordinary is there's someone else that lives in that house besides Radleigh and his sister."

"Who?"

"Dunno, sir. Whoever it is, they has apartments in the old part of the house. That dry old stick of a housekeeper holds the key and she's the only one in or out. No one else knows about it, or if they do, they're being tight-lipped."

"An invalid, perhaps," Jardine mused. He refused to countenance the theory that sprang eagerly to mind.

He'd hoped beyond reason that Smith would be one of the guests at this house party. But things were never that simple, were they?

Who was this unknown occupant?

"Show me these apartments."

Their situation on the ground floor supported Jardine's theory that an invalid occupied them, but he couldn't be sure. He and Ives skirted the house silently. The mysterious apartments were on the opposite side of the house to the orangery.

A heavy curtain shrouded the window. There was nothing to be seen from outside. Jardine gestured for Ives to take care of the casement. In seconds, Ives had the window open.

Jardine eased himself inside, stood behind the curtains, listening. Nothing, not even the deep breathing of someone who slept. He peered into the room, saw that it was an antechamber of some sort, not the bedchamber itself.

The door to the corridor lay open. The double doors opposite it were closed. Jardine crossed the room and pressed his ear to the panels.

Angry voices rumbled within. Radleigh and . . . another man. Older. Could it be Smith?

Heavy footsteps stomped toward him. Jardine only had time to sidestep and press against the wall before the door was flung open and Radleigh strode out.

There was a whiff of something as he passed. The glimpse of dark patches on his coat.

Blood?

Fury exploded inside him, made him want to leap for Radleigh's throat. But he couldn't afford to let his passions rule him. That was what separated him from the common herd, the ability to stop before he acted.

The ability to think.

How long had he been parted from Louisa? Only a few minutes at most. Enough time to hurt her, then traverse the length of the building and engage in some sort of argument with whoever lurked in these rooms?

He didn't think so. It was possible, but not likely. And what reason would Radleigh have to harm Louisa?

He padded after Radleigh through the dark house. It must have been nearing dawn by now.

He hoped to God Louisa had returned to her room. But if she hadn't, at least by following Radleigh, he could ensure that she was safe from him.

Radleigh ignored the central staircase and continued along the first floor, toward the orangery. He wasn't going back to his bedchamber, then. Nor to Louisa's.

Jardine kept to the shadows as Radleigh paused and shrugged out of the silk dressing gown he wore. He rolled the dressing gown into a ball and shoved it behind a solid workbench.

He continued walking, his stride more purposeful. Strange. Radleigh was dressed for riding.

Ducking behind the workbench, Jardine picked up the discarded robe. The moonlit darkness leached color from the garment, painting it in shadowy grays. The stains looked almost black. But that rich smell was unmistakably blood.

Lots of it.

He dropped the garment and went after his host.

WHEN they finally reached the inn, a glimmer of dawn lit the horizon and the birds had begun to call.

Louisa alighted from the cart and, with the help of Saunders, assisted Harriet down. They took care to avoid touching her injuries. The sharp cry Harriet gave told her they hadn't entirely succeeded. Harriet's knees gave out as Saunders released her.

"Oh, she's fainted," said Louisa.

The secretary caught Harriet and lifted her in his arms, surprising Louisa with his strength. Ignoring the lone ostler who looked on, he carried their patient into the inn.

Louisa had no coins to give, so she nodded at the ostler and said, "Stable these, my good man. Mr. Saunders will attend to you in a minute."

She followed Saunders into the inn, to see that he'd laid Harriet on a couch in the vestibule and was speaking with the landlady.

"Set upon! In these parts? Good gracious!" The mistress of the establishment rushed to Harriet's side, her eyes wide with shock.

"Will you send for a doctor, please," said Louisa. "Immediately."

"I can, ma'am, but he's up to his elbows delivering twin babies tonight. He won't be here till morn."

"Well, ask him anyway. In the meantime, I need clean sheets cut into strips for bandages, hot water, brandy, and something to use as swabs," said Louisa in a low voice. "We need to take her somewhere quiet. The lady's guardian is staying here. A Mister . . ."

She trailed off, wondering what on earth Faulkner called himself when staying here. He wouldn't use his real name, would he? But she didn't think Jardine had mentioned it.

"Miller." A voice from the stairs made her look up. The man himself.

Her heart pounded. How had he known they were here?

Of course. Faulkner would make it his business to be informed of any untoward occurrences. He'd probably set a spy to watch.

The head of operations took in the situation at a glance. "Upstairs."

He turned, clearly expecting her to follow, but halted when she said, "Wait."

Louisa licked her lips. "She cannot climb those stairs unaided. I need help."

She dashed a glance at the taproom. Where had Saunders disappeared to?

Shaggy eyebrows raised, Faulkner looked down at himself. He'd assumed the guise of a much older man, doddering and decrepit. She'd been so glad to seem him, she hadn't noticed until now. A fine spy she was.

Faulkner nodded to the landlady. "Find someone to carry my niece up, please."

The landlady called for the ostler they'd seen outside.

Harriet lay in a dead faint, which was not a bad thing, given her fear of men at the moment, the pain she was in, and what must have been the torture of her conscious thoughts.

Allowing the ostler to carry her, Louisa turned and followed Faulkner upstairs.

Louisa directed him to place the injured young woman on the bed. The landlady bustled in with such medical supplies as she'd been able to gather. Louisa thanked them both and ushered them from the room. She turned to Faulkner.

He bent over Harriet with a knife in hand. Without mercy or delicacy, he ripped her bodice open, to further reveal the bloody mess.

Louisa let out a cry and flew to the bedside. She'd known

it was bad, but without proper lighting in the temple she hadn't gauged the full extent of Harriet's wounds. She'd cleaned them as best she could, but during the drive to the village they'd started bleeding again.

A series of deep cuts over Harriet's décolletage and the rise of her breasts had slashed her shift to tatters, but her stays seemed to have protected her from even worse mutilation.

Faulkner's jaw set, grim as granite. "Someone has had a grand old time. Radleigh, most likely." He cocked an eyebrow at her. "Rape?"

Softly, Louisa answered, "As far as I could tell, she hasn't been interfered with in that way." Ah, pray God she was right.

She took up the flannel and the bowl of water and gently sponged the blood away. Harriet's eyes were closed, her face showing a deathly pallor, at least on one side. On the other, her eyelid was purple and so puffy, Louisa doubted Harriet would be able to open her eye when she woke.

"She has been missing for two days," said Louisa. "Was she with him all that time?"

"Hard to say. I don't think so, or she'd be in a worse case than this. But you never know; she was a tough little bird."

He strode to the window and stood looking out. "One more score to settle," he mused. "Does it ever end, do you think?"

Louisa didn't venture an answer, and it appeared none was expected of her. She hadn't considered the question from this perspective before. It must be a heavy burden to bear, this continual fight against villainy on every front. Radleigh was ready to betray his own country for money and prestige. He had taken pleasure in inflicting indescribable pain on Harriet Burton.

How had she escaped? Had Saunders saved her? She hadn't thought to ask.

Saunders. Where was he? Perhaps he'd returned quietly

to the house, now that he'd done his duty. He wouldn't want to be seen to interfere with his master's affairs, gruesome as they were. She wondered why he'd remain in Radleigh's employ after this. Was it so difficult to find other work?

"I think you're right, Mr. Faulkner. I think Radleigh did this," she said quietly. "His secretary, Mr. Saunders, found her. He came to me in great distress and bade me help, for she wouldn't let him touch her. I fear that her mind has been damaged."

Faulkner turned and she looked him in the eye. "Radleigh is dangerous. You knew it, yet you asked me to become close to him."

Slowly, he nodded. "Yes. I knew it. But you, Lady Louisa, were never in danger. A man like that will treat his aristocratic wife like a precious ornament while she is of use to him. Simultaneously, he will use whores and streetwalkers with unparalleled viciousness. Men like that slot different aspects of their lives into compartments, you see. When he is with his wife, his innocent children, he is not the same man as he is when he kidnaps and brutalizes other women."

She shuddered at the cold, authoritative analysis. "Strangely, that doesn't make me feel better."

Louisa decided then and there. Jardine had the matter of the agent list well in hand, or so he said. She would take the wiser course and withdraw from the game.

She took up some gauze and dipped it in hot water. "I want to look after Harriet. Will you give up this room to us and move to another? When she is well enough, I will take her home with me."

Silence reigned while she worked and while Faulkner presumably calculated how this change in circumstances affected his plans.

"How will you get hold of that document now?" asked Louisa, when she'd done all she could to ease Harriet's pain. "The list of operatives?"

Faulkner turned his head. "One always has a fallback plan."

He wouldn't tell her what that was, of course, but she knew. Jardine was the only alternative. Why hadn't Faulkner commissioned Jardine with this job in the first place? Hadn't he been confident Jardine could secure an invitation to the house party?

"I must go out," said Faulkner abruptly, reaching for his hat and walking stick. "Do what you can here and I'll get another room for myself. I'll arrange transport to take you and Mrs. Burton to safety when you judge her well enough to travel."

At the door, he hesitated. "It had better be today. Regardless of her injuries, she'll be safer away from this place."

"In the meantime, I would like you to give me a pistol, if you please." She was stupid to have left the house without her own, but events had moved too quickly.

Faulkner raised his brows in surprise. He didn't know everything about her, then.

She lifted her chin. "You don't think I mean to remain here unprotected?"

Faulkner snorted. "You wouldn't have the gall to shoot a man. Ladies, I find, aren't fond of loud noises."

Her jaw set. "Don't be too sure of that. Rather a loud noise than . . ." Her gaze slid to Harriet, and she shut her eyes at the imagined pain of that torture.

Faulkner tilted his head, considering her with a sharp, speculative gaze. "You surprise me, Lady Louisa. You are not such a delicate flower as I'd supposed. But there will be no shooting here. The last thing we need is to draw more attention to ourselves." He put on his hat. "I won't be gone long."

Louisa locked the door behind Faulkner and dragged one of his trunks against it for good measure. It wouldn't hold a determined intruder at bay, but at least a break-in would create noise and attract the other guests' attention.

A low murmur from the bed brought her to Harriet's side.

The girl cracked open an eye and cried out. The pain must have been intense, indescribable.

Louisa quickly picked up the small glass of laudanum the landlady had brought. She slid an arm beneath Harriet's shoulders—thank heaven Radleigh hadn't touched her back—and held the glass rim against Harriet's cracked, swollen lips.

"Drink, my dear," she murmured. "It will take away some of the pain."

The liquid went down in tiny doses, in fits and starts, some of it running in rivulets from the sides of Harriet's mouth.

Carefully, Louisa wiped the spillage and stroked the hair from Harriet's brow. Harriet's hair had been gold and lustrous. Now, it was matted with dirt and blood, and . . . had some of it been cut off? A short, choppy lock at her temple was a noticeably different length from the others.

The horror of it dawned on Louisa, making her stomach churn. All those locks of hair she'd found. *Not* lovers, as she'd assumed, as Saunders had also believed.

Victims.

Shock clutched her throat. Radleigh. It must have been him. Only now did she fully believe him capable of such brutality.

Louisa shuddered. She had become engaged to a man who collected locks of hair from victims of his torture, and perhaps worse? She had let him touch her hand, had considered allowing him further liberties for the good of King and country.

She felt soiled, revolted that she'd come so close to pure evil. But she'd done it in the name of getting a vital document. That list of agents in the wrong hands could spell disaster, death, and torture for goodness knew how many operatives and the ruin of countless operations. Harriet had been prepared to die to retrieve it, that much was clear.

Did she, Louisa, have the right to shirk that burden now?

Harriet sighed, and her breathing became less frantic. The laudanum must have taken effect. Grimly, Louisa set to work again, smoothing salve on Harriet's injuries, mourning the once-flawless skin that would now be scarred forever.

Despite the warmth in the room, Harriet shivered, so Louisa covered her with blanket and sheet, careful to keep the weight of them off her wounds.

Soon, long, even breathing told her Harriet slept. Louisa exhaled a relieved sigh. There was little more she could do until the doctor arrived in the morning, but she'd have to remain vigilant against infection and fever.

For the moment, Louisa needed rest. She edged her chair closer to the bed, laid her head on her crossed arms, closed her eyes . . .

An insistent tap on the door startled her awake. She shot to her feet, wondering how long she'd slept. Wildly, she glanced around the room for a weapon and settled for one of the candlesticks on the mantel.

The brass was hard and cold in her grip. She raised it, ready for whoever it was to break open the door.

"Lady Louisa? It's me, Saunders."

Louisa's shoulders sagged with relief. She put down the candlestick moved toward the door.

"LADY Louisa?" Faulkner shook his head. "What makes you think she came here?"

Jardine ground his teeth in frustration. He'd lost her. How could he have lost her like that?

He'd followed Radleigh to a village in the next county, watched him knock on the door of a private house and be admitted. A private house that stood next to the church. A rectory? What could Radleigh want with a vicar?

He swore under his breath as Radleigh emerged with an

older man. After exchanging a few heated words, they left together in Radleigh's curricle.

Jardine followed them, cursing, all the way back to Radleigh's house. The notion that leaped to his mind was scarcely tenable, yet what other explanation could there be? Did Radleigh intend to force Louisa to marry him? Was this vicar complicit in the plan?

When Jardine checked Louisa's room, she wasn't there, although she'd pulled the curtains around her bed so that no one could tell she was missing just by looking through the peephole.

Dammit! Where could she be?

He shouldn't have left her alone, even for a second, out there in the dark. Someone must have been watching, but who?

Panic rising, he'd searched the house but not found a trace of her. Finally, he asked at the stables and heard the strange tale of Louisa going off in a cart with Radleigh's secretary and an unknown woman. They'd headed in the direction of the village.

The only establishment open at this hour was the Bird in Hand. Before he'd had a chance to ask for Louisa, he'd caught sight of Faulkner in the taproom and collared him.

Now, he glanced at the head of operations, who remained expressionless, as always. He stabbed a finger at him. "I hold you responsible for this. Lady Louisa's missing, and Radleigh came in last night covered in blood."

"You would be unwise to leap to conclusions on that score," said Faulkner. "She's a resourceful woman. Perhaps she's doing a little digging of her own. Perhaps you don't give her sufficient credit for taking care of herself."

"And perhaps you would like me to slowly disembowel you with a fruit knife," snarled Jardine. "She is a gently bred female and you were totally out of order sending her into Radleigh's sphere. You will help me find her, or by God, you'll wish you were—"

He stopped. His eyes narrowed. The near-feral side of his nature prowled very close to the surface. Faulkner knew something. He could smell it. "Where is she?"

Faulkner snorted, shrugged his shoulders. "How should I know?"

Jardine sniffed out a hint of uncertainty. Silkily, he said, "Do you know how I operate in the field, Faulkner?"

"Can't imagine."

"If I have to kill, the kill is always quick and clean and silent. But sometimes . . . Sometimes the slow, inexorable infliction of pain is necessary, isn't it, to extract information? I think this might be one of those occasions."

A flicker of emotion shook Faulkner's stern features. "You forget who you're talking to, Jardine. Your position would not save you if you harmed me."

"And nothing on this earth will save *you* if you have caused harm to one hair on that lady's head."

Jardine lunged for Faulkner, who put up his hands. "All right, all right! She is upstairs, in my bedchamber."

"What?"

"Tending to one of my operatives." Faulkner waved a hand, his face ashen. "Go up, go up. It's the second floor, first on the right."

Jardine took the stairs, two at a time, and kicked open Faulkner's door.

A girl with tangled blond hair lay on the bed. She looked vaguely familiar, and her injuries made his stomach rise up, not with revulsion, but fear. *That animal.*

He moved toward the bed. Ordinarily, he'd have more compassion, but he couldn't afford delay. He touched her hand, then squeezed it gently until her good eye opened a crack. Her head tossed a little, and he had to repeat his question twice.

"Where is Louisa?"

Her torn lips moved silently, then came a scrape of sound. "Radleigh . . . took her."

"Christ!" He turned to go, but her hand shot out to grab his wrist. He looked back.

"Smith. Smith's here."

The effort seemed to have taken all her strength. She was white to the lips, and her good eye fluttered closed.

No more. Jardine charged downstairs to Faulkner. "Louisa's not there. You tell me where she is, old man, or—"

The genuine shock on Faulkner's face stopped him. "But . . ." Faulkner kneaded his wiry eyebrows with a thumb and forefinger, then looked up at Jardine. "Dear God. She wanted a pistol—"

"Where would Radleigh take her?" Jardine rapped out the words.

Mutely, Faulkner shook his head.

"You are a dead man, Faulkner."

Jardine was gone on the words.

Nineteen

LOUISA woke with a painful throb in the back of her head that was so severe, darkness threatened to overtake her once more. Tears gathered in her eyes as the motion of the carriage she rode in exacerbated the pain. The scant light that filtered into the vehicle hurt her eyes, and the image of Radleigh sitting opposite her blurred and swayed.

Radleigh.

It took all her strength to muster the will. She opened her mouth and screamed, and the sound tore into her skull like hot shards of glass.

Nausea welled, threatened to rise. She clamped her mouth shut and breathed in and out deeply through her nose to quell the sick feeling. She *would not* cast up her accounts in front of him.

"There's no one to hear you." Amused, Radleigh surveyed her critically. "Otherwise I'd have made sure you were gagged."

Her wrists were bound. He'd left her feet free, but in soft slippers she couldn't do much with those.

Radleigh's slow, wide smile made her stomach churn anew.

"Saunders has been very sly, hasn't he, my dear? I must say, I never knew he had it in him. He was very loyal to you for a time. But pain, I find, makes most men weaken. Very soon, they can't tell you what they know fast enough. Eventually, they betray everything they hold dear." His smile grew. "It makes *women* do all sorts of interesting things. As you will see."

She thought of those locks of hair, and of Harriet. The damage he'd done to Harriet's body would heal, albeit leaving scars. But the nightmare of enduring what Harriet had endured . . .

Panic all but choked her. She *couldn't*. She'd do anything to avoid that fate.

Yet, the only knowledge she could offer Radleigh in return for her freedom was that she'd been working for Faulkner, that Harriet had been working for him also, that Jardine wanted that list of names on the government's behalf. That her brother's name would be among those listed.

Betraying any one of those people was out of the question.

Will you still think that when you are cut to ribbons, lying in your own blood?

Through stiff lips, she forced herself to ask, "What do you mean to do with me?"

The carriage slowed and swept around a bend. The hard hazel eyes glinted.

"Why, Lady Louisa, I mean to marry you. What else?"

Oh God. But she would not show him fear. Pointedly, she looked down at her bound hands. "I regret to say that I believe we should not suit."

He threw back his head and laughed. "Do you know, I'm beginning to think you're wrong about that."

"You'll never get away with it. No clergyman would marry an unwilling bride."

A cynical expression fell over Radleigh's features. "How odd that I needed only to travel to the next village to find just such a cleric."

He patted his pocket. "I have the special license right here."

Desperate, she licked her lips. "I shall make an outcry. One of your guests will come to my aid."

"Unfortunately, a rumored outbreak of typhus in the village has sent my guests fleeing for the hills and my servants hurrying home to their families. There will be no one in my house except you and me, the vicar, and the witnesses we need for the ceremony."

He flicked a glance over her. "A pity you are so shabbily dressed for your wedding day, my dear, but it cannot be helped."

She'd worn a simple dimity gown and a straw bonnet when she'd wed Jardine, and he hadn't cared a button.

She curled her lip. "You are so fastidious? I wonder that you could bear to be seen with such a rag-tail specimen as I."

He waved a careless hand. "It's a closed carriage, after all."

A sense of unreality shimmered around her. He couldn't get away with this. He was mad.

The suspicion that Radleigh truly was unhinged and not simply evil crept into her brain. Such a wedding as he proposed would never stand up to challenge given Radleigh's coercion and her prior marriage to Jardine, but legal challenges took time. One day as Radleigh's wife would be one day too many.

"My brother is a duke. He will never take your word or the word of a corrupt clergyman or a hundred witnesses over mine. He'll move heaven and earth to sunder this marriage. He'll destroy you." If Jardine didn't beat Max to it.

Radleigh's smile tightened. Her logic made some impression, then. To any but the most irrational mind, it must.

Clearly, he'd been caught unawares by this latest development with Harriet and had made his plans hastily. He'd thought he had time on his side, but now that Louisa had seen his handiwork, there was no point in continuing to woo her.

His alternative scheme was flawed. He was off balance, and although that made him more dangerous, it also made him more vulnerable.

This marriage was vitally important to Radleigh. How could she use that?

Louisa stiffened. *She could bargain to get that list.*

She licked her lips. "Perhaps we might come to an arrangement."

They lurched over a rut in the road. Radleigh gave a faint smile, spread his arms along the top of his seat. "You are in no position to bargain."

"Oh, but I think I am." She tried to give him a relaxed smile, but she wasn't sure if she succeeded. "I cannot see this marriage will work the way you want it to unless you have a quiescent wife. And it so happens that you hold a certain piece of paper which is of great interest to me."

His head jerked up. So he hadn't guessed why she'd betrothed herself to him. He didn't know of her connection with Faulkner, then.

"For that list," she continued, "I would be prepared to wed you."

Shock flared in his eyes. "I've rarely heard of such altruism," he drawled. "Who told you about this document?"

It was easy to tell half-truths convincingly. "Your latest victim managed to tell me. She was looking for the list when you caught her, you see."

A gleam came into his eye. He crossed his ankles. "Was she, indeed? It seems everyone is after that precious document." He fingered his mouth a little, thoughtfully. "I should have killed her, of course. But that damned busybody must needs spoil my fun."

No doubt he meant Saunders. How had the secretary managed to make him stop?

With heavy irony, Louisa said, "She might yet die of her wounds, if that's any consolation."

"Well, that is something," Radleigh admitted.

She couldn't quite believe she was having this conversation. *As long as he wants me as his wife, he won't hurt me.* She held fast to that thought.

"Do you agree to my terms?"

He sighed. "Oh, very well. I agree to your proposal, Lady Louisa. I'd shake hands on it, but . . ." He indicated her bindings with an airy wave of his hand and laughed.

Perhaps she wouldn't wait for Jardine to take Radleigh into custody. Perhaps she'd shoot the blackguard herself.

"A pity I sent Beth and all my guests away," he mused. "We could have made quite an occasion of it. However, now that I have your agreement, *you* will have the opportunity to rest this evening and make yourself presentable. I shall content myself with anticipating our wedding night."

Louisa barely suppressed a shudder. She certainly would shoot him if he tried to lay a finger on her with amorous intent.

The carriage slowed and finally came to a stop. Between her teeth, she said, "Perhaps you ought to untie me if you wish me to look like a willing bride."

Laughing, he did so, not troubling to be gentle. She hissed with the sting of small nicks from his knife as he sawed through her bonds. Eventually, the ropes fell away and Radleigh opened the carriage door and got out, leaving Louisa chafing her wrists. Even through gloves, the rope had burned.

Though it took a great force of will to allow Radleigh to

touch her after all she'd seen last night, she gave him her hand and alighted.

He kept her hand and kissed it with gallantry that would have been romantic coming from another man. Thank goodness her glove stood between his lips and her bare skin. She thought of the pistol under her bed. If he came near her tonight . . .

"One more condition," she said. "I don't wish to see you until the wedding tomorrow."

"You are a coy damsel, aren't you? Very well, then. I suppose I might curb my impatience for twenty-four hours if that is your wish." Spreading his hands, he added, "You see how well we will deal together, my love? How accommodating I can be? I trust you won't mind if I lock your bedchamber door."

She swallowed, then managed to say lightly, "Not at all. Until tomorrow, then."

He smiled into her eyes. "Ah, but the wait will be an eternity."

RADLEIGH had been right. The wait *was* an eternity.

Louisa slept for some hours, the weariness of her body finally overtaking her spirit. She woke to the fading light, wondering where Jardine could be. She hoped he was safe. Part of her longed for him, yet part of her wanted him to stay away and not disrupt her plans.

Apparently, not all of the servants had left their posts due to the typhus rumor, or some had returned upon finding that it was untrue. Merry came in shortly before the dinner hour to ask Louisa what she needed.

According to the maid, Radleigh had left the house and was not expected to return for dinner.

Merry gazed at her with sympathy at such shabby treatment by her prospective spouse. Louisa could hardly restrain a skip of joy.

"A quiet night, I think." She ordered a bath and a dinner tray to be brought to her room.

The bath was pure, unadulterated heaven. A Chinese screen blocked the view from the peephole, in case Radleigh returned unexpectedly.

Louisa trailed a hand through the water and watched the drips fall from her fingertips. She turned her head to speak to Merry. "Thank you. I can manage for myself now. Lay out my night rail, please, and then you may retire."

The door soon closed behind the maid, and Louisa sank deeper into the steaming water.

The lavender scent she'd poured in soothed and calmed her a little. She closed her eyes, and her aches loudly voiced their presence in her joints and muscles. She massaged them, kneading deeply with her fingertips. She made herself concentrate on the physical, every sensation, every twinge, every slow release of pain.

Worries and doubts clawed at her mind, but for this brief space, she refused to allow them purchase. She needed calm and rest to face the following day.

The water temperature had dropped a little. Louisa was in that languorous state where getting out of the bath seemed far too much effort, while staying in the gradually cooling water would spoil the entire effect.

A scrape of sound made her eyes snap open, to find the candlelight snuffed, the room plunged into darkness. She gasped as two hands shoved under arms and plucked her from the bath as if she weighed no more than a child's doll.

"Damn you, Louisa." The soft growl was all she heard before a savage, beautiful mouth found hers.

I thought you'd never come. The bleat of her little girl self drowned in a flood of pleasure. He filled her senses, beat like a drum in her heart, throbbed in her blood.

His arms enfolded her, and the damp chill down her

back was a sharp contrast to the furnace inside her, to the heat of his mouth and hands.

He feasted on her, claimed her mouth as he'd long ago taken her heart. She gave him back everything with equal force, slid one hand up to his nape and urged him to delve harder, farther.

He kept kissing her as he palmed her breasts, kneaded her peaked nipples, caressed and traced his fingertips over them until excitement snapped and fizzed through her bloodstream.

She groaned softly as his mouth replaced his fingers. His hands slid down to hold her hips firmly, forcing her to surrender to this delicious assault. He gave no quarter, drove her into a frenzy of desire.

Between her thighs, sensation heated and pooled, intensifying to a sweet ache. This was heavenly, sublime, but it wasn't enough. When he touched her there, it wasn't enough. He went to his knees, put his mouth on her, licked into her, and no, it wasn't enough, wasn't . . .

She shuddered, her climax powerful, overwhelming, rocking her body. And he was merciless, prolonging the agony when she begged him to stop, sending her over again.

He let her go, briefly, to shuck his clothes. She turned from him, panting, clutching at the edge of the bed to steady herself.

She felt his presence behind her, solid and silent. His flesh touched hers as he bent over her. She felt the warmth of his breath in her ear, the faint roughness of the hair on his chest brush her back. The smooth, incendiary heat of his skin, his erection pressing against her. The strength in his hands as he gripped her hips, silently urged her to climb on the bed.

She crawled over the coverlet and would have turned, but he stayed her, pulling back a little so that she supported herself with her elbows, her rump high, presented to him.

In the darkness, he couldn't see her, but she felt vulnerable all the same. She twisted a little and gave a soft cry of protest, but he held her there, without speaking, waiting for her submission.

"Jardine," she whispered, but one hand covered her mouth while the other parted her thighs a little wider, then spread the folds between her legs, caressing, exploring with gentle, insistent fingertips.

The tip of his member nudged into her, and she moaned, forgetting her dignity, opening her mouth against his hand, feeling the heat and wetness of her own harsh breathing.

He eased into her, letting her feel every slow, hard inch. She moaned again and licked the hand that covered her mouth, grazed the flesh of his palm with her teeth.

His agonized groan in response made her bold. She squeezed him with her inner muscles, longing to take more of him, while she laved his hand with luxurious abandon.

His other hand came down on her lower back, pressing, holding her still. He was determined to draw this out. She wished she could touch him, but in this position, exploration was impossible.

The hand against her mouth relaxed and lifted, then his fingertips ran over her lips. She licked the pad of his thumb, heard his breathing become harsher. His thumb pressed, insinuated into her mouth. On instinct, she closed around it and ran her tongue along it, stroking him as he stroked his hard length into her.

She made love to his hand as he made love to her, sucking each finger in turn, glorying in his possession.

Shifting a little, he thrust into her, and Louisa gasped as he hit a particularly sweet spot. Both hands gripped her hips now, holding her steady as he plunged and stroked deep that same place that had drawn her gasp.

The fast build of sensation scattered her senses. She

could only focus on the heat and slide of him, the beat of blood, the inevitable surrender. She wanted it, yet it was too much.

Illogically, she tried to move away, but his hands anchored her and she had to take it—take *him*—beyond her endurance, beyond reason or thought.

Finally, she surrendered, shuddering with it, allowing herself to be carried away as the pleasure swept over her in wave after wave.

His release came then, and he collapsed over her, biting hard into her shoulder to stifle his own cry.

When his shudders had subsided, he shifted his body from hers to lie beside her, his lungs heaving.

She ran her palm over the hard muscles of his chest in a gesture of wonder and thankfulness. He turned to her, lashed an arm around her waist, and kissed her softly.

"My wife," he said, a husky rasp to his cut-glass accent. *"Mine."*

A thrill pierced Louisa's pleasure-struck haze. She'd known it, hadn't she? Deep within her, she'd known he'd lied that awful morning at his house. Their marriage had been legitimate; they were husband and wife. They were one.

She couldn't seem to muster the fury she ought to feel.

They lay side by side, face-to-face, long legs tangled. Louisa could discern the barest outline of him in the deep black of night. If only she might transport them to another time and place. There was no leisure for rebuilding foundations or for planning the future.

If they could get out of this mess . . .

She reached up and smoothed the inevitable stray locks of hair from his brow. "You bastard, Jardine."

Silent laughter shook him. "Such language!"

"No, it's not funny. Why did you lie to me about our wedding? It was unnecessary and cruel."

He growled. "I was trying to keep you safe."

"And yet, here I am, betrothed to a traitorous sadist," she murmured. She wouldn't stoop to apportioning blame, but the chain of events was irrefutable. She would not have been so unwise and adventuresome had Jardine not rejected her, cast her adrift.

Did she regret the intervening incidents? Perhaps not, if they brought her this. *Him.* Assuming they didn't both die ugly deaths here, of course.

Softly, Jardine said, "Despite his disgusting tendencies, Radleigh is a small-time villain. There's someone mixed up in this who is far more dangerous than Radleigh could ever be. He's after that list."

"How do you know that? Was he one of the guests?"

Grimly, Jardine said, "No. But the woman you know as Harriet Burton saw him here."

"You spoke to her? When?"

"Today. She couldn't say much. I asked her where you'd gone and she said the name 'Smith.' It was enough."

Jardine bent his head closer. "He wasn't one of the guests. I'd have recognized him. But I think he's nearby. I'll get that list—"

"I don't think Radleigh had any intention of selling it to you. He has agreed to give it to me if I wed him tomorrow. I'll go through the ceremony, but since I'm already married . . ."

"Forget it. I'll not have you compromise yourself like that. Do you want to be labeled a bigamist?"

"I had no choice," Louisa said coolly. "It was either agree to marry him or be forced. Or perhaps shredded to ribbons like Harriet. I don't think he'd decided which."

Jardine's hold tightened around her. "He would have double-crossed you, anyway. If I sum up Radleigh correctly, he would have taken back the document and sold it to me later."

"Why are you so intent on finding this Smith?"

"It's a long story, one I don't intend to regale you with now. But while Smith lives, you and everyone . . . close to me are in danger."

How convenient for you. The treacherous thought seemed to come from nowhere.

"Jardine—"

"Shh." He tensed and laid a finger over her mouth. What had he heard? She strained to hear but couldn't discern any noise beyond her own breathing.

He launched out of bed and pulled on his shirt in one swift motion. The faint glimmer of moonlight caught the whiteness of the fabric as he listened at the door, then opened it.

Louisa scrambled to cover herself with the bedclothes as a swift exchange of murmuring ensued. Then Jardine closed the door.

He bent toward her, spoke in her ear. "That was my man-servant. Radleigh's back, heading upstairs. Get dressed, Louisa. I need to finish this now." Before she could protest at his high-handedness, he added, "I'll need your help. Pin up your hair."

He yanked on his breeches, hunted for his boots.

The click of a pistol being primed reverberated through the silence.

What was he going to do? Louisa scrambled up, fumbled through the darkness for some garments.

Finally clothed, she straightened and reached for her hairpins. "What now?" she whispered, quickly twisting her hair into a makeshift coiffure.

Jardine shifted the Chinese screen she'd used to protect her privacy while she bathed. His hands gripped her hips and he maneuvered her to a spot that would leave her in full view of Radleigh's peephole. "Now I want you to stand here and begin undressing. Very slowly."

Light flared, illuminating the room, throwing long shadows against the opposite wall.

She glanced back at the lit lamp.

Jardine had disappeared.

Twenty

JARDINE liberated a candle from its sconce outside Louisa's door and moved toward the curiosity cabinet next to her bedchamber.

He glanced at the clock. The night wasn't so very advanced. The household would still be up and about, but it couldn't be helped. He had to get Louisa out of here now.

According to Ives, Radleigh had been drinking heavily at the tavern in the village. What was the bet he'd visit his fiancée before going to bed? At the very least, he'd stop in the curiosity room to see whether he could catch a glimpse of her.

Jardine lit two branches of candles, left the door wide open. Glassy, dead eyes stared back at him from the cabinet with all sorts of stuffed animals in them. He shrugged off a frisson of distaste and located the peephole.

He bent to look through it, to ensure that Louisa had obeyed him. Instantly, he was captivated by the sight of Louisa, slowly unpinning her hair. One shining silvery blond lock after another fell down her back like moonlit rain, cool and alluring.

When all the pins were out, she ran her fingers through the straight mass, lifting it from her nape and letting it fall. The graceful sensuality of her movements made him hard for her all over again.

They'd never had leisure for slow exploration, had they? Everything was always rushed, explosive. Exciting, but ultimately not enough.

The longing to see her in his bed, in his home, pulled at him so strongly, the temptation to forget this whole business and steal her away almost gained the upper hand over duty.

But he was doing all this so they could have that leisure, grow old together, wasn't he? After all these years of hiding their association, of being hunter and prey, such an existence seemed as distant and unattainable as a mirage.

He drew a long breath as Louisa daintily lifted one stockinged foot onto a chair, smoothing her skirts back up her leg to reveal the prettiest garter he'd ever seen. All lacy and beribboned, it was pure white, but no whiter than the slender thigh it encircled.

He thought of Louisa's legs, the strong, elegant length of them wrapped around his waist, and more blood left his brain. Slowly, she slid the garter down, and he imagined pressing his mouth in its place, making love to that sensitive, soft skin on her inner thigh.

Still, no Radleigh.

Louisa's stocking, robbed of its anchor, fell easily to her ankle. She bent to pluck the stocking from her foot, giving him a perfect view of her small breasts swinging forward, moving freely against the fabric of her gown and shift. There hadn't been time to lace her corset.

She repeated the slow operation with her other garter and stocking. Clearly, she was drawing this out to delay undressing fully. Sensible of her to remain clothed. Though it was stupid to pant like a dog for the revelation of one more hint of flesh when he'd just licked and touched every naked inch of her, he willed her to reveal something. Just a little more . . .

Footsteps approached the room. "What the hell are you doing there?"

Outrage filled Radleigh's tone. *Bastard.*

Jardine smiled, put a finger to his lips. "You don't know? I would have thought . . ."

He motioned Radleigh forward. "By all means, see for yourself." He allowed his smile to broaden. "Allow me to compliment you on your taste." He kissed his fingers. *"Exquisite."*

Ignoring the furious snarl on Radleigh's face, he bent again to the peephole.

It took a second to register what he saw.

Or didn't see.

Louisa wasn't there.

The moment of distraction made him a little slow to react. Radleigh grabbed his shoulder and yanked him away from the wall. Jardine dodged the blow aimed at his chin and drove his fist hard into Radleigh's stomach.

The breath left Radleigh in a loud "Oof," but he kept on, a powerful battering ram in contrast to Jardine's quick agility.

Jardine could have used his pistol, but a shot would bring servants running. Besides, he wanted Radleigh alive so he could force him to reveal where that list was hidden. The time for strategic maneuvering was past. He'd have that list if he had to kill Radleigh to get it.

The heat of the fight was in his blood now. He had his rhythm and his opponent's measure.

With a snarl, Jardine spun away from a blow aimed at his solar plexus. Radleigh might know some dirty tricks, but he didn't know as many as Jardine.

Radleigh reached out and bunched his big hands in

Jardine's coat, made as if to throw him across the room. Jardine's foot shot out, sweeping Radleigh's legs from under him.

The big man crashed to the floor, hitting his head on the edge of the stuffed animal display.

Jardine stood over the unconscious body of his opponent, panting, his fists clenched.

The sharp sound of someone clapping made his head jerk up.

Jardine froze as the man he had sought all these years strolled into the room.

"Smith."

He was flanked by a heavy, a big, thickset man who looked like he belonged on the streets of London, a knife in his hand and ugliness in his eyes.

Jardine maintained his sangfroid. "I wondered how long it would be before we met."

Another thug arrived, shoving Louisa before him, crowding the small room. He had a handkerchief wrapped around his upper arm, and it was rapidly staining red.

"Stuck you, did she?" Jardine's eyes flickered to Louisa, warning her to be silent. "My compliments, Lady Louisa." Where had she found a knife?

Smith turned, his smile broadening.

Louisa's eyes widened as she saw Smith. "Oh, Mr. Saunders. Thank heaven! Jardine, it's Mr. Saunders, Radleigh's secretary, the man who helped me—"

"No, Louisa. He's not here to help us. And his name is not Saunders." Jardine drew in a long breath. "It's Smith."

Smith threw back his head and laughed.

"Such a trusting little thing, isn't she?" Smith's lively brown eyes sparkled with amusement, glinted with a malice that shocked Louisa to the core.

Confusion flooded her brain. Mr. Saunders, who'd

taken such tender care of Harriet, was the villain Jardine sought? She'd pictured Saunders screaming in pain as Radleigh tortured him into revealing her and Harriet's whereabouts. He appeared in excellent spirits now. So Radleigh must have lied about that. Was he in collusion with Smith, after all? She stared at Saunders—no, Smith—trying to fathom it.

Smith tilted his head, examining her in his turn. "Clever and brave and true. Yes, I like her. I am not, now, surprised at your choice, Jardine, though I admit to my initial bafflement. Your *other* mistress is so very . . . *different*, isn't she?"

Louisa couldn't restrain her gasp. Her gaze flew to Jardine's. His expression was flinty, giving nothing away.

Saunders—Smith—had shed his mild-mannered veneer. The transformation would be remarkable, impressive, if it weren't so terrifying.

He held out a commanding hand. "Bring her here."

The man she'd wounded with the knife left on her supper tray shoved her in front of him, none too gently.

She lifted her chin, met Smith's gaze. "When my brother hears of this, you'll be sorry."

Smith's firm lips trembled, as if he were finding it difficult to contain his mirth. "Shall I? I wonder."

A groan sounded from the floor. Radleigh was waking up. That made the odds even higher against them.

"Ah, alas, poor Radleigh." Smith shook his head. "He was panting to enjoy the social status you would bring as his wife, wasn't he, Lady Louisa? But after the regrettable incident last night, I fear our friend's ambition to turn respectable must be at an end, don't you? Stupid of him. If he'd played his cards right, he could have had everything he wanted, just as I promised."

The dark, deep-set eyes turned opaque as they scanned her from head to toe. "Shall I let him have *you*, my lady?"

Louisa swallowed hard. The picture of Harriet lying

bloodied and haunted in that horrid temple rose in her mind's eye.

She didn't answer, just stared at him doggedly, tried to block out the desperation that gripped the back of her neck, hammered in her chest.

They had to get out of this mess. Why didn't Jardine do something?

Muttering obscenities, Radleigh slowly raised himself to his hands and knees. There was a swift movement, and his head snapped up, the momentum flipping him over. He crashed to the ground and lay still.

Jardine shrugged. "Sorry. Foot slipped."

Smith gave the kind of indulgent smile a father might give at a young son's playful antics. He turned to his henchmen. "Take them down."

"A moment." Jardine fixed Smith with his gaze. "This is between you and me, Smith. Let's settle it now. Alone."

"And miss all the fun I'm going to have?" Smith's smile broadened. "I don't think so."

"You like to take out your inadequacies on women—"

Smith placed a hand over his heart. "Now, there, you wrong me. Not just *any* women, Lord Jardine. You are confusing me with an indiscriminate boor like Radleigh." Dreamily, he said, "*How* your lovely Celeste screamed when Radleigh's knife cut into her flesh. Oh yes, he was with me, even then."

Jardine took a hasty step forward. With a warning growl, the thug's hold on Louisa tightened. His knife pressed harder to her throat. She couldn't stop the cry of pain and fear.

Jardine halted at the sound. With a furious glare at Louisa's captor, he backed away, holding his palms outward.

Smith's hateful deep voice went on. "Does Celeste still bear the scars? I thought so. Such a ripe beauty. Such a terrible waste. As I recall, she had the most glorious hair." He smiled. "Radleigh liked it, at any rate."

His gaze flickered toward Louisa. Nausea made her stomach pitch. She'd been right. Those locks of hair she'd found in Radleigh's desk were trophies, not keepsakes. Had this Celeste's tresses been among them?

Jardine's clipped accents cut through the room. "You haven't thought this through, have you, Smith? Faulkner knows you're here. The net's closing around you, and yet you waste time boring us all to tears, prosing on about how clever you are."

He gestured in Louisa's direction. "If you kill the daughter of a peer, you'll create an uproar. Lyle would hunt you to the ends of the earth. Even the bigwigs who currently protect you will wash their lily-white hands of you once you cross that line."

"And yet . . ." Smith put a fingertip to his lips. "And yet, the satisfaction of seeing you suffer while your lady love goes under the knife would be so delicious, so exquisite, that I simply cannot forgo that pleasure, come what may."

Smith stood a head shorter than Jardine, but at that moment, he looked every bit as lethal. "Since the day you killed my brother it has been my life's work to find a punishment befitting that crime." He made a sweeping gesture toward Louisa. "And now, my lord Marquis, here it is."

TERROR rose so thick and fast in Jardine's throat it nearly choked him. *Louisa.* God, why did she have to get mixed up in this? Why hadn't he forced her to get away when he'd had the chance?

"Let her go. She's innocent."

The hooded lids half closed. "My brother was innocent, Lord Jardine. Yet he was not spared."

"Your brother sold children into prostitution. He was lower than vermin." Jardine sneered. "Lower even than you."

"I'll pretend for your lady's sake that I did not hear

that." Smith paused, then said softly, "You ought to take more care of her, my lord."

Jardine ignored the fierce agreement in his churning gut.

"Who told you? How did you know what Lady Louisa is to me?"

"Why, I believe it was Celeste."

Celeste? How? The shock, the swift anger at her betrayal must have shown on Jardine's face. Smith looked like a man savoring a fine wine.

"Never underestimate the fury and resourcefulness of a woman scorned," said Smith. He jerked his head at his henchmen. "Take them down."

Here was Jardine's only chance. The curiosity cabinet was a small room. Only one person might pass through its doorway at once, creating a bottleneck. Jardine waited, shifting his weight to the balls of his feet as the dirty great brute stepped forward, directly into Smith's line of fire.

Jardine sprang, yelling, "Drop! Louisa, drop!"

He ducked the man's fist, drove his own into his stomach, then kneed him in the groin. Catching the howling oaf off balance, he shoved him into Smith and barreled his way toward Louisa, who was on the floor, scrambling for the door with the second thug lunging for her.

Jardine booted the thug's arse, sent him flying into a display case full of Indian treasures. Glass shattered, showered around them as Jardine reached down, grabbed Louisa's hand, and ran for the stairs.

A shot rang out, too late. They flew down the staircase, ran across the hall, and burst through the front door.

"Good man!" yelled Jardine at Ives, who held his horse, waiting patiently outside.

Jardine swung himself up and pulled Louisa up behind him. She accomplished the ascent without fuss, and he gave her a hard, desperate, thankful kiss as her arms wrapped around his waist. With a swift kick to the flanks, he spurred his mount onward, leaving Ives to vanish in a cloud of gravel dust.

Ives would win to safety. He was like a rat. Survival was second nature to him.

Instead of heading down the drive, Jardine steered his horse west, into the forest, as more shots rang out.

Smith's ruffians would be in pursuit. Did they have shot-guns? He and Louisa would be out of pistol range by now.

Exhilaration and terror shot through him in a heady rush. First, he needed to get Louisa to safety. He had an escape mapped out.

But he still didn't have that list.

"I have to go back," he shouted to Louisa, as the wind whipped through them, as a low-hanging branch brushed its leaves over his face.

He shook his head and pressed on, aware that the crack of gunfire had resumed.

Louisa's arms tighten around him. "Not you," she called, breathless, but determined. "*We* have to go back. It's my mission, too."

Stubborn chit! Brave, too, and he was proud of her, but he'd rather die than subject her to the possibility of recapture.

He made a quick decision. "You take the horse and ride south to the next village. Don't go to Faulkner. Take the first conveyance you can find and get yourself back to London."

Her arms tightened around his torso and he wished circumstances were far different.

"I won't leave you." Her words were hot in his ear. "You can't ask me to leave you now."

"Listen, Louisa. Part of being a good agent is to know when you have to retreat, regroup. Ives will bring reinforcements."

That was a bare-faced lie, of course. When Ives returned—if he returned—he would come alone. The situation was far too sensitive to involve the local militia. Besides, Smith was Jardine's and no one else's.

His jaw hardened. "You don't have to worry about me. Get to safety, that's all I ask."

They flew out of the forest, jumped a low wall, and galloped across country toward a stand of trees. Jardine risked a look over his shoulder. No one had yet followed them out of the wood.

He halted them and turned. Louisa's blue eyes were fierce with tears that shimmered in the pale moonlight.

"I won't leave you," she whispered, but he knew she'd do the sensible thing.

"Head west to Barsby and hire a carriage there." He thrust a small purse of coins into her hand. "Don't go back to the village."

"I love you, Jardine." In her voice there was mettle and terror and a distinct challenge. "Don't you *dare* get yourself killed."

He gathered her to him and kissed her, and the kiss was hard and fierce and strong, everything they were together. His heart burned in his chest, a fiery agony, a glory that transcended life and death. There was no term in any lexicon for what he felt. Love was too tepid a word.

Ah, Louisa. You shouldn't love me. Look where it's brought you.

But he couldn't deny her any longer, couldn't hold back any of himself from that kiss. It might be the last one they ever shared. She understood. For this moment, at least, there was honesty between them.

She pulled away first, her breath coming in sobbing pants. With a brave jut of her chin, she said, "Go. If we delay any further, it will be for naught."

He gripped the back of her head and brought it close to his own, so that their gazes locked, their faces almost touching. "I will come back for you. Nothing will stop me from coming back."

Handing her the reins, he slid down. The stallion was a brute and he wouldn't trust any other lady to handle him, but Louisa, as in everything, was exceptional.

"There's a pistol in the holster. Use it if you have to."

"What about you?"

"Never mind about me." He slid a knife into his boot.

Jardine slapped the stallion on the rump and the horse started forward.

She was a straight, elegant figure on his big horse, despite the awkward hike of her skirts rucking above her knees. With a quick, staccato salute, Louisa cantered off.

Jardine grimaced, beating back the pain in his chest. He watched until she disappeared, swallowed by darkness. Then he began the solitary walk back.

Twenty-one

"HARRIET." Louisa touched the sleeping woman's shoulder.

The gray eyes snapped open. Automatically, one small white hand dived under the pillow and brought out a pistol.

It seemed Harriet had recovered somewhat. Louisa raised her hands, palms outward, in a conciliating gesture. "Don't shoot. It's Louisa."

The pistol didn't lower. The hand that held it shook. Harriet's chest rose and fell quickly. She licked her cracked lips but said nothing.

"Where's Faulkner?" said Louisa.

Harriet's eyes flickered but she still didn't reply.

Couldn't she speak? "Oh good God, what did he do to you?" whispered Louisa. "My dear, I mean you no harm."

Cautious, careful not to make any sudden movement, she edged toward the far side of Harriet's bed. Jardine's pistol rested deep in the pocket of the cloak she had bought from the landlady with the money Jardine had given her. It hit her thigh as she sidled one hip onto the hard mattress.

Slowly, she put out a hand, intending to touch Harriet's cheek, but the girl flinched back, gripped the pistol with more determination.

Stupid! Badly done, Louisa. She ought to have known Harriet would still shy away from touch.

In a low voice, she said, "You must help me. There isn't much time. I have written a letter that I want you to post if I don't return by tomorrow afternoon." She bent a little to look into Harriet's eyes, trying desperately to make out if she understood. "Yes?"

Louisa held out the letter, a hastily scribbled note to her brother outlining the situation. If the worst occurred, Max would come for them.

Jardine would be furious. He wanted her to stay out of it. But how could she simply ride off and leave him? She didn't trust Ives to bring help. She needed to do something to make sure Jardine came back alive. How could she bear to lose him now?

Harriet took the letter with the tiniest nod and slipped it under her pillow. Louisa prayed that meant she understood, that she agreed to do as Louisa asked. Harriet's muteness tore at Louisa's heart. The courageous, clever, slightly contemptuous young woman was gone.

Would Harriet regain the power of speech? Or had the treatment she'd suffered somehow turned her brain?

The door opened, making Louisa jump. Faulkner seemed unsurprised to see her there. Someone must have told him.

She straightened, her heart hammering against her ribs. The fact he remained here told her he hadn't retrieved the list by any other means.

She started up. "Mr. Faulkner. I have bad news."

The bulldog face displayed no surprise at her appearance. Did he ever show emotion?

She quickly explained all that had happened. "I fear for what they'll do to Lord Jardine if you don't help him."

His eyebrows climbed. "He went back, you say?"

"Yes, to get the list. He is but one man against at least four. They have weapons."

Faulkner watched her with a hard, searching expression. He clenched his fist and lightly tapped his other open palm with it. "Very well. I'm going in for him. But I'll need your help."

Louisa's entire body clenched with fear. Go back there? Her gaze flickered to Harriet. Much as she had faith in Jardine, she did not want to suffer Harriet's fate.

Taking her silence as acquiescence, Faulkner said, "I'll get my coat."

Louisa's overwrought senses nearly crumbled. Go back? Did she have that much courage in her? She didn't think so. She was almost certain that she did not.

What help could she be, anyway?

She turned back to Harriet. "Do not forget the letter. Please."

Warmth crept into the gray eyes like the flicker of firelight in winter. Harriet put on the safety catch and turned the pistol in her hand so that she gripped the muzzle. She held it out to Louisa.

Louisa hesitated.

"Take it. I have another." Harriet's voice was a dry rasp, barely audible, but hope for her eventual recovery blossomed in Louisa's heart. She gripped the pistol butt with a murmur of thanks.

Harriet would recover from Radleigh's barbarism. She was strong. If it came to it, could she, Louisa, be equally strong?

Faulkner returned, raised his brows. "Ready?"

"I don't know what you think I can do." She felt craven admitting it. The need to do *something* to help Jardine battled with common sense. Jardine had a plan. He didn't want her there. It was smart to stay away, not cowardly. But what if—

Impatiently, Faulkner said, "This is spy work, Lady Louisa. Secret. There is no cavalry riding over the hill to save the day. There's only us." He fixed her with his perceptive stare. "You and me."

Swallowing hard, Louisa nodded. She forced herself to move to the door and down the stairs, out to the stable yard, where their horses awaited them. A pistol jostled against each leg as she walked.

When they'd mounted their horses and cleared the busy inn yard, Louisa said, "What am I to do? How are you planning to rescue him?"

"That depends on what I find," said Faulkner. He looked sideways at her. "Have faith, Lady Louisa."

She wanted to argue. She wanted to know exactly what her role in this maneuver would be. She didn't like the unpredictable nature of this work. Once again, it was borne in upon her that she was not cut out for the life of a spy. What the *Devil* had ever made her think she might be?

Faulkner remained resolutely silent for the rest of the ride back to the house. Without conversation to distract her, Louisa tried to calm herself. She was frightened, nauseous with it. Her stomach pitched so hard as she bobbed in time with the horse's trot, she clamped her mouth shut, willing the sick feeling away.

Soon, they came upon familiar territory, the edge of the estate.

"We should approach from this direction." Louisa indicated the path through the woods that ran past the Hindu temple, but Faulkner turned his horse toward the temple itself.

"Our meeting place is the temple, not the house. It's all been arranged."

Louisa gave a swift look over her shoulder. "Shouldn't we conceal ourselves?"

"I've not the slightest need to scurry around in the shadows. Smith knows he can't touch me."

She wasn't so certain about that. Smith seemed to believe he was invincible. Why would he give up a sensitive document for the mere asking?

They drew rein outside the house, and a surge of terror shot through her. She slid down from her horse and tethered him with shaking hands.

"This way," said Faulkner, starting up the hill.

Louisa nodded. As she followed, she put her hand in her cloak pocket and felt the reassuring shape of a pistol butt.

JARDINE swore silently and viciously from his hiding place. The full moon had risen, flooding the landscape with light. He could pick out every detail on Louisa's damnably in-the-way form. The proud tilt of her head, her straight carriage, the tall, slim elegance of her, as she approached the temple.

A lamb to the slaughter.

Fury boiled over again. He raised the shotgun to his shoulder, squinted, and took aim.

But Faulkner moved into his line of sight, damn him. So this was what Smith and his cohorts had adjourned to the temple for. A meeting with the head of the secret service. Faulkner must be desperate for that list if he'd risk coming here openly.

Desperate enough to sacrifice Louisa?

Jardine looked around for a better position but there was none. The temple stood alone on this hill beside the stand of shrubbery in which Jardine now hid. He'd have to break cover to get a clear shot.

Smith appeared at the temple entrance, but Louisa and Faulkner both stood in front of Smith. There was no way to eliminate him from this vantage point.

A document changed hands. Then, events seemed to accelerate. Louisa stepped back, simultaneously producing two pistols and pointed them at Smith and his men.

Jardine was already on his feet, crouched low, running, when Faulkner suddenly dropped to the ground, rolling toward the hill's descent.

There was a blast of gunfire and one of Smith's thugs fell.

Jardine hissed through his teeth. He couldn't approach, or she might turn, lose her focus, and be overpowered.

"Easy, there, sweetheart," he muttered, easing forward. "Save your last shot."

But another explosion rang out. The second henchman reeled backward. There was only Smith left, and Louisa turned to run, but Smith dived and caught hold of her skirts, dragging her down.

Dammit to hell but he couldn't get a clear shot. Jardine bit out an oath and broke cover, running for the struggling pair.

"Get away from her!" Jardine aimed the shotgun, but Smith grabbed Louisa by the hair and jerked her head up, holding a knife at her throat.

"Put the gun down, Jardine," he said, breathing hard. There was a fierce grin on his face.

Dimly, through the pound of fear in his head, Jardine registered that Faulkner was on his feet now, slipping and sliding down the hill. He had what he came for. No help there.

The document wasn't important. Getting Louisa away from Smith was the only thing that mattered.

"You won't do that," he said to Smith, taking one pace forward. "You want me to see her suffer. Slicing her throat now would be far too quick."

"You're right," said Smith. "And if I kill her, you'll tear me to pieces." He gripped Louisa's hair harder, yanked her head so her face tilted up toward him.

Jardine's insides cringed at her ragged cry of pain, at the wild fear in her eyes.

"What if I use my knife on this strong-boned face?" He held the point of his weapon a mere inch from her cheekbone. "Eh, Jardine? Seems a shame to mar such perfect—"

"Stop." The air hissed between Jardine's teeth. He put down the shotgun, slowly, at his feet.

Smith looked up, beyond Jardine, and smiled. "Ah. Here's Radleigh. Just in time."

JARDINE groaned as he woke. They'd bloody well had their fun, hadn't they, before throwing him into this anachronism of a dungeon. Lord, it could have starred in a play from Shakespeare with its dank, dripping walls and its rats and its god-awful stench.

Reality hit him, and the roaring started in his ears. They meant to torture Louisa while he watched.

He had no illusions about his own courage. No man clung to his principles when he was roasting over a fire or his balls were ceremoniously crushed.

How much worse would the torture be when he was here, whole and unharmed, watching Louisa slowly and thoroughly maimed?

This was the calamity he'd spent eight years apart from her to avoid. Eight years wanting her, starving for her touch while he hunted the man who threatened to rip their world apart. By pushing her away to protect her, he'd somehow led her straight into the danger he most feared.

The exquisite bloody irony of it made him want to howl.

Footsteps and a desperate scuffle sounded on the stairs. Someone snarled an oath and then the footsteps continued toward Jardine's cell.

One of the apes who guarded him unlocked the cell door and flung it wide.

A bedraggled creature stumbled inside, blond hair hanging in tangles about her head.

Louisa. Oh God, *Louisa*.

The cell door slammed shut, leaving them alone.

She stood there for a moment, her hair falling down around her face, obscuring her expression. Then her chin lifted.

Those blue eyes were solemn, haunted. "I'm sorry." She drew her bloodied lip into her mouth and sucked, wincing a little. Releasing, it she said, "Faulkner has the list. At least he got away."

"I know." When Jardine got out of here, he'd find the head of operations and hack off the man's balls with a blunt cleaver.

"Smith says he's going to let Radleigh have me."

She shuddered, and Celeste's bloody, mauled face rose before his mind's eye.

Ives. Ives was at large still. Jardine had sent him to that cottage in the woods, but he'd be back by first light. Ives would find a way to get them out, but would he be in time?

"I told you to go home." He couldn't believe how even his tone was. He wanted to wring her neck. He wanted to kiss her.

Kiss first, wring later.

Bloody hell.

"I'm sorry," she repeated. "I was stupid. But Faulkner said he had a plan. And . . . I couldn't leave you. Never again."

Awkwardly, she ran to him, sank to her knees where he sat on the hard stone floor. She stared into his eyes, her gaze communicating the depth of her love. She took his face between her hands and kissed him. It was a ginger kiss, their lips clinging lightly because of their injuries. But it struck down his defenses, reached into him, and gripped his soul.

She sank into him, and he strained against the manacles that shackled his wrists, wished he could enfold her in his arms. Her warmth was like a drug, her lips and tongue a tender balm, yet they barely touched the cold terror he felt on her behalf.

He kissed her hungrily and tasted blood. Hers, his own, he didn't know. With a muttered apology, he gentled the contact, touched soft kisses to her cheeks, tasted salt. Raged again at her folly in refusing to stay safe.

"You beautiful idiot, why did you come?" he murmured against her ear.

"A fine way to talk after the way you just greeted me," she whispered, a spark of indomitable humor lightening her moist eyes.

She sobered again. "I'm sorry. I was stupid to be taken in. Faulkner said he needed me." Bitterly, she added, "Well, I suppose he did need me, didn't he? As a distraction. As a shield. *His* plan worked, at all events."

"You shouldn't have listened to him. You should have refused to go."

"I did at first. But, oh, Jardine, I love you. He knew I could not leave you here alone."

His mouth set in a hard line. "It's *my* duty to protect *you*, not—"

She put up her hand and lightly stroked his face with her fingertip. "There is no need for you to feel responsible for this. It was all my own doing, my own folly in trusting him. Part of me isn't sorry that I did."

She took a deep, shaky breath. "I've lived in comfort and safety for eight years, but that existence suffocated me, Jardine. I'd much rather be here with you than safe at home not knowing where you are, whether you're dead or alive. That was no life at all. *That* was torture."

"Rather be here?" Jardine gave her an incredulous look.

She looked away. "Oh, you would never understand."

"You're right. I don't."

Did she truly fail to see the gravity of the situation?

Fury boiled up, but he reminded himself of all she'd been through and repressed the urge to give it free rein.

Louisa removed herself from his embrace, and he was powerless to stop her. Stepping over his outstretched legs, she inspected the damp stone floor beside him. Then she sank down beside him in one elegant movement, arranging her skirts as if she were on a bloody picnic.

He was stung into saying, "Do you *know* what Radleigh will do to you?"

She laid her head back against the wall next to him and stared at the curved stone ceiling above. She swallowed convulsively. Her hand went to her stomach, as if the thought sickened her. But her eyes were dry and her face had taken on that firm set of determination he knew well by now. She was making a Herculean effort to show no fear.

He regretted his words. She'd seen Harriet; she needed no reminder of Radleigh's capabilities.

You don't have to be brave with me, he wanted to say. But something told him that she needed to preserve this front, even with him, or she'd shatter.

After a time, she spoke. "I think I killed one of Smith's men."

He nodded. "Good."

"You seem unsurprised."

He turned his head to look down at her. "You're a re-markable woman. I've always known it."

WARMTH spread over Louisa, like the glow from a good brandy. But she didn't feel remarkable. For all her swagger, she was afraid. Terrified of ending up like Harriet.

Or worse. Harriet had been tough, tenacious, despite her fragile exterior. Louisa hadn't a fraction of Harriet's experience or training. She was a miserable coward, in fact.

But she'd brought this on herself, trusting Faulkner, and the last thing she'd do now was snivel to Jardine.

She glanced at him. Despite the bruises and the dirt, he still looked gorgeously disheveled, as opposed to the utter guttersnipe she must resemble. "My remarkableness doesn't extend to thinking of a plan to get us out of here, unfortunately. Any ideas?"

"Ives." The word was barely a whisper. "Tomorrow."

Tomorrow? Her stoic mask slipped.

An eon of pain could lie between now and tomorrow. She and Jardine might both be dead by then. They might be yearning for death to come.

The crease between his angled black brows showed her Jardine was putting that powerful, Machiavellian brain to work. This was what he did best, wasn't it?

"There's a way," he said at last. "It would mean giving Smith something he wants. The only thing he wants more than seeing me suffer."

A surge of hope died. Grittily, Louisa said, "You will not sacrifice your principles for me. If Smith wants something badly, the chances are it would hurt a lot of people."

"Principles? I have no principles where your safety is concerned. But just to assuage *your* offended principles, what I propose is not likely to hurt anyone."

He hesitated. Then he shifted a little, making the chains that bound his hands sway and clank. "Smith mentioned a woman he called my mistress—"

The blow came from nowhere, knocking the breath from her lungs. It was a dread she'd barely acknowledged to herself, and now . . .

She threw out her hands to ward off more of these crippling words. "I don't want to know," she blurted out. "I don't want to know who you've been with while we were apart."

"But I—"

"No!" Stricken with the pain of it, she forced down a sob. In a halting, trembling voice, she continued, "I always knew there'd be other women. Eight years—how could

there not be others? But I don't want to know, Jardine. Let me have that dignity, at least."

Jardine let out a furious oath. "By God, Louisa, if I weren't chained to this wall, I'd shake you. How dare you? How *dare* you say that to me?"

Jardine's voice was fury itself. Louisa gasped, half affronted, half intrigued. "What? What do you mean?"

"I've had no other woman since we married. I said you were remarkable, Louisa. Incomparable would be closer to the mark. No one could ever measure up to you. Why would I want them to? I gave my oath to honor and protect you. I gave my word."

Her entire being was suspended in wonder. She couldn't speak.

He must have taken her silence for doubt. "Dammit, why do you think I've been in a foul mood for eight years?"

She wanted to laugh. She wanted to weep for days. She wanted to leap up and caper about the cramped, cold room. That nagging suspicion, that undercurrent of distrust had been her companion for a long time, she realized. It had eaten away at her, eroding her confidence and her faith in him.

Suddenly, it was as if the gates to her heart had been flung open. She'd tried so hard not to love him. Then she'd finally accepted that her love had no limits or conditions. No matter what he'd done, she was helplessly in love with this man.

Now, it seemed she need not have suffered so greatly. If only her pride had not stopped her ever alluding to this question, she'd have saved herself years of agony.

She blinked hard. *Do not cry.* If she started weeping now, she'd never stop.

She remembered Smith's mention of Celeste. "But . . . there was a woman, wasn't there?"

Jardine gave a curt nod. "Before I met you. In fact, when I met you I was still involved with her. Celeste was my mistress, but I never went back to her. One look at you . . ."

He sucked in a harsh, shaken breath. "You were like a blinding light, and everything else fell into shadow. I forgot about her. To my regret. If I'd done the decent thing and broken it off, perhaps they wouldn't have . . ."

He bowed his head, and Louisa wanted to draw him into her arms. But she let him finish what he had to say.

"She was living in a house I'd bought for her. She was a high-flying courtesan, very beautiful. Everyone knew she was my mistress."

Louisa put a hand on his arm. "Radleigh."

"Yes. Apparently. Smith hates me. He thinks I'm responsible for his brother being tried and hanged. Smith had a finger in every rancid pie in the London underworld. His younger brother Elias worked for him, overseeing a particularly nasty ring of brothel owners. Elias peddled children, sold them into a life of prostitution, degradation, and pain. That alone would not have occasioned much remark, but he chose to blackmail a government minister."

Jardine's lips curled into a cynical smile. "*That* galvanized the authorities as the rest could not. Max and I put together a very complicated operation. We arrested Elias Smith and closed down the ring. The minister was innocent and Faulkner tried to hush up the investigation, saying we didn't want to drag the minister's name through the mud. But Max and I wouldn't stand for that. We managed to get Smith's brother convicted on other charges, with no mention of blackmail. Faulkner arranged for the sentence to be commuted and he was transported to one of the colonies. We were told Elias Smith died en route to New South Wales."

"So he's dead and Smith wants revenge."

"I had thought so. Except . . . I've had suspicions about Faulkner for some time. After the affair with Kate's diary last year, it became clear how far he was prepared to go to keep the present government in power. I've had him watched. There is a cottage in the next county that is heavily secured and guarded. And its sole prisoner is a man who looks very like Elias Smith. The man we all thought had perished."

Louisa frowned. "Does Smith know his brother is alive?"

"It seems not. So, the question is, why does Faulkner hold him? Could it be that he is keeping him in reserve as a bargaining chip? Perhaps he means to ransom the fellow to fund his retirement, I don't know. But he didn't use him to get that list back, did he?"

Hope glimmered on the horizon. Louisa licked her lips. "It gives us something to bargain with."

Jardine's mouth hardened. "It gives us bait."

He sent up a shout in the direction of the door. "Ho there! Tell your master I want a parley with him. Tell him I've a proposition he can't refuse."

There was a long wait, and Louisa dug her nails into her palms, tense with apprehension. A door slammed. They heard footsteps approach. The door swung open.

The man who stood on the threshold was not Smith.

Twenty-two

RADLEIGH hulked in the doorway, filling the space, a swelling bruise covering his left eye. The part of Radleigh that had connected with Jardine's boot.

Any flicker of satisfaction Jardine might have felt was swiftly doused by the way Radleigh's hungry gaze took in every inch of Louisa's appearance.

If he objected, it would only serve as fuel to Radleigh's enjoyment. He kept his mouth shut, fighting to contain his rage.

He smelled Louisa's fear, a tang that tinged the air. Yet, she remained silent and composed in the face of this monster. Jardine marveled at her courage. By God, when he got his hands on Radleigh . . .

It almost killed Jardine to be conciliating, but he'd swallow his pride for Louisa. He gave Radleigh a nod in greeting. "I was rather hoping for a chat with Smith, old man. Any chance that he's about?"

"He's not here." Radleigh stood over them, clearly itching to stamp on Jardine's face while he was unable to return the favor.

Something held Radleigh back, however. Perhaps Smith had threatened dire retribution if he harmed Jardine. He wanted his old enemy fully in possession of his wits while he tortured Louisa.

Radleigh's gaze turned again to Louisa. "Smith wants me to wait. Anticipation being torture all in itself. But . . ."

He pulled a knife with a wicked-looking blade from his pocket. "I'm impatient, you see. And I don't relish taking orders from the likes of Smith."

He tilted the knife blade this way and that. Light from the lantern slid along the mirrorlike surface.

Louisa was breathing hard. *Courage, sweetheart.*

"How does your sister, Radleigh? Fled from the rumors of typhus, did she?" Jardine spoke conversationally, but Radleigh's head jerked toward him.

The sensual lips curled in a snarl. "You'll be too dead to go after my sister."

"Will I?" Jardine smiled. "But I have a proposition for Smith that I believe will set me free as a bird. Lay one finger on Lady Louisa and your sister will suffer the same treatment."

"Ha! Wouldn't that be against your *gentlemanly* code?" Radleigh spat out the word *gentlemanly* as if it were an oath.

"Oh, I ceased laying any claim to gentility long ago."

Radleigh gazed at his knife, then at Louisa, as a starving man would view a feast. "I have to. I simply *must* . . ."

He reached down, grabbed Louisa's arm, and pulled her to her feet. He looked like a man in a daze of anticipated ecstasy.

Louisa struggled like a wild animal but Radleigh easily overpowered her, clamping her against him with her back pressing along his front.

The knife poised a small distance from her face.

The blue eyes pleaded, grew moist. Jardine strained at the manacles but to no avail. Louisa opened her mouth and screamed.

Jardine heard an inarticulate roar and realized that it howled from deep inside him. He strained at the chains that manacled him to the wall, felt such a fury of strength pour into his body that he almost could have ripped the iron links asunder with his bare hands.

The manacles bit savagely into his wrists, but they were bolted securely to the wall. Panting, he gazed at Louisa, agonized, more terrified than he'd ever been.

Footsteps running in the corridor. Thank God, thank God, thank—

Louisa's scream changed key from terror to agony as the knife point slashed slowly down her cheek.

"LET her go, Radleigh." Smith's bored tone sounded from the doorway.

Louisa sagged in Radleigh's hold, relief threading its way through fear and sickening pain. The warm flow of blood from the wound dripped down her face, onto Radleigh's sleeve, and she felt a perverse satisfaction in ruining his perfect tailoring.

Crazed laughter bubbled inside her. Lord, she was hysterical. She needed to calm herself. But the harsh sting of that cut made her whimper. Another scream welled in her chest. She forced it down.

Despite his brave words in Smith's absence, it appeared Radleigh wouldn't challenge Smith's authority to his face. She felt him relax, and the next second the constraining support of his arms vanished. She dropped to the ground like a stone.

Jardine swore viciously. "By God you'll pay for that."

Radleigh laughed. Even Smith smiled a little. "Radleigh,

you exceeded your orders. Later. I promise you, you will have her. All in good time."

His eyes twinkled as if he was offering a small boy a bonbon if he ate his dinner. Then his voice grew curt. "Leave us."

The smug look Radleigh threw at Jardine made Louisa's fingers curl with the longing for her pistol. "Just don't let him talk his way out of here."

A twinge of irritation crossed Smith's features. "Confine yourself to your own peculiar talents, Radleigh. You are decidedly de trop here."

Radleigh shrugged and sauntered out.

Smith watched him leave and shut the door behind him. Then he turned to Jardine and Louisa. "You must excuse Radleigh, Lady Louisa. He is quite vulgarly eager to amuse himself with you."

He tilted his head and looked inquiring. "Now, why do you wish to see me, Lord Jardine? To plead for clemency? You, of all people, must know that I haven't a spark of mercy in my soul."

Jardine's face was stark white. "Get her something clean to staunch the wound and some brandy and I'll tell you."

Smith paused, considering. "Very well."

He gave the order to an underling and the supplies were duly brought. The guard smirked at the damage to Louisa's face, and she recognized the ruffian she'd knifed upon her initial capture.

She took a deep breath and doused her cut with the brandy, her muscles rigid, her breath a sharp hiss as the flare of agony nearly swamped her senses.

For an instant, the world receded almost to black. She gulped in air, willing herself not to faint. Raised the brandy flask to her lips and took a hearty swallow. A ball of fire burned down her throat, warmed her stomach.

The dizziness faded. She pressed the clean gauze cloth

to her wound to staunch it. The sting intensified to an agonizing throb.

Through stiff lips, she said, "Pray, continue." The sooner they made this bargain, the sooner they'd be free.

Jardine spoke. "I've a proposition for you, Smith." Though obliged to tilt his head and look up at their captor, Jardine lost none of his dangerous presence.

Don't provoke him. She couldn't bear it if Jardine brought another beating on himself, or worse. She was coward enough to admit she didn't wish to be on the receiving end, either.

She pressed harder on her wound as it bled and bled. Every movement of her face stung with a needle-sharp pain.

She would bear a scar . . . *No.* She refused to countenance such frivolous thoughts now. Not when she might not live to see morning.

Smith gave a soft snort and the lines bracketing his mouth deepened. "You took away the one person I cared about in the world. What could you possibly offer me to atone for that, besides the blood of someone *you* love? You see, my lord, I'm going to let you live."

His merciless black eyes drilled into Louisa and she couldn't help a shudder of fear as he continued. "Long after Radleigh has finished raping her and cutting her, long after she is dead of her wounds, I am going to let you walk free."

He turned his head and fixed his gaze on Jardine. "And you will have to live. You will live with the knowledge that not only did you lead your beloved into this agonizing death, you failed to protect her, to stop it from happening."

Jardine's lip curled. "A fine oration. You should run for Parliament, Smith. May I speak now?"

Smith inclined his head. "Go on. Amuse me. I'm all ears."

"Your brother is alive."

Smith stilled, his eyes widened, his nostrils flared. "What?"

"Your brother is alive and well."

"A trick. A damned lie," muttered Smith. He shook his head, staring at Jardine as if trying to divine the truth. Then his gaze sharpened. "Where?"

Jardine shrugged. "That, I don't know. I know how you can find out, but the price of telling you is our freedom."

His sangfroid returning, Smith lifted his thick black brows. "Why should I believe you?" But he wanted to, Louisa could tell.

Jardine shrugged, making the chains that constrained him rattle and chink. "No reason at all."

"Does Faulkner know about this?"

"Now, why would Faulkner know? He would have offered your brother in exchange for the list, wouldn't he?"

There was a long silence. Finally, Smith nodded. "I'll consider it."

At the door, he turned his head to bend his piercing stare on Jardine. "Were you aware that my brother was alive all this time?"

Jardine shook his head. "No. And when you get him out, I'll hunt both him and you until the day I die."

A grunt that was almost a laugh escaped Smith. "Oh yes, I'm sure you will. I'll look forward to it."

"He didn't believe you." There was a slightly fretful note in Louisa's voice that made Jardine's gut churn.

"I didn't expect him to take my word for it." He wished he could hold her, but these damned chains kept his arms spread wide. His back ached and the muscles in his arms screamed with fatigue.

"He'll want to check my story, try to discover for himself where his brother is held. He'll hunt down Faulkner."

"Do you think he'll find him?"

"That old fox? No, Smith won't find him. But Smith will come back to talk terms."

"You seem confident."

"I am. You see, this is a gambit, but it has the advantage of being true." He looked at her. "Come here."

She sidled over to him. After a brief calculation, she sat side-on, on the space of floor between his legs. She nestled into him, her good cheek resting on his chest.

Her hand still pressed the gauze to her face. Despite their reprieve, Louisa's entire body trembled. Again, he wondered at the courage of her, raged against his own impotence.

Jardine muttered a foul curse under his breath. He'd tear Radleigh apart with his bare hands when he got hold of him.

Louisa heaved a shaky sigh, and he turned his head to kiss her brow. His hands flexed with the need to touch her, but instead, all he could do was talk.

When we get out of here . . .

He talked and talked, painting a picture for her of sunlight, happy families, and sweet contentment, all the things she'd said she wished for in that long ago confrontation at his house. They'd live out their days together, have babies, watch them grow.

Live in a cottage, if a vast estate and a house that could accommodate a hundred children could be termed as such.

He didn't believe it, not a word.

He'd failed. Not only had he failed to put an end to Smith's ridiculous vendetta against him and those he loved, he'd failed to protect Louisa. If he couldn't protect her, he didn't deserve her. It was that simple.

But as he wove this dream with nothing to support it save the air that formed his words, he heard her breathing slow, felt her head grow weightier against him. That halcyon future became vivid in his mind.

He wanted it. God, how he wanted to be with her, always, in peace and calm. Away from the sordid life of a spy.

While Smith survived, neither peace nor calm were possible for them. Smith wasn't the type to forgive and forget. In fact, it might be wise to ship Louisa off to the Continent once they got out of here, put her entirely out of Smith's reach.

One corner of his mouth kicked up. He could just imagine how she'd take that news.

Twenty-three

THE pillow beneath Louisa's head was hard and warm. It was also moving, a slight rise and fall. A large hand stroked her hair with lulling gentleness. She sighed, not wanting it to end.

"Jardine?" She opened her eyes to find herself dragged up a solid male chest for a soul-searing kiss.

One side of her face throbbed with pain. She gasped and he drew back. "Christ, did I hurt you?"

"No, no. My face, though . . ." She stopped as the horror came flooding back.

Then, she realized. "Your hands are free." She looked up at him in wonder. "Smith is letting us go?"

Briefly, Jardine nodded, but he looked grim and her elation dimmed a little. "What is it?"

"Nothing. Just . . . Let's go."

It must have been daytime by now but they were in the bowels of the house, the cellars, where no light penetrated.

Smith must have been in an exceptionally good mood. He'd left them a lantern.

She scrambled to her feet, stiff and sore from her extended rest in such an uncomfortable pose. She rubbed the back of her neck, kneading aching muscles. How much worse must Jardine feel?

He was so tall, he couldn't quite stand upright in the confined space. Bending his head so as not to hit the barrel ceiling, Jardine rolled his shoulders, evincing no sign of pain beyond a soft grunt and a flex of his hands. He picked up the lantern and started toward the door.

Louisa followed, scarcely believing they were free.

Jardine held the lantern high enough that it illuminated her path as well as his own. They climbed stairs, encountering no one in the cellars as they made their way through a forest of wine bottles, past a warren of storerooms alive with the scuttle of small feet. Finally, they found the entrance to the kitchens and emerged into daylight.

The scent of yeast, beeswax, and a faint whiff of cinnamon made Louisa's stomach clench with hunger. When had she eaten last? No time for that now. Who knew how many of his men Smith had left behind. Was Radleigh here? She shivered.

Jardine doused the lantern and set it on the kitchen table. Clearly, the staff had not yet returned after Radleigh's announcement that typhus had struck the village. It was strangely eerie to see the kitchen with rolling pins and bread dough abandoned, as if its occupants had vanished.

A scuttle and squeak told her some of the kitchen's occupants had *not* disappeared.

Jardine was scanning benches and riffling through drawers. "Knives, where are the knives? It's a kitchen, for God's sake."

"Over 'ere." One of Smith's thugs stood in the doorway,

a large knife gripped in one meaty fist. Louisa couldn't contain her whimper of fear at the sight.

The ruffian smiled and the fierce light of anticipation in Jardine's eyes intensified. "Louisa. Get behind me."

She made no argument, backing until her hips hit the kitchen table. She gripped the edge, feeling the soft, powdery texture of flour beneath her fingertips. She ought to turn and scuttle back toward the larder like one of those rats, but she couldn't keep her eyes off the two men.

Taunts and filth spewed from the cutthroat's mouth as Jardine moved slowly toward him. They both crouched a little as they circled in the confined space.

Jardine sprang. The big ruffian lunged. They clashed together in a desperate struggle, Jardine's hand clamped around the man's wrist, arresting the plunge of his knife.

His fist smashed into the ruffian's face. The big man staggered back. Jardine's leg kicked out but the bigger man somehow regained his feet and spun away.

The ruffian's hulking body brushed Louisa's as he passed, and she shuddered at the contact, at the sour stench of male sweat and unwashed linen. He paid no heed to her; his intention was fully engaged with Jardine. The bully feinted and slashed and his blade came away bright red.

Jardine bit out an oath, but the wound on his arm didn't seem to slow him. Instead, he took more risks; Louisa feared he'd take a deeper wound before too long.

Terror for Jardine mobilized her brain, heightened her awareness of her surroundings. *Weapon. Weapon.* She needed something. . . .

Fingers scrabbling, she groped behind her on the table, encountered the cool ceramic surface of a mixing bowl, the crumbling remains of bread dough that had never made it to the oven. *A rolling pin.*

She gripped the heavy wooden utensil and waited for her chance.

The two men scuffled again, locked together in a battle

for the knife. Blood dripped and smeared over the black-
and-white chessboard floor. The ruffian stumbled, tripped,
and fell backward. Jardine crashed to the floor with him.

Louisa couldn't fathom how Jardine kept going. His
arms must have ached from his incarceration. The attacker
was twice his size.

Jardine straddled the big man, managing to pin one arm
to the ground with his knee. He punched the villain in the
face with one fist while he gripped the ruffian's forearm in
the other, holding the knife at bay. As Jardine pummeled
him, blood spurted from a nose that had already been broken several times, but the cutthroat didn't release his grip
on the knife.

In a desperate show of strength, Jardine finally succeeded in pinning his knife hand to the floor. Seeing her
chance, Louisa darted forward, brought up the rolling pin,
and smashed it down on the fellow's hand.

With a howl of pain, he dropped the knife and Louisa
kicked it out of his reach. Jardine kept punching him, until
the ruffian's massive hands reached up to close around Jardine's neck.

Louisa cried out, but Jardine didn't falter. He picked up
that big, bald head and dashed it against the hard tiled floor.
Once. Twice. On the third smash, those meaty hands fell
from Jardine's throat, and the light went out of his eyes.

Both breathing hard, they stared down at the inert
form.

"Is he dead?" Louisa whispered. The rolling pin dropped
from her fingers and clattered on the floor.

"Yes." Jardine sat back on his heels and nursed his fist
with one hand.

Slowly, panting hard, he drew to his feet. His eyes still
blazed from the fight, and his mouth was grim.

Once, she'd called Jardine a murderer, turned away from
him in horror and disgust.

Now, she could only be glad Jardine was capable of

killing a man. She closed her eyes and shuddered at the thought of that knife.

More than anything at that moment, Louisa wanted Jardine to hold her, but he made no move toward her. Still breathing hard, he watched her for a few seconds in silence, then he turned away, stripping off his ruined coat.

"You're hurt. Let me see."

He shrugged off her hand. "Flesh wound. Nothing to concern you."

"Let me bathe it at least."

"No. I'll attend to it." He eyed her from head to foot. "Go upstairs and change. We'll need to look respectable if we don't want to cause any fuss."

Why was he being so curt with her? "What is the matter, Jardine?"

He sent her an incredulous look, then gave a quick shake of his head. "Go and get dressed. Pack everything you need into a bandbox."

She hesitated, and he said, "Look lively, there, Louisa. We don't have much time."

WHEN he found Louisa in her bedchamber, she was dressed only in her shift. She was clean and her hair combed and dressed. She smelled of lilies and his craving for her intensified.

But she was gazing into her mirror at the gash down her face. Guilt burned his soul like acid. When this was over, she would turn from him, just as Celeste had. And she'd be right to do so.

"Aren't you dressed yet?" Pain lent an edge to his tone. He didn't want to see Louisa like this, so fragrant and tempting. Not now.

She rose from the dressing table and walked gracefully to the counterpane, where a gown and other accoutrements were laid out. "I need help with my stays."

He grunted and walked forward. Snatched up the corset and fitted it around her lithe body. The delicate turn of her neck called to him, the elegant line of her shoulder blade. The exquisitely sensitive spot behind her ear.

His hands itched to rove, but he made himself concentrate on lacing and pulling until the corset hugged her slender form.

"Thank you." Her voice was crisp, clipped. She didn't, as he hoped she might, sink back against him, throw her head back, offer her throat to his lips and teeth.

She stepped away to pick up her gown and whisked it over her head. With a twitch and a shake, she was ready.

"Louisa."

She pulled on a pelisse and began to button it. "Yes?" She didn't meet his eye.

He looked away at the spectacular view from her window. The memory of the view Radleigh had enjoyed from the peephole opposite made his fury burn anew.

"What is it?"

He turned his head to look at her. "I hope you're not going to grow soft about that fellow now that it's over," he said harshly. "He would have killed both of us."

Louisa picked up a bonnet and fitted it on her head, carefully avoiding the long gash that ran from cheek to jaw.

"I know that, Jardine," she said quietly. She tried to tie the wide, green ribbons at her chin and winced as one brushed against her wound. She let the ribbons flutter free.

Louisa turned her face to the mirror again, and he realized she'd chosen a bonnet with a poke that almost entirely concealed the cut on her face.

She'd cleaned it and it had finally stopped bleeding. Thank God it wasn't quite as deep as he'd thought.

She would bear a scar, though. *She would bear a scar.*

Fury and remorse twisted inside him, rose in his throat, in his eyes, blinding him. He turned back to the window, bracing himself with one fisted hand against the embrasure.

He wanted to hit something. The drubbing he'd given that bastard minion of Smith's hadn't been release enough.

But he made himself think of what needed to be done. "We'll go to a house I know. It's not far."

He blew out a breath. "At least the list is safe. No one will even know it existed. Faulkner would have burned it by now."

There was a tense pause. "Someone else knows," said Louisa.

He turned. "What?"

Louisa's eyes were wide, uncertain. "I—I gave a letter to Harriet. I didn't tell her what was inside it, but I asked her to post it to Max if I didn't come back by next morning."

Jardine shook his head. "The letter won't have reached Max, Louisa. Harriet's a professional. She'd have read it and then destroyed it. It's what I would have done."

"But—"

His fury boiled over. In biting accents, he said, "The work we do is secret work, Louisa. That means we're on our own. We don't write to our brothers, asking them to rescue us when we're in a tight spot."

"Max was one of us."

"Not anymore. Do you know how sensitive that information was? What if someone else had intercepted your message? Do you know what damage you could have done?"

Her eyes flashed. "I see what this is. Your pride is hurt. You cannot accept that I went to someone else for help. I was desperate, Jardine. You were heading back into the Devil's lair and I was about to follow. It was insurance, in case we were captured."

The knowledge that jealousy and shame at his own failure to protect her fed his fury enraged him even more. "This nation's security is more important than my life, don't you understand?"

She gave him a long, sober look. "Not to me."

He broke inside, then, sundered in two, creaking and

cracking open like a ship dashed against jagged rocks. She loved him. And in his love for her lay his greatest weakness.

Smith knew that. Their present freedom was but a temporary reprieve.

"Come on. We'd better leave this place." He picked up the bandbox she'd packed and walked out the door, leaving her to follow.

THE cottage was charming, a half-timbered house with a thatched roof, a pretty garden, and smoke curling from the stone chimney. A house straight from a fairy tale. A house from her dreams.

At the door, a woman with shrewd eyes greeted them. Jardine exchanged a few odd sentences with her about the weather, which were patently untrue. Some sort of password, Louisa gathered. Satisfied, the old woman handed him a large bunch of keys and left.

"The larder's stocked and the sheets aired. I trust you'll be comfortable." The woman, who looked like someone's benign old nanny, picked up her basket and bustled on her way.

Louisa blinked. "Is *she* . . . ?"

"Oh yes." Jardine looked about him. Then he went through the house, methodically checking windows and doors.

Louisa stripped off her gloves and carefully removed her bonnet before going in search of the kitchen. The old woman's mention of food reminded her she hadn't eaten for a long time. No doubt Jardine was similarly ravenous.

As she busied herself boiling water on the range and raiding the larder for supplies, she fought to keep the hurt at bay.

Jardine seemed more distant from her than ever. An unwelcome sense of futility pervaded her. Had all this been for nothing?

That thought made her pause. Was that the true reason she'd accepted Faulkner's mission? Not to save those many unknown souls on the fatal list, not even so much to save Jardine, for she'd always placed faith in his almost supernatural ability to survive.

No, she'd done it to prove herself worthy of his love. To show him she was brave enough to share his life, not merely wring her hands on the fringes of it, waiting for him to decide when it was safe for her to join him.

Yes, it had all been for nothing. She was not a natural at spy work like Harriet. She'd made far too many mistakes. And Jardine still saw her as the helpless damsel in distress.

If only she hadn't been caught. If only she'd managed to get that list and escape with it, Jardine would have to accept her as an equal, let her into his life.

Now, he'd locked her out as he prepared to do battle with Smith. And all she could do was make sure he was fed.

The soup was hearty, flavored with dried herbs culled from the stillroom. There was no fresh meat in the house, to her regret, but she'd added thick chunks of chopped bacon, which lent a smoky richness to the meal.

Jardine surveyed her with a gleam in his eye as she set a place for him at the small table in the parlor. Did it amuse him to have her play housekeeper for him?

She dipped her own gaze to hide how much she longed for such domestic normalcy. Then she reminded herself that even if he accepted her and brought her into his life, she would not be cooking for him like this.

"Delicious." Jardine eyed her in surprise. "How did you learn to cook like that?"

"I taught myself."

"Life in the country was that dull?"

She made herself speak calmly. "I did it out of necessity, if you must know. Our father left us without a penny to bless ourselves with and a mountain of household debt. I had to let all but two of our staff go simply to survive."

His black brows drew together. "You told me you wanted for nothing."

"That's right, I did." *But you never came to see for yourself, did you?*

"Did Max know about this?"

She snorted. "Of course not. And I had the Devil of a time keeping him ignorant. He worked himself to the bone to send us what money he had. He'd sacrificed everything so that Alistair could stay at Cambridge. I wasn't about to add to his burdens. I managed."

Jardine slammed his fist on the table. "He should have done something." He pushed away from the table a little and pointed his finger at her. "And *you* should have used the money I sent."

She remained silent a moment, while she tried to bring her feelings under control. "How could I have explained my sudden affluence to my mother?" But that wasn't the real reason she hadn't spent that money. She'd been so furious and full of pride, she'd disdained to take it. "I have not complained, so I don't see why *you* are making such a fuss."

"Bloody hell, Louisa. You're a marchioness, for God's sake! And you tell me you were reduced to making your own dinner!"

"I *shot* my own dinner many a time," she said, with a perverse desire to twist the knife. She shrugged. "My mother was prostrate with vapors nine days out of ten; we kept no company; I'd read every book the house contained, including my father's hunting annuals. I'm cow-handed at embroidery and equally bad at the pianoforte. What else was there for me to do?"

He almost started up. She hoped he would shake her. Then he sat back in his chair, one long, tapered index finger circling his wine glass. "You are no longer in such straits, now that your brother is the Duke of Lyle."

"True." She sipped her own wine. It was rough and robust, and perhaps it wasn't wise to drink such strong liquor on an empty stomach. It made her reckless.

She took another long sip.

Changing the subject, she said, "You will go after Smith, of course."

He returned to his soup. "No. I'm going to get you out of the country, while there's still time."

She blinked at him. "Out of the *country*? Are you mad? Where would I go?"

He waved a hand. "Calais. Dieppe. It depends. We'll make for the coast and then we'll see whether we can book a passage. In any case, there'll be smugglers who'll take us."

She'd rather eat dirt than scuttle off to France, but she let it pass for the moment. She needed to marshal her defenses. She needed a plan.

"What will happen to Smith?"

"My hope is that he'll try to snatch his brother and get himself killed in the process." He didn't meet her eye.

"You'll go back for him, won't you? Once I'm safely out of the way."

"I must."

"You think he will still wish to harm you after you've given him his brother back?"

He raised a sardonic eyebrow. "Don't you?"

"I think perhaps his thirst for revenge will be assuaged. He might even be grateful to you."

Jardine rested his spoon in his empty bowl. "I did my level best to get his brother hanged, Louisa. Once he's free, I shall go after him and Smith again. Smith knows that."

"But—"

"I'm *not* taking any more chances. Not where your safety is concerned."

Twenty-four

WITHOUT a word, Louisa rose from the table to collect their bowls.

As she reached for Jardine's his fingers gripped her wrist. "Leave it."

"I was just going to—"

"Leave it, I said. You're not a damned footman."

She took a pointed look around her. "Well, I don't see anyone else here to do it, do you?"

She tried to pull herself free from his grip. He snatched the bowl she held and hurled it across the room. It shattered in the empty fireplace.

Louisa let out a breath in an outraged hiss. She didn't know why she was so furious. It wasn't because of the bowl or the mess he'd made.

A sudden, ungovernable rage rushed up inside her. She picked up his wine glass and dashed its contents over him. In awe-filled horror, she watched the ruby liquid arc out of the glass and drench his face.

He recoiled, swearing viciously, but he didn't loose his grip on her wrist. His clasp tightened as he dashed the liquid from his eyes.

Panting, she watched wine drip down his pale skin like blood from a wound, bemused at her behavior.

There was a taut, fulminating silence. Then his mouth crashed down on hers. She gave a muffled gasp, but whether it was a protest or a cry of satisfaction, she didn't know and he didn't pay attention.

He tasted of the wine and a hint of the rosemary she'd used to flavor the soup. His firm lips crushed hers as his tongue dominated her mouth.

A sweep of his hand sent the tablecloth and everything upon it sliding off the table with a clatter and crash. Her bottom pressed against the table edge as he slowly bent her back over his arm.

Jardine feasted on her mouth with a greater appetite than he'd shown over their meal, and his hands were everywhere, ripping at her clothes, as if desperate to feel her.

The wound in her cheek throbbed in protest. It might even have been bleeding, but she wanted this so badly—his dark, unfettered passion, his physicality—that she didn't care.

His mouth left hers to travel lower, and the sensations he orchestrated in her body with his hands and lips and tongue soon overwhelmed the sharp beat of pain.

He picked her up and deposited her on the table, his hand rucking up her skirts until he found the hot, moist place between her legs. He touched her there, his fingers swift and urgent, pressing, rubbing, bringing her quickly to a peak.

As she began to climax, he freed his member from his trousers and thrust into her, sinking his teeth into the sensitive side of her neck. He kept that wolfish hold on her while he stroked, and her climax erupted again, coursing like a hot, pulsing current through her body.

She gripped the hair at his nape, threw her head back, and cried out.

"Oh God. Louisa." He gave an agonized groan as he emptied himself into her.

He laid his forehead against her neck as he shuddered, and his warm breath flowed over her skin.

Tenderness swept over her, and in its wake flowed aching regret. For all the years they'd wasted, for the black chasm of loneliness that yawned before her. *France, for God's sake!*

Despite her frustration and anger, she let her hand drift upward to stroke his silky black hair.

And knew that this heated coupling had solved nothing at all.

JARDINE trailed his hand slowly down Louisa's side and let it rest on her warm, lithe flank. She lay in his arms in a proper bed this time. They'd made love as if the world was ending. In every way that mattered, it was.

Could he ever get enough of her? Despite the pressing need to send her away, he couldn't resist stealing as much time with her as possible before the daylight faded.

He thought of Smith and another operation that would proceed tonight. He'd no doubt Smith would act quickly, decisively, to free his brother from his prison. He wouldn't want to take the chance that Jardine might alert the guard or have Elias moved.

Jardine's inability to stop it gnawed at him, but he couldn't be in two places at once. Ives hadn't turned up, nor had Faulkner. In any case, Jardine didn't trust anyone else to guard Louisa while he was off foiling Smith's rescue.

Desperate as he was to get his hands on Smith, Louisa's safety must come first. He wouldn't make the same mistake twice.

"I'm not going to France, Jardine." Those fiery blue eyes blazed into his.

The hand that had been stroking along her flank stilled. She only made it harder by protesting, didn't she know that? But she would go, whether she wanted to or not.

She seemed to read his thoughts. "And if you force me to go, I'll find a way to come back."

He let his thick black eyelashes come down to shutter his eyes and concentrated on her body. He said nothing, simply resumed his caresses, giving the languid movements all his attention.

"We need to finish Smith, once and for all," Louisa persisted. "You'll never have a better chance than now to do it. By the time you pack me off to France, he'll have gone to ground and taken his disgusting brother with him."

Anger shook him at the thought. But he'd made his peace with that, hadn't he? He'd risked Louisa's safety on that last roll of the dice and she'd narrowly escaped torture and death. It was time to cut his losses.

He might never have her, but she would be safe. There'd be some comfort in knowing she was alive and well.

He slid his hand up to cup her shoulder. "I can't pursue him tonight. I can't leave you here, without protection, where he might find you before I find him. I can't take the risk."

He touched her hair, where it tangled around her ear, close to the slash on her face. It was a featherlight touch, painfully careful of her wound. His hand trembled.

A harsh breath that sounded shamefully close to a sob escaped him. "Your face . . ."

She gripped his wrist. The blue eyes hurled lightning bolts. "Don't you *dare* pity me, Jardine."

That fierce warrior woman leaped in her eyes. "I have felt more alive in the past few days than I have in eight years and I've no intention of losing you now. Go after Smith. I'll come with you. I promise I'll stay out of your way. Give me a shotgun and I'll hide somewhere nearby. At the least, I can even the numbers."

No. He couldn't possibly allow it.

In a rasping voice, he said, "Louisa, I have lost everyone who was ever close to me." She blinked at the change of subject, but he went on. "My parents were loving and gentle and kind. They died of typhus fever while I was away at school."

"It must have been dreadful for you."

"They were my world," he said simply. "I had no siblings, or at least none that survived infancy. It was just the three of us. And suddenly, there was only me. I was brought up by schools and servants, and then as a young man I ran wild. I was good at finding trouble and even better at getting out of it. Faulkner discovered me, trained me, and I thought I'd found direction. For a while, it was exciting and I believed passionately in what I did. But that life isolated me even more than before."

He looked into her eyes. "And then I met you. It was as if I'd been adrift all those years, rudderless, sailing through an endless night. You, Louisa. You were the sun on the horizon, lighting the way home." He gripped her dear, determined chin. "I cannot lose you. If I lose you, then I am lost, too."

"There are more ways than one to lose someone." She said it quietly, but he detected the tremor in her voice. "If you send me away now, it must be over between us, Jardine. When this threat is past, there'll be another, and another. There'll be more excuses for you to avoid risking your heart."

The accusation stunned him. "You think I'm a coward?"

"Yes, I think you are. You don't want to see me hurt, I know that. But I've lived with that same fear for you. I've lived for eight years with the knowledge that I might hear news of your death at any moment, or worse, that I might never hear at all. What do you think that has been like? I've been a prisoner to your fear, like a princess in a tower. You've made me alone, just as you are."

She sat up, hugging her knees. "That's no way to live, Jardine. I'm not going to live like that anymore."

A drum of desperation beat in his brain. She'd leave him. She'd find someone else. After all she'd been through. After all he'd done in her name.

He gritted his teeth. "All right, I'll go. You stay here with the shotgun. I'll tell the old woman to look out for you."

She shook her head. "I'm coming with you."

JARDINE'S eyes snapped. Flatly, he said, "The hell you are."

Louisa made what was possibly the most momentous decision of her life, next to marrying him. "If you go without me, Jardine, I won't be here when you get back."

She lifted her chin, her heart beating hard in her chest. She was afraid. The memory of their recent incarceration, of Radleigh's blade slicing into her flesh, was all too vivid in her mind. With iron will, she repressed a shudder, gripped her hands together so they wouldn't tremble.

He tilted his head, considering, and she swiftly forestalled him. "If you are thinking how you might tie me up and put me in a cupboard until you get back—"

"The thought crossed my mind," he muttered.

"—Then think what will happen if Smith has sent another of his cutthroats after me. Or if you do not come back . . ."

The place behind her eyes stung and grew hot. She would *not* cry. She despised women who used tears to get what they wanted.

His features were so taut with anger, she thought the pale mask of his face might crack. "You will be safer here than in the cross fire."

But she wouldn't back down now. She'd leave him no choice. "If you go without me, I shall return to London and go to work for Faulkner. If I'm going to live my life in fear, without you, then I'll turn it to good account. I won't die waiting for you, Jardine."

Hours might have ticked past as they stared at each other. He was white to the lips, his eyes fiery and dark as hot coals.

Finally, he launched from the bed and reached for his shirt. "If you're coming with me, you'll damned well do as I say."

THE ride was a long one, and by the time they arrived at their destination, her mare was almost blown. Silently, Jardine dismounted, then reached up for her.

The warmth of his hands spanning her waist was a small comfort. She wished she could stop shaking. She would go through with this. She must.

Jardine checked the shotgun he'd brought and handed it to her. Then he motioned her to the edge of the stand of trees.

Below them, in a dell overrun with shrubs and weeds, stood a small stone cottage. The house had bars on the windows and a sturdy-looking door. An odd place to hold a dangerous criminal.

Two guards played cards at a crude wooden table under the eave, tankards at their elbows and rifles propped against the benches on which they sat. A large lantern swung gently from a beam overhead, casting its glow over the two men.

Jardine hissed in disgust. "Ripe for the picking," he muttered. He glanced back at Louisa. "Stay here and cover me. If anyone approaches you, shoot them on sight."

Ducking low, he made his way through the thicket, and she realized he meant to circle the house, rather than approach it directly.

Louisa lost sight of him almost immediately. She turned

her gaze to the clearing around the cottage, her heart beating in her throat.

What she needed to do was give herself as much cover as possible and present the smallest target she could to anyone firing back at her. A prone position would be best.

She managed to find a suitable spot that had the added advantage of a large boulder behind which she could retreat in case of return fire. She sat on the grass with her back to the boulder, to wait.

The day waned and the sun hung low in the sky. How long would Smith wait to make his move? Until nightfall? With the summer twilight, that was likely to mean an extended vigil.

She didn't know how many men Smith could command. Three of his rough henchmen were already accounted for. Radleigh was still on the loose, though.

She shivered and clutched her shotgun tighter.

Suddenly, there was a loud crack. Louisa twisted and peered around her concealing rock, to see one of the cardplayers jerk and fall backward, toppling his chair. The other player leaped up, grabbed his shotgun, and ducked out of the lantern light. She could see his outline as he dived for cover behind the table.

The shots came from the other side of the house, about three o'clock to where Louisa now waited. She didn't return fire immediately, however. She waited until a dark-headed figure she recognized as Jardine slipped from the undergrowth.

Louisa didn't know exactly where her target lay, but she knew the general direction. She sighted, fired, bit off a grunt of pain at the hard kick of the butt against her shoulder. She reloaded and fired again.

Jardine had made it to the house.

There was no answering shot. Perhaps whoever was out there was too surprised by the unseen opposition.

She listened, but all was still.

Then a crunch of boot on fallen leaves sounded behind her. She swung around, shotgun at the ready.

And there, in her sights, stood Radleigh.

JARDINE heard a shot and a startled cry behind him as the second guard fell.

What had happened to Louisa? The cross fire from her hiding place on the ridge had ceased. Was she having trouble reloading? He hoped to God that's all it was. A string of oaths ripped from his lips.

The front of the house was entirely exposed. Jardine flattened himself on the ground to present and slithered to wrest the rifle from the fallen guard. It was loaded. That was something.

From the ground, he sent a shot in the direction from which the enemy fire had come. No time to find more ammunition. He threw down the spent rifle and drew his pistol.

Then he took his chance and ducked around the side of the cottage.

A shot whistled so close, he imagined he felt its tail wind brush his ear. But he reached safety, crouching behind a large beer barrel. Smith, or one of Smith's minions, would have to come out in the open to rescue his brother. Jardine would pick them off, one by one.

"My lord Marquis." The deep, resonant voice sounded close by. Smith emerged from the thicket, holding his hands up high.

"Don't move." The need for information warred with the impulse to simply kill Smith and be done.

Smith spoke again. "I sent Radleigh after your sharpshooter, Jardine. Judging from the lack of fire from that direction, it seems he must have caught him."

Rage roared in Jardine's ears. Louisa! No, Louisa had a gun and she knew how to use it. He had to put his faith in her. He must.

He heard scuffles, then, coming from within the cottage. The back door . . .

A swift glance toward the sound, that moment's inattention, brought Smith into action.

As Smith whipped his own pistol from his pocket, Jardine's instincts kicked in. Without hesitation, Jardine fired. The villain's entire body jerked and flailed as he fell.

Smith's pistol went off, and the barrel beside Jardine split. Beer gushed from the hole in the barrel's side, the scent of hops mingling with the acrid stench of gunpowder and blood.

Jardine dropped to his knees beside the dying man and gripped his lapels. "The list. Who wrote it? Who gave it to you? Tell me!"

Smith's response was a choked laugh. "That, my dear Jardine," he panted, "is the cream of the jest."

The crack of wood splintering caught Jardine's attention. He dragged Smith toward the back of the house, but he was too late. A man, presumably Elias Smith, shot out of the door, stumbled, regained his feet, and kept running.

"Elias! Elias, help me!" Smith's hoarse cry arrested the fellow in his tracks. He looked back, hesitating but an instant, recognition illuminating his thick features. Then he turned and kept running.

Jardine took one look at Smith's stunned, ashen face and gave a grim smile.

Twenty-five

"RADLEIGH." It amazed Louisa that she could speak at all, yet her voice held not a tremor.

The taste in her mouth was an acrid mix of gunpowder and fear. The only sound she heard was her own heart's frantic beat.

There was a brilliant, excited look in Radleigh's eye, the one she'd seen shortly before he'd cut her. Only, now she held a gun on him and all he had was that pathetic little knife. He hadn't even bothered to arm himself with a pistol. That oversight infuriated her.

"You look awfully cocky for someone who is about to die." Her finger caressed the trigger. The butt of the gun felt solid and sure against her shoulder.

"Ha. You won't kill me. Even if you could hit a barn at ten paces with that thing, which I doubt, you wouldn't have the mettle to kill me."

His words touched a chord of doubt. This confrontation

was far beyond the range of her experience. Hunting was one thing. Could she shoot a man?

He stepped closer. She had to act. One step more and he'd reach out and take the gun.

One more chance. She threw as much authority into her voice as she could. "Stop now. Turn and lie facedown on the ground. Or I *will* kill you."

He paused, tilted his head. "I've never met a woman like you. The others . . . they all sniveled and cried. Except the last one, and Smith put an end to my fun with her far too soon. But *you*, my dear. You are strong. And I've learned I like strong women. They're so much more amusing to break."

Fear reached up to grab Louisa's throat. Despite the fact that she was the one holding the gun, she was petrified.

She made herself speak. "I don't want to hear this. I might shoot you just to stop your mouth."

"You know, I really don't think you would."

Could she? Before this moment, she hadn't doubted she could pull the trigger to defend herself, to end a life force as evil as Radleigh.

But her body was cold with fear, paralyzed with it. The same feeling of helplessness when he cut into the tender flesh of her cheek pervaded her now.

"See? You can't shoot me. Despite your courage, you're a woman, and women's hearts are too tender for killing. *Now*." He smiled. "I'm going to tell you all about what I did to your little friend." He took a step, reached out. "And then I'm going to do it to—"

The shot blasted, obliterating his final word. Louisa had no memory of pulling the trigger, but she must have, because the stench of gunpowder filled her nostrils and the recoil of the shotgun knocked her off balance. As she regained her feet, Radleigh staggered back, crumpled to the ground with a heavy thud.

She watched him, saw the stain of blood spread over his chest. He didn't move.

Louisa swayed, put her hand out to clutch the tree next to her to hold herself steady.

Her mind was blank. Breathe, she told herself, but she felt as if she were sinking beneath water, suffocating, drowning.

Gunfire cracked below.

Jardine.

Her numb mind snapped into action. She fumbled in her pouch for a powder cartridge, took it out, and ripped it open with her teeth. Her hands were shaking; it took too long to load the gun, but finally, she was ready, stretched out at her vantage point.

She could make out nothing at first. The two guards lay dead in front of the cottage. Jardine was nowhere to be seen.

Footsteps running toward her along the ridge caught her attention. She scrambled to her feet and aimed, ready this time to shoot without hesitation.

"Louisa." Jardine erupted into her hiding place, grabbed the shotgun from her, turned, and fired. She couldn't even make out a figure, but an agonized cry told her he'd found his mark.

He gripped her hand and yanked her along, and they ran full tilt through the wood. She stumbled over her skirts, and he jerked her upright, giving her no quarter until they came to their horses.

"Up with you." He threw her into the saddle and mounted his own horse.

"Smith?" She choked out the word.

"Dead. I think we've accounted for the rest. We'll make for the cottage. Come on."

JARDINE doubted Smith's remaining henchmen would follow once they realized their master was dead, but he took no chances, riding across country most of the way, eschewing major thoroughfares and high streets.

Finally, they arrived back at the cottage, weary, their horses blown. They stabled the horses and walked toward the house. Neither spoke, but anticipation crackled between them like twigs in a bonfire.

Jardine breathed in the soft summer air with a sense of freedom he hadn't experienced in eight years. The twilight had all but softened into night. Birds still twittered madly in the trees.

He stopped and turned to Louisa, drew her into his arms.

She clung to him, shaking. "I killed him, Jardine. I shot him and I—He's dead."

"I'm so sorry, sweetheart. Not sorry he's dead, not that. Sorry that you had to be the one."

Violently, she shook her head, shuddering again. "I'm glad he's dead. I don't feel one speck of remorse." She lifted her face to look at him.

He regarded her with understanding. "It is no small thing to kill a man." He thought of Smith, of the look on his face when his brother turned his back and left him to die. The brother he'd waited eight years to avenge. "Not even to me."

"I know." She swallowed hard. "Jardine? I—"

"Never mind that now." He slid an arm around her waist and they walked together toward the cottage.

At the door, Jardine halted, frowning. He thought he'd seen movement within. A flutter of curtains.

Louisa stopped also, tilting her head. "Ives?" she mouthed.

"Perhaps." But he didn't think so. He didn't think he'd mentioned the location of this house to Ives.

Maybe it was their friendly landlady, come to see that they had everything they required. But she was in the service's employ. She ought to know better than to enter the house when it was in use.

A face appeared at the window. Louisa gasped. "It's Faulkner."

Of course. It had been Faulkner who had told him of this place, after all. Grimly, Jardine said, "He's got a hide showing up here."

"I suppose I ought to be glad that he got the list, even if he did leave me for dead at that confounded temple."

Grimly, Jardine jerked his head, opening the door. "Come on. By the time I'm through with that bastard, he'll . . ."

Left her for dead . . . Jardine froze on the threshold. He had wanted to tear Faulkner apart with his bare hands for that piece of callous stupidity. Why bring someone like Louisa into the middle of that business? Why ask for her help in the first place?

Faulkner always had a reason for everything. Nothing he ever did was on a whim.

What if involving Louisa in this mess hadn't been stupidity at all? What if . . . ? What if Faulkner had delivered them both to Smith in exchange for that list?

"Jardine, what is it?"

Smith's final words, his smug laughter. That's what he'd meant. Lord, why hadn't Jardine seen it for himself? Faulkner had involved himself personally in this business because that list was his death warrant. He'd written it. He'd been one of the few men in a position to know the information it contained.

"Bloody *hell*."

"What?" Louisa stopped, and Jardine turned her in his arms so that he was between her and the small entryway.

He pretended to kiss her, whispering in her ear. "Faulkner betrayed us all. He wrote that list. He's here to find out what we know. He might be here to kill us."

A rumbling cough sounded from beyond the open doorway. "When you're quite finished, Jardine, I'll have my report."

So this was how he was going to play it. Jardine took his time finishing the kiss. Then he lifted his head. Ignoring Faulkner, he said to Louisa, "I'm famished. How about some more of that soup, darling?"

His voice was light but his eyes were fierce on hers.

For once, she obeyed him, moving quickly toward the kitchen.

With a short exhalation of relief, Jardine turned and went to lean on the doorjamb of the small parlor where Faulkner sat.

The place no longer seemed cheerful and cozy; the lengthening shadows as much as the man who sat there in the semidarkness made Jardine's hackles rise.

Faulkner's brows lifted. "It seems you and Lady Louisa are better acquainted than I was aware."

You know exactly what our relationship is, you bastard.

Jardine had had enough of talking. He went to Faulkner, picked him up by his shirt, and planted him a facer that sent the older man hurtling back into his chair.

Hell, but Jardine wanted to kill the traitor then and there. But all he had was suspicion, circumstantial evidence. Without proof, he had no recourse against Faulkner. Better to let him think them both ignorant, then Louisa would be safe.

He gripped Faulkner's coat in his fists. "You took Lady Louisa into a hopeless situation and left her there. What the hell were you thinking of?"

Jardine saw the exact moment when Faulkner registered that Jardine had failed to make the connection between him and that list.

Satisfaction burned in those hard gray eyes. "You, of all people, know that we do what must be done, no matter what the personal cost."

Not anymore. With a contemptuous sneer Jardine loosed his grip on Faulkner's coat and let him fall back in his chair.

The older man warmed to his theme. "The trouble with most failed operatives, Jardine, is that they want a private life. They want family, a safe haven from the ugliness of corruption and betrayal. You and I both know that simply isn't possible. Once you have soiled your hands with the blood of your own countrymen, you can never live in innocence again. Everyone you love.leaves, or is lost, or damaged or tainted." Faulkner smiled grimly. "Just look what happened to Lady Louisa."

Rage boiled inside Jardine at this blatant attempt at manipulation. Corrosive remorse and anger had been wearing at his soul ever since Radleigh had made that terrifying incision on Louisa's face. Faulkner sought to capitalize on that weakness, just as Jardine had taken advantage of Radleigh's social ambitions to bargain for the agent list.

But for the first time, underlying all the guilt and self-recrimination was a sweet, wholesome sense of certainty. Louisa had not only survived the past few days but emerged stronger, his wonderful warrior woman. Strong and steadfast. She would not fail him. Her innocence was gone, and he would never forgive himself for it. But while she loved him, he had hope of forging something good and lasting between them.

Faulkner gave a snort and half closed his eyes. "Ah, you're all the same."

That cynical complacency galled Jardine so much he wanted to rip the man apart. Quietly, he spoke. "Do not rest easy, old man. For what you did to Lady Louisa, I will make it my life's work to bring you down. Now get out."

Faulkner sneered. "Might I remind you that this house is Crown property—"

"I said get *out*!"

Louisa returned at that point with brandy and glasses. She handed a glass to Jardine and glanced inquiringly at their unwanted guest.

Faulkner rose a little unsteadily, but Jardine just knew the bastard was dancing a jig inside.

The old man gave one of his rare smiles. "That's quite

all right, Lady Louisa—or should I say, Lady Jardine? I have what I came for."

He left the room and closed the door quietly behind him.

Jardine hurled his glass at the wall.

LOUISA left the mess. She poured a brandy for herself and sank into an armchair, took a long, fiery gulp, and rested her head back against the chintz-covered cushions.

She ached in every conceivable part of her body. The wound in her cheek throbbed like the Devil. At least she seemed to have escaped infection. That was a boon, indeed.

Her mind drifted, and the events preceding this night seemed to haze and blur into unreality until her brain couldn't grasp even the merest wisp of reason. She needed to think, but that required too much effort. She needed to talk to Jardine, too, but he'd gone off somewhere, too furious for company, even hers.

Perhaps he was avoiding her. It was possible, after all, that he still thought they had no business being together. How like him to withdraw from her after they'd faced such a danger, even though they'd won.

But she was tired, battle-weary, and sore, and she couldn't deal with him now. It was getting harder to think every moment.

She closed her eyes, and at the last instant before she slept, Louisa knew a deep satisfaction.

Everything would be all right. This time, she would fight for him. This time, she'd win everything she'd dreamed of for so long.

WHEN Louisa roused, there were hands on her body. Large, elegant hands, gentle hands, smoothing away her clothing, releasing her torso from stays, easing her shift over her head.

She lay on sheets that smelled of sunshine. She murmured and turned her face into the pillow. Strong arms dug into the ticking beneath her and lifted her up, and her heart swooped and soared.

She opened her eyes and saw a steaming hip bath before the fire. Turning her head, she looked up at the stern, troubled face of her bearer and couldn't stop her smile bursting forth.

He'd done this for her. While she'd slept he'd built a fire, drawn water and boiled it, carried it to the bedchamber so she could sink into this delicious bath.

A lift of his lips acknowledged her smile, but his eyes remained dark and bleak.

He lowered her gently into the bath, wetting his own cuffs as he did. He was travel-stained and rumpled, yet he exuded masculine beauty so vivid and powerful that it hurt her to look at him. Yet, she couldn't look away.

"Soap," he muttered, hunting around in her discarded garments. "Here. I couldn't find a flannel or a sponge."

She thought he'd give her the soap, but instead, he dipped the small cake in the water and lathered it between his hands.

"Hold this."

She took the slippery cake and watched as his hands slid over her, giving particular attention to her breasts, laving their peaked nipples, skating over their swells, palming them, squeezing gently.

She arched back with a cry, her lips parted and moist. He touched her, skillfully, sinfully. He parted her legs and used his fingertips inside her and out until she shuddered and gave a gasping cry.

Later, warm and dry in those sun-drenched sheets, she felt the mattress depress as he climbed in next to her.

She ran her hand over his chest. *My love.* She smiled. *You don't have to be alone anymore.*

He rolled toward her and sighed, and he slept in her arms like a dead man until morning.

JARDINE woke and found himself staring directly into a pair of startling blue eyes. No matter how often he looked at her, every time, those eyes pierced him anew.

They were fierce, those eyes, and he couldn't quite believe he was waking up with them and the person who owned them next to him. Perhaps it was selfish, but nothing would stop him claiming her now.

"I owe you an apology," she said, and with delight, he realized why she looked particularly fierce this morning. Louisa hated to admit she was wrong.

He lifted himself on one elbow, and his gaze dipped. For a moment, he was distracted by the lushness of her mouth. Her lips pressed together in a determined line.

Jardine forced himself to raise his eyes to hers, dutifully ignoring the stir in his nether regions. He didn't want to miss this. "Yes?"

"I—I never quite understood what it was that you did. When he forbade us to marry all those years ago, Max told me you were a cold-blooded killer." Her brow puckered. "But that's not the case, is it?"

He said nothing, merely waited for her to go on.

"All I knew was that your Home Office work stood between us. Like a child, I only thought of myself and what I wanted. I wanted you to stop."

"Understandable. Louisa, really, you don't have to—"

She held up a hand. "Don't interrupt me, Jardine. You know how I hate to be wrong, so let me get this over with."

She snagged her underlip between her teeth, then released it. "I know now that your work is important and worthy of respect, that you have killed, but it wasn't easy and never cold-blooded."

She paused. "I know you didn't murder that boy, I knew it in my heart at the time, but I was so furious and hurt that you continued to choose this life over me . . . Everything became hopelessly tangled."

She raised her eyes to his. "I won't be so selfish again. Let me share your life in any small part I can. You need to do this work, I understand that. I won't stand in your way if only you will let me in."

Jardine took an unsteady breath. He'd never even registered the shame he'd felt at her accusations until now, when it lifted. "It means a lot to me to hear you say that."

He reached out and took her face in his hands. "I love you. My only thought in holding you at arm's length all this time was to shield you from that side of my life."

Her eyes softened, pleaded. "Don't shield me. Love me, and let the rest fall as it may." She took a shuddering breath and it caught on a sob. "Don't send me away again."

"My dear Lady Jardine." He gathered her into his arms. "*You* are not going anywhere."

He kissed her, and it was as if a world that had been careering beyond his control for eight years suddenly righted itself. He would spend the rest of his life loving Louisa, aye, and protecting her, too.

There was just one thing he needed to do first.

Twenty-six

———— ✦ ————

THE notice was brief, barely a paragraph, but it could have been a hand grenade exploding in Almack's for the stir it would create.

The Marquis of Jardine and his wife, formerly Lady Louisa Brooke, announce the resumption of their marriage. They will be at home to no one for the foreseeable future.

Louisa laughed as she walked in to Jardine's study with the *Gazette* in her hand. "That will set chins wagging."

"Yes, but we won't be in town for some time yet."

"They will all come here and plague us. Mama was agog."

His impossible brows twitched together. "*She's* not coming here, is she?"

"No, she's staying in Paris for a month or two yet, never fear."

Louisa rested her hip on his desk and gazed out with bottomless satisfaction at the park beyond the long windows. She belonged here, with Jardine, at Claybourne Abbey.

At last, at last, she was home.

Jardine had been sifting through files and papers as she came in. Louisa turned to him. "Anything yet?"

"The evidence is mounting." He sat back and pushed his hands through his hair. He'd allowed his black locks to grow a little longer, the way she liked. At the moment, they were irresistibly disheveled, and the need to run her own fingers through their thick softness gripped her.

Would she ever grow tired of touching him?

Jardine met her gaze, and his eyes darkened with answering heat. He pushed his work aside.

"Come here," he said softly.

And she went.

ONLY a select few were invited to attend the Marquis of Jardine's study in his Mayfair house one cold autumn day.

Max, Duke of Lyle, had traveled up from his country estate, quarreling with his heavily pregnant wife all the way. Kate had refused to miss whatever treachery was afoot. Louisa knew her friend would dance with joy to see Faulkner get his comeuppance. She hoped all would go to plan.

Harriet Burton was there, looking pale and composed. She wore a high-necked gown, presumably to cover the scarring that marked her décolletage.

Louisa sat with her, talking quietly. She'd placed Harriet in the care of a competent nurse and no longer feared for her health. But while her physical recovery was complete, Harriet's heart and mind were different matters.

"Tell me again how Radleigh looked when you shot him," Harriet whispered, with relish.

Louisa pretended not to hear.

Jardine conferred in low murmurs with Lord Nicholas Morrow. Nick had become some sort of aide-de-camp to him recently, ferrying documents and files back and forth.

On her own account, Louisa would be glad to leave all that subterfuge and danger behind. She was no Harriet Burton, and the small life that might even now grow in her womb deserved every protection she could give. The faint, wistful yearning for complete contentment was one she resolutely pushed aside. Not even for a child could she demand that Jardine turn his back on his duty.

The butler ushered two more men into the room. Sir Henry Frampton, Secretary to the Home Secretary, and Faulkner.

Louisa rose and forced herself to be civil as they exchanged greetings. "Won't you sit down, gentlemen?"

"What's all this about?" Faulkner bristled with impatience. "You told me you wanted to see me alone, Jardine."

There was a pause before Jardine answered. He nodded to Nick, who took a seat at his right hand. Then he said, "As to that, there've been . . . developments. I'm sure Sir Henry will forgive the liberty, but I've invited various interested parties here to witness what I'm about to say."

He placed his fingertips on the desk, on either side of the files in front of him. "The work we do in secret is sometimes dangerous, often dirty, but most of the time, it involves sheer, intellectual drudgery: painstakingly piecing the puzzle together, sifting through information until we find a vital fragment of intelligence that fits with something else."

From the corner of her eye, Louisa saw Faulkner's hand clench.

With his gaze fixed on Faulkner, Jardine lifted a thick file and let it fall back on the desk. "Reports from operatives, dossiers on important figures, and expert assessments on everything from the possibility of foreign invasion to civil unrest within the country."

He flicked a glance at the head of operations. "You know all about civil unrest in this country, don't you, Faulkner?"

"Get to the point, will you?" Faulkner barked.

Jardine stared at the man for a moment, then shook his head. "How you will wish you hadn't rushed upon your fate. My point? Ah yes. My point is that above all else, the single most important quality I bring to the service is the kind of brain that retains facts and makes connections."

He tapped the file with a fingertip. "When you drew Lady Louisa into your scheme to retrieve a certain document from one Duncan Radleigh, I was stunned. But your explanation for her involvement seemed plausible enough." He gave a short laugh. "I admit, I was a dupe. You wove an elaborate scheme to bring the two of us to Smith. Handed us to him on a platter, didn't you? Did Radleigh go along with your plan or was he, also, a dupe?"

Faulkner rose. "I don't have to sit here and listen to this. You're mad, Jardine! What's more, you're divulging secret intelligence to civilians. I'll have your *head* on a platter for this."

Jardine's face darkened. "*Sit down.* The only reason you are still alive is that I have respect for the office you so tenuously hold."

Sir Henry's shrewd eyes narrowed. He leaned forward in his chair. "What is this, Jardine?"

Jardine walked around his desk and handed Sir Henry the file. "*This* is all the evidence you need to arrest and convict Mr. Faulkner here for treason and corruption of the highest order."

Louisa, watching Faulkner quite openly now, saw that he'd lost a little of his bluster. His sangfroid didn't waver, however. He sat grimly silent, turning his heavy gold signet ring around his finger.

Sir Henry bent his gaze to the pages in front of him and read. The quiet stretched, punctuated only by the occasional crinkle of a turning page.

Louisa's nerves drew taut. Her heart pounded. She could only imagine how Faulkner, in his guilt, must feel.

Finally, Sir Henry sat back, pale and grim. "This is appalling. This file alone could bring down the government. Collusion with a known head of organized crime over *decades* . . . Betraying your colleagues to keep your nefarious activities quiet. It beggars belief!"

He glared at Faulkner under shaggy brows. "For an intelligent man, you've dug yourself a very deep hole."

Faulkner rumbled. "I don't know what is in that file, but I can assure you, sir, it's a pack of lies. Fabricated by an embittered, washed-up operative who should get out of the game before he embarrasses more than himself with these trumped-up charges."

Jardine stared at Faulkner for a long moment. Then he said, "I thought you'd say something like that." He nodded to Nick, who now lounged at the doorway. "Bring him in."

"Is there no end to this charade?" Faulkner wondered aloud. "Really, I don't have time for th—"

He broke off when he saw who stood, manacled, between two burly militia guards.

"Hello, Faulkner." Elias Smith grinned.

Faulkner's face paled to ash. Satisfied, Jardine gave the nod and the guards muscled Smith away.

"The betrayer betrayed," said Jardine softly.

Perfect. Utterly perfect. Louisa's fingertips lightly touched the scar on her face. Operatives dead, missions compromised, evil allowed free rein. She looked around and saw her satisfaction reflected in the faces of their guests. Almost everyone in this room had a score to settle against Faulkner.

"*Now,*" Harriet whispered, her small fist clenched.

Suddenly, Faulkner raised the back of his hand to his lips and sucked on his gold ring.

"Prussic acid," murmured Harriet. "Fast acting. Very tidy. Painful, messy, but no more than he deserves, the filthy traitor." She rose quickly, placing her hand on Louisa's arm. "Come, Louisa. You won't want to watch this."

Louisa half rose, then stared in horror as Faulkner toppled from his chair, convulsing and gasping, writhing as if he were having a fit.

"Someone do something!" She started toward him. "Help him, for God's sake!"

Max stood and brought Kate to her feet. "There's nothing we can do, Louisa. He'll be dead in less than a minute." He slid an arm around his wife's waist and together, they left the room.

The others were filing out also. Louisa stood there, helpless, as foam spilled from Faulkner's horribly grimacing mouth. She looked to Jardine. He must have foreseen this result, surely?

Jardine was pale, his dark eyes glittering like jet. "He's a traitor, Louisa, and you know the penalty for treason. It's a better death than he deserves. I could have thrown him to the wolves, but I let him go in his own way." Jardine curled his lip. "For once, he did the decent thing."

Shuddering, she nodded. He was right. She hated it, but he was right.

Jardine gathered up his papers. "Sir Henry, if you'll come this way, I believe we have matters to discuss."

He looked down as Faulkner's convulsions finally came to a halt, then glanced at his butler, who stood waiting at the door. "There you are, Emerson," he said calmly. "Have someone clean up this mess."

Louisa lay in Jardine's arms, quiet and sated—for the moment at least. The novelty, the sheer luxury of being with him every day was one she'd treasure as long as it lasted. Soon, he must resume his dangerous calling.

She splayed her hand against his bare chest, felt the reassuring beat of his heart. "When will you go back?"

He sucked in a long breath. "Tomorrow. I'm needed." He glanced down at her obliquely. "Do you mind?"

Swallowing past a lump of apprehension in her throat, Louisa did as soldiers' wives do everywhere and shook her head, lifted her chin, and smiled.

A gleam stole into his eyes. "You don't want to come with me? We need people like you."

She shivered. "No, thank you!" Her recent experience had been hair-raising enough to last a lifetime.

Hesitating, she licked her lips. "Jardine?"

"Yes, my love?" He knew how she adored hearing him call her that. His thick black lashes lowered as he drew her palm to his lips for a kiss.

She caught her breath. "Don't you dare die."

Jardine grinned. He stretched, his lean muscles flexing as he put an arm around her and hugged her close. "Don't worry about me, sweetheart."

She touched his chest again with her fingertips, traced a pattern among the scattering of black hair there. "Don't joke about it, Jardine. I think if you're going to risk your life every day, we ought to talk of it seriously, just this once."

"But I'm not risking my life. It's a boring desk job—"

"Oh, tell that to the cat!" Fury shot through her. "After all I've been through, I deserve the truth, Jardine!"

He laughed. He actually laughed, and it was the most carefree, joyous sound she'd ever heard from him.

He hauled her into his arms and flipped so that she was beneath him, pinning her to the bed with his hips.

"Jardine!"

He kissed her ear, then took the lobe between his teeth.

"Stop. No. *Ohhh*." He pressed his lips, warm and soft, to her throat.

His mouth moved lower, igniting fires that danced and flared beneath her skin.

"You're trying to distract me."

"Mm. Is it working?" He gave her nipple a generous lick and ecstasy speared through her body.

Summoning all her willpower, she reached down to

clamp her hands around his upper arms and tugged. He was impossible to move.

"Come up here," she commanded.

He swirled his tongue around her navel. "No, I rather like the view I'm getting from this angle."

"Jardine!"

He sighed, crawling up, looming over her body like a predator. He looked into her eyes. "Sir Henry has asked me to take over Faulkner's job. I've accepted."

She frowned. "You mean it really *is* a desk job? No time in the field?"

"Exactly."

The flood of relief and joy in her heart must have shown in her face, because he laughed again.

In a moment, his laughter died and the light in his eyes warmed. "You would have borne it, wouldn't you? You wouldn't have stopped me going back."

"The work you do is necessary," she said. "I would have borne it. I would have been miserable, but I would have borne it for you."

"I wish I could be so magnanimous, but let me tell you that I'd have you manacled to this bed rather than allow *you* to go back into the field, my lady."

She smiled up at him. "I don't want to go back to the field."

"In my capacity as head of operations, I regret the loss of a damned good operative. As your husband, I can only applaud your excellent sense."

She sighed. "All I've ever wanted was to make a home, a family, with you. However," she added, twining her arms around his neck, "I will, on occasion, give you the benefit of my advice. . . ."

He smiled as she brought him down to her. "You're a formidable woman, Lady Jardine."

JULIA St. Clement had never tried to eat soup through a mustache before. It was dashed difficult, she found. No wonder the awful embellishment had gone out of favor with modern men. Three days now she'd hidden behind the blasted thing, and already she felt weak and malnourished from struggling to strain any decent sustenance through it. Why ever had she let Papa talk her into this dreadful disguise?

Because she'd had no other choice—that was why. Papa had whacked off her long dark hair, fashioned a sorry little mustache from a lock of it, and threw a pack of clothing at her.

"Change quickly, *ma chérie!*" he'd ordered. "Fitzgelder will know my face, but he's not seen you before. With this, he'll never suspect who you are."

And it was true. The man they both feared—for good reason—had been completely deceived. He'd not caught a glimpse of Papa, and Julia had faced Fitzgelder alone. She was properly introduced as Mr. Alexander Clemmons, and the foul little man had no reason to guess his new friend was as much a sham as the shabby facial hair. Papa had escaped. This bloody mustache, it seemed, had saved his life.

And now, God willing, it would save a few others. Hopefully, Julia's would be one of them. Provided, of course, she didn't succumb to starvation first.

"You've got soup on your whiskers," her pretend wife, Sophie, announced with a girlish giggle.

"Of course I do," Julia grumbled. "I've got soup on my chin, soup in my cravat, soup everywhere but in my mouth. Blast this disgusting mustache!"

"But you look quite dashing, you know," Sophie said as she daintily spooned plenty of soup safely into her own mouth. "Really, it's a pity mustaches aren't more the style."

"I feel wretched, and I look worse," Julia assured her. "It's a monstrous thing, and Papa will never hear the end of it when we finally meet up with him again."

"*If* we meet up with him," Sophie corrected, her sweet voice quavering. "The coachman has been so slow, miss. What if Mr. Fitzgelder catches us?"

"He won't. Surely that locket you stole from him isn't so important he'd come chasing us all the way out here."

"I didn't steal it!" the girl insisted for at least the dozenth time. "When he attacked me, it must have torn off in the struggle and fallen into my apron."

"Little that will matter to him, will it? But I doubt he'll be looking for you, Sophie. That locket is the least of Fitzgelder's worries just now. He's got bigger things on his mind, I'm afraid."

"Such as killing your friend, you mean."

Julia shushed her. They were sitting off alone in the crowded common room of the posting house, but still it couldn't hurt to be cautious. There was no telling who might be listening in. Fitzgelder had men out and about, and they could be anywhere right now. The room was quite full of strangers, not all of them respectable-looking.

"Anthony won't be killed if I can help it," Julia muttered under her breath.

Sophie gave a dreamy sigh. "He must be very special to you."

Lord, she'd quickly disabuse the girl of that deranged notion. "The man is a selfish lout who doesn't have an honest breath in his body," she announced. "He very nearly deserves to be murdered."

Sophie wasn't swayed. "Then why have we spent the last three days traveling all the way out here to warn him?"

"I said *nearly*," Julia had to admit. "No one deserves what Fitzgelder has planned for him; murdered on the highway by cutthroats and left there to rot."

Sophie shuddered, momentarily forgetting her soup. "Are you sure we shouldn't just find the local magistrate and tell him? I'm not too keen on all this cutthroat business."

"I told you to wait back in London, didn't I?"

Now the girl was offended. "What? And leave you to come out here alone? I couldn't do that, Miss Clement! You saved my life."

"Well, I certainly didn't save you from Fitzgelder just so his hired thugs could do you in on the road," Julia said and stared longingly at the two shriveled potatoes in her bowl. "It's getting dark. I think we should let the mail coach go on without us and spend the night here."

"Here? But surely we're getting close to—what's that place where your gentleman friend is staying?"

"Hartwood; it's likely some musty old estate. The lord of the manor had Rastmoor stand up at his wedding, and no doubt they're all still reveling. Since we've not yet passed through Warwick, and as difficult as the roads have been, it's bound to be another full day's travel for us."

Sophie sighed. "Well, I suppose we ought to stay here, then. I just hope, for the sake of that selfish lout you want to rescue, we get there in time."

"So do I, Sophie," Julia agreed, making another brave go at the soup. "So do I."

Almost as irritating as this blasted mustache was the worry that Fitzgelder's men had already reached the destination and accomplished their goal. True, she and Anthony, Viscount Rastmoor, had not parted on the best of terms, but she'd give anything right now to see that he was alive and well. If he could just walk through that door safe and sound, she'd . . . well, she'd be very relieved.

Then she'd knock him on his arse and ask what in the hell he'd been thinking three years ago when he'd wagered—and lost—her at the gaming table. Good God, as if she was chattel he could own and barter at will! Well, he'd owned her, all right—owned her heart and soul—right up until that night when Fitzgelder marched up to Papa, waving Anthony's vowels and claiming that *he* was her fiancé now. As if such a thing could be legally binding.

But it was the fact that Anthony had done such a thing, even as an angry jest, that had broken Julia's heart. She knew what it meant. Anthony had found out the truth about her identity and wanted no part of such a wife. He'd cast her off like the rubbish he believed her to be and Julia had never seen him again.

Indeed, Anthony Rastmoor simply had to remain alive. If Fitzgelder's men got to him first, how would Julia ever get her revenge?

"It's broken," Anthony, Lord Rastmoor, said as he inspected the underside of their carriage.

"Damn," his companion, the Earl of Lindley, fumed. "I just bought this phaeton three weeks ago. Quite a piece, don't you think?"

"I think you got taken." Rastmoor dusted the dirt off his hands and trousers. "Most of the higher-quality conveyances have axles that actually attach to the wheels."

"It certainly was doing that when I bought the blasted thing," Lindley said, fairly diving onto his hands and knees to crawl under the carriage. "Are you saying there's been shoddy workmanship here?"

Rastmoor was perfectly content to let his elegant friend get muddy. It was, after all, Lindley's carriage. He should have been the one down there investigating in the first place, although what Lindley would have investigated, Rastmoor couldn't say. The stylish earl likely wouldn't have known the difference between a broken axle and a hay rake. Still, Rastmoor was happy enough not to be the only one with dirt on his knees.

Lindley swore, and Rastmoor had to chuckle. While most men might let out a string of colorful words over the condition of the axle, Lindley was more likely upset over what he'd just done to his clothes. He probably wouldn't even notice it was some very shoddy workmanship, indeed, that put them in this predicament.

In fact, it hardly looked like workmanship at all. No, if Rastmoor didn't know better, he might even wonder if the damage to Lindley's carriage was intentional. But that was ridiculous. Who would tamper with Lindley's carriage? Unless, of course . . .

But that was ridiculous, too. Surely dear cousin Fitzgelder would not stoop to something like this, would he? No, this had to be merely an accident.

Damn, but it was rather coincidental, wasn't it? Mother sent a message warning he'd best get himself to London for some unnamed trouble Fitzgelder was stirring up, and now something so unusual as this threatened to delay him. Could it be mere coincidence? He wanted to believe so, but somehow he just couldn't.

What was Fitzgelder about, this time? The terms of Grandfather's will had been well settled these two years. Surely his cousin couldn't think to dredge all that up again, could he? Then again, Rastmoor had learned the hard way not to put anything past Cedrick Fitzgelder.

"What rotten luck," Lindley said finally, uttering a few more oaths and crawling out from under his carriage. "I don't suppose you have a spare axle or whatever you said that was?"

"No, I don't," Rastmoor said. "But if you have some straps or the like, we might be able to bind the thing well enough to get it back to that posting house we just passed. We won't be riding, though."

Lindley bit his lip and glanced around at the dusky trees

lining the road on either side of them. "That's slow going, isn't it?"

"I suppose, but with that axle broken, we're done for the night, I'm afraid."

"Yes, it appears that way, but I'm not sure my horses are up for pulling dead weight. Even if we bind it, that axle won't turn very well, will it?"

So Lindley did have some basic understanding of the mechanics of the thing. Well, he couldn't very well blame the man for not wanting to overtax his cattle. The only thing finer than Lindley's wardrobe was his stables, and these two goers were as good as they got. It would be a shame for such proud horseflesh to be dragging a lame carriage all the way to that posting house.

"All right, help me loose them, then. We'll walk the horses and send someone back to get your precious phaeton."

Lindley agreed, then noticed his muddied condition. "Bother. My valet will have my hide over these trousers."

Oh, not the valet, again. Rastmoor rolled his eyes. "I don't see how you abide the man. From what you say, he sounds like a ruddy tyrant."

Lindley smiled. "That he is, but I assure you I'd never make it without him. Which reminds me."

He left Rastmoor with the horses and went around to the back of the carriage. He dug through a box stowed there.

"Ahem, but we unharness the horses up at this end," Rastmoor called.

"Yes, but the weapons are back here."

"Weapons?"

"Here, take this," Lindley called out, tossing Rastmoor a lethal little pistol.

"What's this?" Rastmoor asked.

"It's a pistol," Lindley informed him.

"I know it's a pistol. What in God's name is it for?"

"For shooting anyone who might come out of those trees after us." Lindley glanced at said trees and shuddered. "You never know what sort of persons are about these days, and it's very nearly dark out."

"Good grief. Is it loaded?"

"Of course. What bloody use would it be empty?"

Rastmoor shook his head, but he accepted the pistol and slipped it into his pocket. He was a bit taken aback when Lindley casually tucked his own pistol into the front of his trousers. This image of the always elegant Lindley with a pistol wedged at his waist was more than a bit humorous.

"What is it?" Lindley asked.

"Aren't you worried that will ruin the lines of your tailoring?" Rastmoor asked, not bothering to hide his smirk. "Whatever will your valet think?"

"Should a highwayman leap out after us, I would prefer to have my weapon where I can get at it," Lindley said, stepping up to help with the horses. "A few wrinkles can always be ironed out. Blood, my valet tells me, is a bit more dicey."

"I'm sure it is," Rastmoor had to agree.

No highwaymen did leap out, though, and they pushed and pulled until the phaeton was safely out of the roadway. Leading Lindley's fine horses, the men headed off to the posting house. The evening was dreary and still, yet not nearly so dreary as the day two months ago when Rastmoor had traveled this same road.

He'd been traveling with his friend Dashford, on the way to what was supposed to have been a quiet house party. Some house party, though. There were floods and fiancées and fiascos until the bloody thing ended with Dashford's wedding. Rastmoor still wasn't sure how he felt about that.

The whole concept of matrimony hadn't exactly worked out very well for him and, to be honest, he was still not convinced any man ought to put much stock in the institution. From what Rastmoor had seen so far, women were an untrustworthy lot. He hoped Dash wouldn't have to learn that the hard way.

Rastmoor sighed as they plodded along. Damn, but with Dashford trussed up and married now, Rastmoor would likely have to settle for Lindley's persnickety company more often. Oh well. For a game here or there at the club or a visit to the races, no one could fault Lindley's sportsmanship or his overall entertainment value. But if Rastmoor had to have one more discussion about where to find the best gloves or which bloody knot would look best in his cravat . . . Honestly, what could Dashford have been thinking to go and get leg shackled?

"You know what I'm thinking?" Lindley said after they'd walked in silence quite a while, the horses plodding nervously along behind them.

He hated to imagine. "No. What?"

"There'll likely be women at this posting house."

"Probably so."

"That suits me just fine. With luck, there'll be a couple for both of us. Which do you prefer, the blonds or the brunettes?"

"The ones who do their job and disappear before daylight."

"I reckon that'll be all of them," Lindley declared with a hopeful laugh. "I think I'd favor a blond tonight. Unless of course there's only one available, and blond is your preference, then naturally I would—"

"No, thank you. Have any woman you want. I think I'll just sleep tonight."

"What? But you've been stuck up there at Hartwood for nearly two months, and I saw the sort of guests they had—not exactly fresh and accommodating, as they say. Surely now that you're getting out and about again, you'd want to prime the old pump handle, if you know what I mean."

"I know what you mean, damn it," Rastmoor grumbled. "But I'm not interested, all right? Good luck to you and your pump handle, but I'd rather sleep. Alone."

Lindley frowned as if that was a foreign concept. "Alone? But you're not ill, are you?"

"No. I'm fine."

"You don't sound fine. You sound—blue deviled. My God, but you can't possibly still be pining after that girl? That little French actress of yours—St. Clem, or something, wasn't it?"

"St. Clement," Rastmoor corrected before he caught himself. The last thing in the world he wanted was to discuss

Julia right now. "And I'm not pining. I'm just not interested in some dirty whore at a posting house, all right?"

Lindley gave a slow whistle. "You *are* still pining! Dash it all, Rastmoor, that was years ago. And didn't she end up marrying your cousin, or something?"

"Yes." By God, what would it take to not have this conversation?

"That's right, and then she died in childbed, didn't she?" Lindley went on.

Rastmoor gritted his teeth. "That's what I heard."

Oh, he'd heard the story, all right. Then he'd gone and gotten roaring drunk. Dashford's father had taken ill and died some short time thereafter, and the two of them were roaring drunk together. Things hadn't gone so well for them after that, as he recalled.

Eventually, Dashford pulled himself together, and Rastmoor had simply learned to pretend. He supposed, in a way, it had been easier for Dash. He'd been mourning a devoted father, a man who left behind fond memories and warm emotions. Rastmoor, however, had been grieving something altogether different.

When Julia St. Clement died, all she left behind were bitter wounds and heartbreak. It was hard enough knowing she'd left him for another man, but with time he might have recovered. It cut deeper than that, though. Julia left him a scar that would never go away. The whore may have died in Fitzgelder's bed, but the child she'd taken to the grave with her had been Rastmoor's. She'd carried *his* child and still left him for another, passing the child off as Fitzgelder's.

How did a man ever recover from that?

"I can't wait to see this Lord Rastmoor's face when he meets you again," Sophie was saying as they finished their supper.

Julia cringed. "Hopefully that will never happen. With luck, we'll find he's safely at Lord Dashford's home, and

I can simply send a warning message. He'll find out what Fitzgelder is about, and you and I can be off to meet Papa."

"You don't want to see him again?"

"Heavens no!"

"We've come all this way, and you're not even going to see the man?"

"Exactly."

Sophie was downcast. "That's so sad. I was hoping the two of you might . . ."

"Sorry, Sophie. That only happens in novels."

It was a shame to disappoint the poor girl, but better she get such foolishness out of her mind now before she started expecting grand romance for her own life. Indeed, women like them should harbor no such hopes—Julia had learned that the hard way. Perhaps the truth would come easier for Sophie.

"We'll be done with this before you know it," Julia went on, hoping her light tone and warm smile would both encourage and distract her young friend. "Then we'll find Papa, and you'll become a part of our troupe. You're quite a hand at sewing, but perhaps we can coax you into acting, as well."

"Acting? Oh, I'm sure I could never be so very good at that. All those lines I'd have to memorize!"

"You've been playacting the part of a blushing bride for three days now, and so far, the audience seems quite enthralled," Julia said, sweeping her arm wide to indicate the patrons of the posting house, a few of whom had traveled this last leg of the journey on the mail coach with them.

Sophie looked around the dim room and frowned. "I believe our audience would be no less enthralled were I simply a chicken tucked under your arm. They've hardly taken note of us at all."

"There, you see? You've played your part to perfection. Who's to say you might not make a memorable Juliet or Ophelia or—"

"Lord Lindley!" Sophie said suddenly.

"Lord Lindley? I don't believe we have any scripts with Lor—"

And then Julia glanced up to realize what Sophie meant. The doorway was filled with the elegant form of a man they had briefly met in London just as they were making their hasty escape. Lord Lindley—a good friend and confidante of the evil Fitzgelder.

Sophie's eyes were huge and terrified, and Julia wanted to slide under the table. Good heavens, if Lindley recognized them, he'd notify Fitzgelder of their whereabouts! They had to hide, to get out of here this very instant.

But there was nowhere they could go, nowhere in the room to hide. They were trapped. Julia's pulse pounded, and she struggled to think up some scheme to protect them. What could she do? Where could they . . . ?

Suddenly all coherent thought ceased.

A familiar broad-shouldered form appeared behind Lindley. Julia's lungs contracted, the air squeezed out of them in a whimper. Around her, the world disappeared, and she was aware of only one thing: Anthony Rastmoor was still alive.

Thank God she wasn't too late! Fitzgelder's men hadn't succeeded in their plan. Anthony still lived and breathed and wore that smile of half amusement, half boredom she'd come to know so well three years ago. Three long, painful years ago.

He was alive, and he was beautiful. And he was cold. When his gaze fell on her, she recoiled, both inwardly and out. The chill that emanated in his hazel eyes was as unfamiliar as the image that had been greeting her in the mirror since she and Sophie had taken up this masquerade. Indeed, the Anthony Rastmoor who followed Lindley into the poorly lit common room was a man much changed from the man who had taken Julia's virtue—as well as her heart.

His gaze didn't last long on her, though. Quickly it moved on, as if she were of little importance to anyone. This surprised her more than even the fact that she was seeing him again. How could she be struggling for air, feeling as if the universe itself would collapse around her, and yet his gaze simply swept over her as if she'd been nothing more than furniture? It was unthinkably hurtful.

Then his gaze did linger, but not on her. She had to physically turn her head to see what he was seeing. The air swept back into her lungs and burned like fire.

He was gazing at Sophie.

Her brain began functioning again. Mostly her thoughts were torn, though. Should she gouge out the man's eyes or grab up a dull knife and castrate him here? God, but how he was staring at Sophie! The nerve of him!

Funny, Julia had never contemplated how fetching the girl must appear to those of the male persuasion. Yes, Sophie was pretty, she supposed. Gentlemen would notice that, of course. But, by God, what was that charming expression forming on Sophie's fresh, youthful face? Why, the little tart was actually smiling at Anthony Rastmoor!

"Why, Mr. and Mrs. Clemmons," Lindley said, noticing them and coming their way.

Julia had given the false name at the spur of the moment as they were leaving London. It had seemed convenient to use as they'd traveled, and now she was glad they had. No one would think it amiss to see the quiet Clemmons couple being greeted by an old acquaintance here, and no awkward explanations would have to be given at mistaken names.

Anthony, too, would likely not recognize the name.

Or maybe it didn't really matter. He'd likely forgotten her altogether, judging by the way his attention was now given entirely to her companion. Indeed, why should he so much as spare a second glance to Julia's severe haircut and soupy mustache, while Sophie was sitting there in front of him, all blond and dreamy and feminine? Damn his eyes.

"How odd to run into you here," Lord Lindley said when he reached their table. "I had no idea you were traveling this way, else I would have invited you to share my carriage."

He, too, had his eye on Sophie. What pigs these men were. Didn't they realize Sophie was supposed to be a married woman? How dare they stare like this! If it kept on, Julia feared she'd end up having to call at least one of them out or risk exposing herself as a fraud. What husband could sit calmly while virtual strangers drooled over his wife? Shame on them. How on earth had Julia ever thought Anthony Rastmoor to be a decent, worthwhile human being?

"We had a rather sudden change of plan," Sophie was saying. "Didn't we, Mr. Clemmons?"

Julia cleared her throat. "Er, yes. We came this way rather spur of the moment." She worked at keeping her voice low and hoped Anthony might not recognize it.

She needn't have worried. His focus was all on Sophie, to the point the poor girl must have noticed and was finally starting to appear uncomfortable.

"Forgive me," Lindley said, at least trying to tear his eyes from Sophie and act respectably. "Everyone has not been introduced. Lord Rastmoor, this is Mr. Alexander Clemmons and his lovely wife, Mrs. Sophie Clemmons. We met a few days ago in London."

Rastmoor made a polite bow and allowed Julia a quick nod before turning his attention back to Sophie. It had been highly unnecessary for Lindley to recall Sophie's first name, but obviously he had. Sophie was looking decidedly anxious now. The girl might be too pretty for her own good, but at least she appeared to have some sense. She knew enough not to trust the flattery of blackguards.

"How do you do," Julia said, not pausing long enough for Rastmoor to speak before directing her next question to Lindley. "Will you gentlemen be staying for the night here?"

Lindley sent a quick look toward his partner, and Rastmoor gave the reply. His voice sliced Julia to the heart. Odd that a voice could have so much power.

"We're undecided as yet, Mr. Clemmons. Will you be staying?"

Julia fixed her eyes firmly on her soup bowl. *Mr. Clemmons.* He still hadn't recognized her. Lord, but that, too, hurt far more than it should have.

"We haven't entirely decided that, my lord," Julia replied. It was true. If she found the men would be here, she'd simply leave a note of warning for Rastmoor with the innkeeper then get herself and Sophie back on the road and far away from the lusty lords.

But Sophie had her own ideas. She smiled brightly for the men. "The roads have been so very difficult, though. I do truly dread getting back in that coach to be jostled along to the next posting house. Perhaps if Mr. Clemmons knew some of his gentlemen friends were to be staying here tonight, I could stand a better chance of convincing him."

Julia gaped at her friend. What was she doing? Now that Lindley was here, they needed to leave, not settle in for the night! He was the one who could unmask them! Maybe Sophie didn't have so much sense, after all.

Lord Lindley gave a rumbling chuckle and turned his gaze onto Julia. "Shame on you, Mr. Clemmons, forcing your young bride to travel under these conditions."

His attention was short-lived. He returned his focus—and a disgustingly warm smile—back on Sophie. "Rest assured, Mrs. Clemmons, if it will gain you a few hours' respite from the torment of travel, Rastmoor and I will do our best to persuade your husband to obtain a room for the night. In fact, I'll go see to making arrangements with the proprietor. Don't worry, Clemmons, tonight will be at my expense."

Lindley made a showy bow then went off in the direction the innkeeper had last been seen. Blast, what had Sophie done? It was true the small purse Julia had on her at the time of their departure was growing a bit thin right now, but certainly she couldn't allow Lindley to assume their expenses. Even more certainly, she couldn't spend the night under the same roof as Anthony Rastmoor! What if the man tried to engage her in conversation? How long could she expect her disguise to hold out if Rastmoor ever did decide to take his eyes off Sophie long enough to question Mr. Clemmons's bizarre mustache and feminine voice?

But so far Rastmoor hadn't reached that point. He was still staring at Sophie and smiling in delight as he called out to Lindley, "See about getting us a private dining room, as well. I'm sure the Clemmonses will wish to join us in a quiet supper."

Oh, Lord. What next?

Lindley nodded and disappeared into a back hallway where the innkeeper had last been seen to go. Julia glanced nervously at Sophie. The girl just batted her wide blue eyes and shrugged. Well, Julia would just have to find a way to get them out of this.

"There's no need for a private room, sir," she protested. "Mrs. Clemmons and I have just finished our meal, as you can see, and now we'd like—"

"Oh, but dearest," Sophie interrupted, innocent and darling. "Surely that little bowl of soup was barely enough for a strapping man such as yourself. Why not join your friend Rastmoor over a hearty meal?"

Ah, so *that* was Sophie's angle. The chit was meddling. Julia would put a quick end to that.

"I assure you, my precious, that soup was quite adequate for my frame," Julia said. "We have no need to remain here any longer. I simply need to give a note to our innkeeper, if you recall." Now she gave Sophie a glare that should have wiped the pink smile from her rosebud lips. It didn't.

"What's our hurry, dear? Surely you can think of *something* interesting to discuss with these fine gentlemen," Sophie suggested.

"No, actually, I'm sure I can't," Julia assured her.

"Fear not, Clemmons," Rastmoor said, leaning casually against a nearby table and leering down at Sophie. "I'm sure we'll find plenty to occupy our time. In fact, a private room will be just what we need. There is a particular matter I'm certain you'll be most eager to discuss."

Now, that erased the pink smile. Sophie slid a nervous glance at Julia. What was Rastmoor hinting at with that glinting eye and ominous tone? Had he found them out? Preventing any hasty escape Julia may have contrived, Lindley returned with the proprietor.

"Yer in luck," the innkeeper said with an eager grin. "I got a nice room just waiting for ye, and my wife'll bring a good, healthy stew."

Julia tried to demur, but Lindley gracefully swooped in to loop Sophie's hand through his arm and assist her up from her chair. When Julia glanced over at Rastmoor, she found him, at last, looking her way.

"Come, Clemmons," he said. "I doubt you'll want to miss this."

Indeed, from the way he spoke, she was fairly certain she *did* want to miss it, whatever *it* was. She was fairly certain, too, he was not about to let her. Helpless, she followed Anthony Rastmoor through the big, safe common area into a private dining room off the dark corner under the stairs.